"Mr. Carr can lead us away from the small, artificial, brightly-lit stage of the ordinary detective plot into the menace of outer darkness. He can create atmosphere with an adjective, and make a picture from a wet iron railing, a dusty table, a gas-lamp blurred by the fog. He can alarm with an alusion or delight with a rollicking absurdity—in short, he can write—not merely in the negative sense of observing the rules of syntax, but in the sense that every sentence gives a thrill of positive pleasure."

—Dorothy L. Sayers

"You can argue as you will about which was the most enjoyable period for a reader of detective stories: My allegiance remains irrevocably fixed to the 1930's, when you could count on four new novels a year by John Dickson Carr."

—Anthony Boucher

"If Agatha Christie was the queen of the murder mystery, Carr was certainly its king. . . . She's fine in her way (I've read all 80 of her mysteries), but when you're looking for an intricate plot and a ghostly atmosphere, you can't do better than John Dickson Carr."

—Walter Kendrick
Village Voice

Novels by
John Dickson Carr
available in IPL Library of Crime Classics® editions:

Dr. Fell novels:
DEATH TURNS THE TABLES

HAG'S NOOK

THE SLEEPING SPHINX

TILL DEATH DO US PART

Non-series:
THE BURNING COURT

Series Consultant: Douglas G. Greene

JOHN DICKSON CARR

HAG'S NOOK

INTERNATIONAL POLYGONICS, LTD.
NEW YORK CITY

HAG'S NOOK

Copyright © 1933 by John Dickson Carr. Copyright renewed 1960 by John Dickson Carr.

Introduction and cover: Copyright © 1985 International Polygonics, Ltd.

Library of Congress Card Catalog No. 85-81384
ISBN 0-930330-28-5

Printed by Guinn Printing, Inc., Hoboken, N.J.
Printed and manufactured in the United States of America
First IPL printing November 1985
10 9 8 7 6 5 4 3 2 1

HAG'S NOOK

DR. GIDEON FELL, DETECTIVE

> He comes striding towards us now, beaming like Old King Cole.
> You can probably hear him chuckle. If he wheezes a little, that's
> due to his weighing more than three hundred pounds....You
> notice the three chins, and the bandit's mustache, and the
> eyeglasses on the black ribbon. He removes his hat with old-
> school courtesy. Don't try to bow, doctor! He is Gideon Fell,
> doctor of philosophy and expert on crime.

In these words, the narrator of one of John Dickson Carr's radio-plays introduced Dr. Gideon Fell. As Anthony Boucher remarked, "the detective story in the grand manner demands a Great Detective," and Dr. Fell is a memorable sleuth. He is larger-than-life both in his appearance and in his actions. Although he is not fiction's most gargantuan crime-solver—that prize belongs to the four hundred pounds of Paul McGuire's Superintendent Fillinger—he puts most detectives literally in the shade. But, to be fair, Carr may have exaggerated Fell's weight for radio audiences; normally he is described as being a relatively svelte twenty stone. It is, however, more than his size which allows Fell to dominate his cases: "A huge joy of life, a piratical swagger merely to be hearing and seeing and thinking, glowed from him like steam from a furnace. It was like meeting Father Christmas." Everything about Fell is in large proportions. He smokes a meerschaum which he fills from an obese pouch. He consumes countless tankards of beer and is fond of whisky ("It would be very interesting to find any whisky that could take the top of my head off"), and he has a tremendous fund of miscellaneous knowledge about obscure subjects.

At the time of HAG'S NOOK, Dr. Fell has been working for six years on his magnum opus, *The Drinking Customs of England From The Earliest Days*. It was eventually published in 1946, Carr said, by a publishing house with the evocative name of Crippen & Wainwright. Fell is also the author of *Romances of the Seventeenth Century* and a book on the supernatural in English fiction. He spends his spare time, he explains on several occasions, improving his mind with sensational fiction.

Dr. Fell's name came from the seventeenth-century bishop and dean of Christ Church, Oxford, who was immortalized in Thomas Brown's famous doggerel:

> I do not like thee, Doctor Fell.
> The reason why I cannot tell,
> But this I know, and know full well,
> I do not like thee, Doctor Fell.

Fell himself sometimes quotes this verse, and so do the murderers he tracks down, but otherwise he does not take after his rather stern namesake. His appearance and personality were based on Carr's literary idol, G. K. Chesterton, the essayist and author of the Father Brown detective stories. The formality of Fell's speech was borrowed from Dr. Samuel Johnson, a fact which probably explains why Fell is described in HAG'S NOOK as a lexicographer. Fell is, as students of his cases know, a historian, Fellow of the Royal Historical Society with degrees from Harvard, Oxford, and Edinburgh. He has occasionally lectured at American universities on such topics as "The Effects of King's Mistresses on Constitutional Government."

In the Mystery Writers of America Anthology, *Four-and-Twenty Bloodhounds* (1950), Carr contributed a "Detective's Who's Who" entry about Dr. Fell. We learn that he was born in Lincolnshire in 1884 the second son of Sir Digby and Lady Fell; his aristocratic connections help us to understand why he never seems to be earning a living during his cases and why he was able to afford several different residences. Besides Yew Cottage in Lincolnshire, where Fell is living during the events of HAG'S NOOK, he resides at Number 1 Adelphi Terrace in London and, later at 12 Round Pond Place, Hampstead. In one short story, he has a house in Chelsea. Carr added a few more details: Fell is the recipient of the French Grand Cross Legion of Honor, and he is a member of the Garrick, Savage, and Detection Clubs — organizations, incidentally, to which Carr also belonged. (The Detection Club is a society of detective-story writers; Carr was the only American member.)

But what is most noteworthy about the "Detective's Who's Who" is how much Carr left unsaid. We hear nothing about his wife, who plays a subsidiary role in HAG'S NOOK and is mentioned in passing in three or four other cases. Nothing is revealed about Sir Digby Fell's first son or, indeed, of Dr. Fell's other relatives. Like Sir Arthur Conan Doyle (but unlike many modern Holmesians), Carr realized that much of a detective's life should be left vague. A larger-than-life character can be part of this world, but he should not be limited by it. It is insignificant that Hercule Poirot must have been as old as Methuselah in his final cases. Poirot, like Holmes and Fell, has gained an immortality that is unaffected by mere chronological considerations. Glimpses of a detective's background are more effective than elaborate biographical details. Thus Doyle referred to Holmes's unrecorded cases, and Carr mentioned that Fell was involved in such matters as the "Weatherby Grange affair," the "six blue coins which hanged Paulton of Regent Street," and "the still more curious problem of the inverted room at Waterfall Manor." Tolkien understood in LORD OF THE RINGS the importance of referring to other events which are not detailed in the narrative. Such hints contribute a feeling of depth and timelessness, what Tolkien called "a large history in the background, an attraction like that of viewing far off an unvisited island."

Carr was only twenty-six years old when he wrote HAG'S NOOK, the first Gideon Fell story. He was born in Uniontown, Pennsylvania, on November 30, 1906. Beginning in preparatory school and continuing through his studies at Haverford College, he wrote detective stories and historical romances along with occasional poems and comic tales. After living in Paris in the late 1920s, he returned to the United States and published his first novel, *It Walks by Night,* featuring the French detective Henri Bencolin. But Carr believed that England — the land of Holmes and Watson, of Fu Manchu and Nayland Smith, of Dr. Thorndyke and Reggie Fortune and the transplanted Belgian Hercule Poirot—was the natural home for a detective-story writer. In 1932, he married an Englishwoman, Clarice Cleaves, moved to England, and began a regimen of writing four or five detective novels a year featuring English sleuths. Under the pseudonym "Carter Dickson" he wrote a series of books about Sir Henry Merrivale, and under his own name he wrote about Gideon Fell, who eventually appeared in twenty-three novels, four short stories, and four radio-plays.

HAG'S NOOK is told from the viewpoint of Tad Rampole, a young American visiting England who clearly represents Carr's own feelings, and it is filled with Anglophilic warmth. I know of no writing that conveys so sensitively the love of England and of the past than the second paragraph of HAG'S NOOK. Rampole will appear in two other Fell cases, *The Mad Hatter Mystery,* and *The Three Coffins,* in which his name is unaccountably altered to "Ted." It is the feeling for the past and how it influences the present that dominate HAG'S NOOK. Carr believed that "to write good history is the noblest work of man," and like Fell he loved the romance of the past. In 1936, he wrote the finest true-crime book, *The Murder of Sir Edmund Godfrey,* about an unsolved murder of 1678, and later in his career he became the master of the historical detective novel. According to Dr. Fell "the talent for deduction developed by judicious historical research can just as well be applied to detective work."

HAG'S NOOK also reflects Carr's affection for the works of G. K. Chesterton. Dorothy Sayers wrote of Carr's novels: "Chestertonian …are the touches of extravagance in character and plot, and the sensitiveness to symbolism, to historical association, to the shapes and colours of material things, to the crazy terror of the incongruous." Not only Dr. Fell's appearance but his love of paradoxes come directly from Chesterton.

John Dickson Carr was famed for the "miracle crime"—the impossible disappearance and the locked-room murder; indeed he found so many ways to explain tricks and impossibilities that as Anthony Boucher remarked, "his own career seems a miraculous event demanding some rational explanation." The seeming impossibilities in HAG'S NOOK are handled subtly, more hinted at than proclaimed. Few tales so perfectly combine atmosphere, mystery, ingenuity, and an extraordinarily well-concealed murderer.

Douglas G. Greene

Norfolk, Virginia
April, 1985

Acknowledgements: I am grateful to Dr. James E. Keirans and to the late Larry L. French for material on Dr. Fell which appears in this introduction.

Series Consultant Douglas G. Greene is Director of the Institute of Humanities at Old Dominion University. Dr. Greene is working on a multi-volume history of the detective story. He has edited two anthologies of John Dickson Carr's work, and is widely recognized as *the* authority on that writer.

Chapter 1

THE old lexicographer's study ran the length of his small house. It was a raftered room, sunk a few feet below the level of the door; the latticed windows at the rear were shaded by a yew tree, through which the late afternoon sun was striking now.

There is something spectral about the deep and drowsy beauty of the English countryside; in the lush dark grass, the evergreens, the grey church-spire and the meandering white road. To an American, who remembers his own brisk concrete highways clogged with red filling-stations and the fumes of traffic, it is particularly pleasant. It suggests a place where people really can walk without seeming incongruous, even in the middle of the road. Tad Rampole watched the sun through the latticed windows, and the dull red berries glistening in the yew tree, with a feeling which can haunt the traveller only in the British Isles. A feeling that the earth is old and enchanted; a sense of reality in all the flashing images which are conjured up by that one word "merrie." For France changes, like a fashion, and seems no older than last season's hat. In Germany even the legends have a bustling clockwork freshness, like a walking toy from Nuremberg. But this English earth seems (incredibly) even older than its ivy-bearded towers. The bells at twilight seem to be bells across the centuries; there is a great stillness, through which ghosts step, and Robin Hood has not strayed from it even yet.

Tad Rampole glanced across at his host. Filling a deep leather chair with his bulk, Dr. Gideon Fell was tapping tobacco into a pipe and seemed to be musing genially over something the pipe had just told him. Dr. Fell was not too old, but he was indubitably a part of this room. A room—his guest thought—like an illustration out of Dickens. Under the oak rafters, with smoke-blackened plaster between, it was large and dusky; there were diamond-paned windows above great oak mausoleums of bookshelves, and in this room, you felt, all the books were friendly. There was a smell of dusty leather and old paper, as though all those stately old-time books had hung up their tall hats and prepared to stay.

Dr. Fell wheezed a little, even with the exertion of filling his pipe. He was very stout, and walked, as a rule, with two canes. Against the light from the front windows his big mop of dark hair, streaked with a white plume, waved like a war-banner. Immense and aggressive, it went blowing before him through life. His face was large and round and ruddy, and had a twitching smile somewhere above several chins. But what you noticed there was the twinkle in his eye. He wore eyeglasses on a broad black ribbon, and the small eyes twinkled over them as he bent his big head forward; he could be fiercely combative or slyly chuckling, and somehow he contrived to be both at the same time.

"You've got to pay Fell a visit," Professor Melson had told Ramphole. "First, because he's my oldest friend, and, second, because he's one of the great institutions of England. The man has more obscure, useless, and fascinating information than any person I ever met. He'll ply you with food and whisky until your head reels; he'll talk interminably, on any subject whatever, but particularly on the glories and sports of old-time England. He likes band music, melodrama, beer, and slapstick comedies; he's a great old boy, and you'll like him."

There was no denying this. There was a heartiness, a *naïveté,* an absolute absence of affectation about his host which made Rampole at home five minutes after he had met him. Even before, the American had to admit. Professor Melson had already written to Gideon Fell before Rampole sailed—and received an almost indecipherable reply decorated with little drawings of a hilarious nature and concluding with some verses about prohibition. Then there had been the chance meeting on the train, before Rampole arrived at Chatterham. Chatterham, in Lincolnshire, is some hundred and twenty-odd miles from London, and only a short distance away from Lincoln itself. When Rampole boarded the train at dusk, he had been more than a little depressed. This great dun-coloured London, with its smoke and its heavy-footed traffic, was lonely enough. There was loneliness in wandering through the grimy station, full of grit and the iron coughing of engines, and blurred by streams of hurrying commuters. The waiting-rooms looked dingy, and the commuters, snatching a drink at the wet-smelling bar before train time, looked dingier still. Frayed and patched, they seemed, under dull lights as uninteresting as themselves.

Tap Rampole was just out of college, and he was, therefore, desperately afraid of being provincial. He had done a great deal of travelling in Europe, but only under careful parental supervision on the value-received plan, and told when to look. It had consisted in a sort of living peep-show at the things you see on post cards, with lectures. Alone he found himself bewildered, depressed, and rather resentful. To his horror, he found himself comparing this station unfavourably with Grand Central—such comparisons, according to the Better American Novelists, being a sin.

Oh, well, damn it! . . .

He grinned, buying a thriller at the bookstall and wandering towards his train. There was always the difficulty in juggling that money; it seemed to consist of a bewildering variety of coins, all of inordinate dimensions. Computing the right sum was like putting together a picture puzzle; it couldn't be done in a hurry. And, since any delay seemed to him to savour of the awkward or loutish, he usually handed over a bank note for the smallest purchase, and let the other person do the thinking. As a result, he was so laden with change that he jingled audibly at every step.

That was when he ran into the girl in grey.

He literally ran into her. It was due to his discomfort at sounding so much like an itinerant cash-register. He had tried jamming his hands into his pockets, holding them up from underneath, walking with a sort of crab-like motion, and becoming generally so preoccupied that he failed to notice where he was going. He bumped into somebody with a startling thud; he heard somebody gasp, and an "Oh!" beneath his shoulder.

His pockets overflowed. Dimly he heard a shower of

coins tinkle on the wooden platform. Fiery with embarrassment, he found himself holding to two small arms and
looking down into a face. If he had been able to say anything, it would have been, "Gug!" Then he recovered himself to notice the face. Light from the first-class carriage
beside which they stood shone down upon it—a small face,
with eyebrows raised quizzically. It was as though she were
looking at him from a distance, mockingly, but with a sym-
pathetic pout of her lips. A hat was pulled down anyhow,
in a sort of rakish good-humour, on her very black, very
glossy hair; and her eyes were of so dark a blue that they
seemed almost black, too. The collar of her rough grey coat
was drawn up, but it did not hide the expression of her lips.

She hesitated a moment. Then she spoke, with a laugh
running under it: "I say! You *are* wealthy. . . . Would you
mind letting go my arms?"

Acutely conscious of the spilled coins, he stepped back
hastily.

"Good Lord! I'm sorry! I'm a clumsy ox; I— Did you
drop anything?"

"My purse, I think, and a book."

He stooped down to pick them up. Even afterwards,
when the train was rushing through the scented darkness
of a night just cool enough, he could not remember how
they had begun talking. A dim train-shed, misted with soot
and echoing to the rumble of baggage trucks, should not
have been the place for it; yet it seemed, somehow, to be
absolutely right. Nothing brilliant was said. Rather the opposite. They just stood there and spoke words, and Rampole's head began to sing. He made the discovery that both
the book he had just bought and the book he had knocked
out of her hands had been written by the same author. As
the author was Mr. Edgar Wallace, this coincidence was
hardly stupefying enough to have impressed an outsider,
but Rampole made much of it. He was conscious of trying desperately to hold to this subject. Each moment, he
felt, she might break away. He had heard how aloof and
unapproachable Englishwomen were supposed to be; he
wondered whether she were just being polite. But there
was something—possibly in the dark-blue eyes, which

were wrinkled up at him—of a different nature. She was leaning against the side of the carriage, as carelessly as a man, her hands shoved into the pockets of the fuzzy grey coat: a swaggering little figure, with a crinkly smile. And he suddenly got the impression that she was as lonely as himself. . . .

Mentioning his destination as Chatterham, he inquired after her luggage. She straightened. There was a shadow somewhere. The light throaty voice, with its clipped and slurred accent, grew hesitant; she spoke low:

"My brother has the bags." Another hesitation. "He—he'll miss the train, I expect. There goes the horn now. You'd better get aboard."

That horn, tooting thinly through the shed, sounded inane. It was as though something were being torn away. A toy engine began to puff and stammer; the bumping shed winked with lights.

"Look here," he said, loudly, "if you're taking another train—"

"You'd better *hurry!*"

Then Rampole grew as inane as the horn. He cried in a rush: "To hell with the train! I can take another. I'm not going anywhere, as it is. I—"

She had to raise her voice. He got the impression of a smile, bright and swashbuckling and pleased. "Silly!—I'm going to Chatterham, too. I shall probably see you there. Off you go!"

"Are you sure?"

"Of course."

"Well, that's all right, then. You see—"

She gestured at the train, and he swung aboard just as it got under way. He was craning out of one corridor window, trying to get a glimpse of her, when he heard the throaty voice call something after him, very distinctly. The voice said an extraordinary thing. It called:

"If you see any ghosts, save them for me."

What the devil! Rampole stared at the dark lines of idle carriages sweeping past, the murky station lights which seemed to shake to the vibration of the train, and tried to understand that last sentence. The words were not exactly disturbing, but they were a little—well, cockeyed. That was the only way to express it. Had the whole business been a joke? Was this the English version of the needles, the raspberry, or any similar picturesque and delicate term? For a moment his neckband grew warm. No, damn it! You could always tell. A train guard, passing through the corridor at this moment, perceived an obviously American Young Gen'lman thrusting his face blindly out of the window into a hurricane of cinders, and breathing them with deep joyous breaths, like mountain air.

The depressed feeling had vanished. This little, swaying train, almost empty of passengers, made him feel like a man in a speedboat. London was not big and powerful now, nor the countryside a lonely place. He had drunk strong liquor in a strange land, and he felt suddenly close to somebody.

Luggage? He froze for a moment before remembering that a porter had already stowed it into a compartment somewhere along here. *That* was all right. Under his feet he could feel the floor vibrating; the train jerked and whirled with a clackety roar, and a long blast of the whistle was torn backwards as it gathered speed. This was the way to begin adventure. "If you see any ghosts, save them for me." A husky voice—which somehow suggested a person standing on tiptoe—drifting down the platform. . . .

If she had been an American, now, he could have asked her name. If she had been an American . . . but, he suddenly realized, he didn't want her to be an American. The wide-set blue eyes, the face which was just a trifle too square for complete beauty, the red and crinky-smiling mouth; all were at once exotic and yet as honestly Anglo-Saxon as the brick staunchness of Whitehall. He liked the way she pronounced her words, as though with a half mockery. She seemed cool and clean, like a person swinging through the countryside. Turning from the window, Rampole had a strong desire to chin himself on the top of one of the compartment doors. He would have done so but for the presence of a very glum and very rigid man with a large pipe, who was staring glassily out of a near-by window, with the top of his travelling-cap pulled over one ear like a beret. This person looked so exactly like a comic-strip Englishman that Rampole would have expected him to exclaim, "What, what, what, what?" and go puffing and stumping down the corridor, had he seen any such athletic activity indulged in here.

The American was to remember this person presently. For the moment, he knew only that he felt hilarious, hungry, and in need of a drink. There was, he remembered, a restaurant-car ahead. Locating his luggage in a smoking-compartment, he groped his way along narrow corridors in search of food. The train was clattering through suburbs now, creaking and plunging and swaying under the shrillness of its whistle, and lighted walls streamed past on either side. To Rampole's surprise, the restaurant-car was almost full; it was somewhat cramped, and smelt heavily of beer and salad oil. Sliding into a chair opposite another diner, he thought that there were rather more crumbs and blotches than were necessary; whereupon he again damned himself for provincialism. The table shook to the swaying of the train, lights jolted on nickel and woodwork, and he watched the man opposite skilfully introduce a large glass of Guinness under a corresponding moustache. After a healthy pull, the other set down the glass and spoke.

"Good evening," he said, affably. "You're young Rampole, aren't you?"

If the stranger had added, "You come from Afghanistan, I perceive," Rampole could not have been more startled. A capacious chuckle enlivened the other man's several chins. He had a way of genially chuckling, "Heh-heh-heh," precisely like a burlesque villain on the stage. Small eyes beamed on the American over eyeglasses on a broad black ribbon. His big face grew more ruddy; his great mop of hair danced to the chuckles, or the motion of the train, or both; and he thrust out his hand.

"I'm Gideon Fell, d'ye see? Bob Melson wrote me about you, and I knew you must be the person as soon as you walked in the car. We must have a bottle of wine on this. We must have two bottles of wine. One for you, and one for me, d'ye see? Heh-heh-heh. *Waiter!*"

He rolled in his chair like a feudal baron, beckoning imperiously.

"My wife," continued Dr. Fell, after he had given a Gargantuan order—"my wife would never have forgiven me if I'd missed you. She's in a stew as it is, what with plaster falling off in the best bedroom, and the new revolving sprinkler for the lawn, which wouldn't work until the rector came to call, and then it doused him like a shower-bath. Heh-heh. Have a drink. I don't know what kind of wine it is, and I never ask; it's wine, and that's enough for me."

"Your health, sir."

"Thank'e, my boy. Permit me," said Dr. Fell, apparently with some vague recollections of his stay in America, "to jump the gutter. *Nunc bibendum est.* Heh.—So you're Bob Melson's senior wrangler, eh? English history, I think he said. You're thinking of a Ph.D., and then teaching?"

Rampole suddenly felt very young and very foolish, despite the doctor's amiable eye. He mumbled something noncommittal.

"That's fine," said the other. "Bob praised you, but he said, 'Too imaginative by half'; that's what he said. Bah! give 'em the glory, *I* say; give 'em the glory. Now, when I lectured at your Haverford, they may not have learned much about English history, but they cheered, my boy, they cheered when I described battles. I remember," continued the doctor, his vast face glowing as with a joyous sunset, and puffing beneath it—"I remember teaching 'em the Drinking Song of Godfrey of Bouillon's men on the First Crusade in 1187, leading the chorus myself. Then they all got to singing and stamping on the floor, as it were; and a maniacal professor of mathematics came stamping up with his hands entangled in his hair—as it were—and said (admirably restrained chap) would we kindly stop shaking the blackboards off the wall in the room below? 'It is unseemly,' says he; 'burpf, burpf, ahem, very unseemly.' 'Not at all,' says I. 'It is the "Laus Vini Exercitus Crucis,"' 'It is, like hell,' says he. 'Do you think I don't know "We Won't Be Home until Morning" when I hear it?' And then I had to explain the classic derivation.

. . . Hallo, Payne!" the doctor boomed, breaking off to flourish his napkin at the aisle.

Turning, Rampole saw the exceedingly glum and rigid man with the pipe, whom he had noticed before in the corridor of the train. The cap was off now, to show a close-shaven skull of wiry white hair, a long brown face, and a general air of doddering down the aisle, looking for a place to fall. He grumbled something, not very civilly, and paused by the table.

"Mr. Payne, Mr. Rampole," said Dr. Fell. Payne's eyes turned on the American with a startling flash of their whites; they seemed suspicious. "Mr. Payne is Chatterham's legal adviser," the doctor explained. "I say, Payne, where are your charges? I wanted young Starberth to have a glass of wine with us."

A thin hand fluttered to Payne's brown chin, and stroked it. His voice was dry, with a premonitory rasp and difficulty, as though he were winding himself up.

"Didn't arrive," replied the lawyer, shortly.

"Humf. Heh. Didn't arrive?"

The rattle of the train, Rampole thought, must shake Payne's bones apart. He blinked, and continued to massage his chin.

"No. I expect," said the lawyer, suddenly pointing to the wine-bottle, "he's had too much of that already. Perhaps Mr.—ah—Rampole can tell us more about it. I knew he didn't fancy his little hour in the Hag's Nook, but I hardly thought any prison superstitions would keep him away. There's still time, of course."

This, Rampole thought, was undoubtedly the most bewildering gibberish he had ever heard. "His little hour in the Hag's Nook." "Prison superstitions." And here was this loose-jointed brown man, with the deep wrinkles round his nose, turning the whites of his eyes round and fixing Rampole with the same pale-blue, glassy stare he had fixed on the corridor window awhile ago. The American was already beginning to feel flushed with wine. What the devil was all this, anyhow?

He said, "I—I beg your pardon?" and pushed his glass away.

Another rasp and whir in Payne's throat. "I may have been mistaken, sir. But I believe I saw you in conversation with Mr. Starberth's sister just before the train started. I thought perhaps—?"

"With Mr. Starberth's sister, yes," said the American, beginning to feel a pounding in his throat. He tried to seem composed. "I am not acquainted with Mr. Starberth himself."

"Ah," said Payne, clicking in his throat. "Just so. Well—"

Rampole was conscious of Dr. Fell's small, clever eyes watching through the joviality of his glasses; watching Payne closely.

"I say, Payne," the doctor observed, "he isn't afraid of meeting some one going out to be hanged, is he?"

"No," said the lawyer. "Excuse me, gentlemen. I must go and dine."

Chapter 2

THE rest of that ride often came back to Rampole as a sinking into the deep countryside; a flight into cool and mysterious places as the lights of towns went out with the hours, and the engine's whistle called more thinly against an emptier sky. Dr. Fell had not referred to Payne again, except to dismiss him with a snort.

"Don't mind him," he said, wheezing contemptuously. "He's a stickler for things. Worst of all, the man's a mathematician. *Pah!* A mathematician," repeated Dr. Fell, glaring at his salad as though he expected to find a binomial theorem lurking in the lettuce. *"He* oughtn't to talk."

The old lexicographer did not even manifest any surprise at Rampole's acquaintance with the unknown Starberth's sister, for which the American felt grateful. Rampole, in his turn, refrained from asking questions about the odd statements he had heard that evening. He sat back, pleasantly padded by the wine, and listened to his host talk.

Although he was no critic in the matter of mixing drinks, he was nevertheless a trifle appalled at the way Dr. Fell poured down wine on top of stout, and followed both with beer towards the close of the meal; but he kept up valiantly with every glass. "As for this beverage, sir," said the doctor, his great voice rumbling down the car, "as for this drink, witness what the Alvismal says: 'Called ale among men; but by the gods called beer.' Hah!"

His face fiery, spilling cigar-ashes down the front of his necktie, rolling and chuckling in his seat, he talked. It was only when the waiters began to hover and cough discreetly round the table that he could be persuaded to leave. Growling on his two canes, he lumbered out ahead of Rampole. Presently they were established facing each other in corner seats of an empty compartment. Ghostly in the dim lights, this small place seemed darker than the landscape outside. Dr. Fell, piled into his dusky corner, was a great goblin figure against the faded red upholstery and the indistinguishable pictures above the seats. He had fallen silent; he felt this unreal quality, too. A cool wind had freshened from the north and there was a moon. Beyond the flying click of the wheels, the hills were tired and thick-grown and old, and the trees were mourning bouquets. Then Rampole spoke at last. He could not keep it back. They had chugged in to a stop at the platform of a village. Now there was absolute silence but for a long expiring sigh from the engine. . . .

"Would you mind telling me, sir," said the American, "what Mr. Payne meant by all that talk about 'an hour at the Hag's Nook,' and—and all the rest of it?"

Dr. Fell, roused out of a reverie, seemed startled. He bent forward, the moon on his eyeglasses. In the stillness they could hear the engine panting in hoarse breaths, and a wiry hum of insects. Something clanked and shivered through the train. A lantern swung and winked.

"Eh?—Why, Good Lord, boy! I thought you knew Dorothy Starberth. I didn't like to ask. . . ."

The sister, apparently. Handle with care. Rampole said:

"I just met her today. I scarcely know her at all."

"Then you've never heard of Chatterham prison?"

"Never."

The doctor clucked his tongue. "You've got something out of Payne, then. He took you for an old friend. . . . Chatterham isn't a prison now, you know. It hasn't been in use since 1837, and it's falling to ruin."

A baggage truck rumbled. There was a brief glare in the darkness, and Rampole saw a curious expression on the doctor's big face, momentarily.

"Do you know why they abandoned it?" he asked. "It was the cholera, of course; cholera—and something else. But they said the other thing was worse."

Rampole got out a cigarette and lighted it. He could not analyse his feeling then, though it was sharp and constricting; he thought afterwards that it was as though something had gone wrong with his lungs. In the dark he drew a deep breath of the cool, moist air.

"Prison," continued the doctor, "particularly prisons of that day, were hellish places. And they built this one round the Hag's Nook."

"The Hag's Nook?"

"That was where they used to hang witches. All the common malefactors were hanged there, of course. H'mf." Dr. Fell cleared his throat, a long rumble. "I say witches because that fact made the most impression on the popular mind. . . .

"Lincolnshire's the fen country, you know. The old British called Lincoln *Llyn-dune,* the fen town; the Romans made it *Lindum-Colonia.* Chatterham is some distance from Lincoln, but then Lincoln's modern nowadays. We're not. We have the rich soil, the bogs and marshes, the waterfowl, and the soft thick air—where people see things, after sunset. Eh?"

The train was rumbling out again. Rampole managed a little laugh. In the restaurant-car this swilling, chuckling fat man had seemed as hearty as an animated side of beef; now he seemed subdued and a trifle sinister.

"See things, sir?" the other repeated.

"They built the prison," Fell went on, "round a gallows. . . . Two generations of the Starberth family were governors there. In your country you'd call 'em wardens.

It's traditional that the Starberths die of broken necks. Which isn't a very pleasant thing to look forward to."

Fell struck a match for his cigar, and Rampole saw that he was smiling.

"I'm not trying to scare you with ghost stories," he added, after he had sucked wheezingly on the cigar for a time. "I'm only trying to prepare you. We haven't your American briskness. It's in the air; the whole countryside is full of belief. So don't laugh if you hear about Peggy-with-the-Lantern, or the imp on Lincoln cathedral, or, more particularly, anything concerned with the prison."

There was a silence. Then Rampole said: "I'm not apt to laugh. All my life I've been wanting to see a haunted house. I don't believe, of course, but that doesn't detract from my interest. . . . What *is* the story concerned with the prison?"

" 'Too imaginative by half,' " the doctor muttered, staring at the ash on his cigar. "That was what Bob Melson said. —You shall have the full story tomorrow. I've kept copies of the papers. But young Martin has got to spend his hour in the Governor's Room, and open the safe and look at what's in there. You see, for about two hundred years the Starberths have owned the land on which Chatterham prison was built. They still own it; the borough never took it over, and it's held in what the lawyer chaps call 'entail' by the eldest son—can't be sold. On the evening of his twenty-fifth birthday, the eldest Starberth has got to go to the prison, open the safe in the Governor's Room, and take his chances. . . ."

"On what, sir?"

"I don't know. Nobody knows what's inside. It's not to be mentioned by the heir himself, until the keys are handed over to *his* son."

Rampole shifted. His brain pictured a grey ruin, an iron door, and a man with a lamp in his hand turning a rusty key. He said: "Good Lord! it sounds like—" but he could not find words, and he found himself wryly smiling.

"It's England. What's the matter?"

"I was only thinking that if this were America, there

would be reporters, news-reel cameras, and a crowd ten deep round the prison to see what happened."

He knew that he had said something wrong. He was always finding it out. Being with these English was like shaking hands with a friend whom you thought you knew, and suddenly finding the hand turned to a wisp of fog. There was a place where thoughts never met, and no similarity of language could cover the gap. He saw Dr. Fell looking at him with eyes screwed up behind his glasses; then, to his relief, the lexicographer laughed.

"I told you it was England," he replied. "Nobody will bother him. It's too much concerned with the belief that the Starberths die of broken necks."

"Well, sir?"

"That's the odd part of it," said Dr. Fell, inclining his big head. "They generally do."

No more was said on the subject. The wine at dinner seemed to have dulled the doctor's rolling spirits, or else he was occupied with some meditations which were to be seen only in the slow, steady pulsing and dimming of his cigar from the corner. Over his shoulders he pulled a frayed plaid shawl; the great mop of hair nodded forward. Rampole might have thought him asleep but for the gleam under his eyelids, the bright shrewd steadiness behind those eyeglasses on the black ribbon. . . .

The American's sense of unreality had closed in fully by the time they reached Chatterham. Now the red lights of the train were sinking away down the tracks; a whistle fluttered and sank with it, and the air of the station platform was chill. A dog barked distantly at the passage of the train, followed by a chorus which sullenly died. Their footsteps crunched with startling loudness on gravel as Rampole followed his host up from the platform.

A white road, winding between trees and flat meadows. Marshy ground, with a mist rising from it, and a gleam of black water under the moon. Then hedgerows, odorous with hawthorn; the pale green of corn stretching across rolling fields; crickets pulsing; the fragrance of dew on grass. Here was Dr. Fell, in a rakish slouch-hat, and the plaid shawl over his shoulders, stumping along on two canes. He had been up to London just for the day, he explained, and he had no luggage. Swinging a heavy valise, Rampole strode beside him. He had been startled, momentarily, to see a figure ahead of them—a figure in a nondescript coat and a travelling-cap, beating along the road, with sparks from a pipe flying out behind. Then he realized it was Payne. Despite his doddering walk, the lawyer covered ground with speed. Unsociable dog! Rampole could almost hear him growling to himself as he walked along. Yet there was small time to think of Payne; here *he* was, singing with adventure under a great alien sky, where not even the stars were familiar. He was very small and lost in this ancient England.

"There's the prison," said Dr. Fell.

They had topped a slight rise, and both of them stopped. The country sloped down and out, in flat fields intersected by hedgerows. Some distance ahead, muffled in trees, Rampole could see the church spire of the village; and farmhouses slept, with silver windows, in the rich night-fragrance of the soil. Near them and to the left stood a tall house of red brick, with white window-frames, austere in its clipped park beyond an avenue of oaks. ("The Hall," Dr. Fell said over his shoulder.) But the American was staring at the promontory to the right. Incongruous in this place, crude and powerful as Stonehenge, the stone walls of Chatterham prison humped against the sky.

They were large enough, though they seemed much bigger in the distortion of moonlight. And "humped," Rampole thought, was the word; there was one place where they seemed to surge and buckle over the crest of a hill. Through rents in the masonry vines were crooking fingers against the moon. A teeth of spikes ran along the top, and you could see tumbled chimneys. The place *looked* damp and slime-painted, from occupation by lizards; it was as though the marshes had crept inside and turned stagnant.

Rampole said suddenly: "I can almost feel insects beating against my face. Does it get you that way?"

His voice seemed very loud. Frogs were croaking somewhere, like querulous invalids. Dr. Fell pointed with one cane.

"Do you see that"—queer how he used the same word —"that hump up there, on the side where there's the fringe of Scotch firs? It's built out over a gully, and that's the Hag's Nook. In the old days, when the gallows used to stand on the edge of the hill, they'd give the spectators a show by attaching a very long rope to the condemned man's neck and chucking him over the brink with a sporting chance to tear his head off. There was no such thing as a drop-trap, you know, in those days."

Rampole shivered, his brain full of images. A hot day, with the lush countryside burning dark green, the white roads smoking, and the poppies at the roadside. A mumbling concourse of people in pigtails and knee-breeches, the dark-clad group in the cart creaking up the hill, and then somebody swinging like an unholy pendulum above the Hag's Nook. For the first time the countryside really seemed to be full of those mumbling voices. He turned, to find the doctor's eyes fixed on him.

"What did they do when they built the prison?"

"Kept it. But it was too easy to escape that way, they thought; walls built low, and several doors. So they made a kind of well below the gallows. The ground was marshy anyhow, and it filled easily. If somebody got loose and tried a jump he'd land in the well, and—they didn't pull him out. It wouldn't have been pleasant, dying with the things down there."

The doctor was scuffling his feet on the ground, and Rampole picked up the valise to go on. It was not pleasant, talking here. Voices boomed too loudly; and, besides, you had an uncomfortable sensation that you were being overheard. . . .

"That," added Dr. Fell, after a few wheezing steps, "was what did for the prison."

"How so?"

"When they cut down a person after they'd hanged him, they just let him drop into the well. Once the cholera got started . . ."

Rampole felt a qualm in his stomach, almost a physical nausea. He knew that he was warm despite the cool air. A whispering ran among the trees, lightly.

"I live not far from here," the other continued, as though he had mentioned nothing out of the way. He even spoke comfortably, like one pointing out the beauties of a city. "We're on the outskirts of the village. You can see the gallows side of the prison very well from there—and the window of the Governor's Room too."

Half a mile on, they turned off the road and struck up through a lane. Here was a crooked, sleepy old house, with plaster and oak beams above, and ivy-grown stone below. The moon was pale on its diamond-paned windows; evergreens grew close about its door, and the unkempt lawn showed white with daisies. Some sort of night bird complained in its sleep, twittering in the ivy.

"We won't wake my wife," said Dr. Fell. "She'll have left a cold supper in the kitchen, with plenty of beer. I— *What's the matter?*"

He started. He wheezed, and gave an almost convulsive jump, because Rampole could hear the slither of one cane in the wet grass. The American was staring out across the meadows to where—less than a quarter of a mile away— the side of Chatterham prison rose above the Scotch firs round Hag's Nook.

Rampole felt a damp heat prickling out on his body.

"Nothing," he said, loudly. And then he began to talk with great vigour. "Look here, sir, I don't want to inconvenience you. I'd have taken a different train, except there isn't any that gets here at a reasonable hour. I could easily go to Chatterham and find a hotel or an inn or—"

The old lexicographer chuckled. It was a reassuring sound in that place. He boomed, "Nonsense!" and thumped Rampole on the shoulder. Then Rampole thought, "He'll think I've got a scare," and hastily agreed. While Dr. Fell searched after a latch-key, he glanced again at the prison.

These old woman's tales might have influenced his outlook. But, just for a moment, he could have sworn that he had seen something looking over the wall of Chatterham prison. And he had a horrible impression that the something was *wet.* . . .

Chapter 3

SITTING now in Dr. Fell's study, on the afternoon of his first day at Yew Cottage, he was inclined to question everything in the nature of the fanciful. This solid little house, with its oil-lamps and its primitive plumbing, made him feel as though he were on a vacation in some hunting-lodge in the Adirondacks, say; that presently they would all go back to New York, and that a car door would slam, to be opened only by the doorman of his own apartment house.

But here it was—the bees astir in a sunlit garden, the sun-dial and bird-houses, the smell of old wood and fresh curtains; not like anything except England. Bacon and eggs had a savour here that he had never fully appreciated before. So had pipe tobacco. The countryside here didn't look artificial, as country has a habit of looking when you live in it only during the summer; nor did it at all resemble the shrubs on the roof of a penthouse.

And here was Dr. Fell, pottering about his domain in a broad-brimmed white hat, looking sleepily amiable and doing nothing with an engrossed thoroughness. Here was Mrs. Fell, a very small and bustling and cheerful woman who was always knocking things over. Twenty times in a morning you would hear a small crash, whereupon she would cry, "Bother!" and go whisking on with her cleaning until the ensuing mishap. She had, moreover, a habit of sticking her head out of windows all over the house, one after the other, to address some question to her husband. You would just place her at the front of the house when out she would pop at a rear window, like a cuckoo out of a clock, to wave cheerfully at Rampole and ask her husband where something was. He always looked mildly surprised, and never knew. So back she would go, previous to her reappearance at a side window with a pillow or a dust-cloth in her hand. To Rampole, lounging in a deck-chair under a lime tree and smoking his pipe, it suggested one of those Swiss barometers where the revolving figures are for ever going in and coming out of a châlet to indicate the weather.

The mornings and a part of the afternoons Dr. Fell usually devoted to the composition of his great work, *The Drinking Customs of England from the Earliest Days,* a monumental labour into which he had put six years of scholarly research. He loved to trace out the origin of such quaint terms as drinking *supernaugulum;* carouse the hunter's hoop; quaff *upse freez crosse;* and with *health, gloves, mumpes, frolickes,* and other curious terms of the tankard. Even in speaking of it to Rampole, he took violent issue with the treatises of such authors as Tom Nash *(Pierce Pennilesse,* 1595) and George Gascoigne *(A delicate Diet for daintie mouthed Dronkardes, wherein the fowle Abuse of common carowsing and quaffing with hartie Draughtes is honestlie admonished,* 1576).

The morning passed, with the blackbirds piping from the meadow and drowsy sunlight drawing all suggestion of evil from Chatterham prison. But the mellowness of afternoon brought him to the doctor's study, where his host was tapping tobacco into a pipe. Dr. Fell wore an old shooting-jacket, and his white hat was hung on a corner of the stone mantelpiece. On the table before him were papers, at which he kept stealing furtive glances.

"There will be guests to tea," said the doctor. "The rector is coming, and young Martin Starberth and his sister—they live at the Hall, you know; the postman tells me they got in this morning. Perhaps Starberth's cousin, too, though *he's* a sullen sort of dog for your money. I suppose you'll want to know more about the prison?"

"Well, if it's not—"

"Violating any confidence? Oh no. Everybody knows about it. I'm rather curious to see young Martin, myself. He's been in America for two years, and his sister has run the Hall since their father died. A great girl, that. Old Timothy died in rather a curious way."

"A broken neck?" Rampole inquired, as the other hesitated.

Dr. Fell grunted. "If he didn't break his neck, he broke

most of the rest of him. The man was fearfully smashed up. He was out riding just after sunset, and his horse threw him—apparently while he was coming down Chatterham prison hill near the Hag's Nook. They found him late that night, lying in the underbrush. The horse was near by, whinnying in a kind of terror. Old Jenkins—that's one of his tenants—found him, and Jenkins said the noises his horse was making were one of the worst things he'd ever heard. He died the next day. He was fully conscious, too, up to the end."

Several times during his stay Rampole had the suspicion that his host might have been making game of him as an American. But he knew differently now. Dr. Fell was plodding through these gruesome anecdotes because something worried him. He talked to relieve himself. Behind the shiftings of his eyes, and his uneasy rollings in the chair, there was a doubt—a suspicion—even a dread. His asthmatic breaths were loud in the quiet room, turning dusky against the afternoon sun.

Rampole said, "I suppose it revived the old superstition."

"It did. But then we've always had superstitions hereabouts. No, this business suggested something worse than that."

"You mean—"

"Murder," said Dr. Fell.

He was bending forward. His eyes had grown large behind the glasses, and his ruddy face looked hard. He began to speak rapidly:

"Mind! I say nothing. It may be fancy, and it's no concern of mine. H'mf. But Dr. Markley, the coroner, said he'd got a blow across the base of the skull which might have been caused by the fall, and then again might not. He looked, it seemed to me, less as though he'd had a fall than that somebody had trampled on him. I don't mean by a horse, either. Another thing: it was a damp evening in October, and he was lying in marshy ground, but that didn't seem to account wholly for the fact that the body was *wet*."

Rampole looked steadily at his host. He found that his fingers had closed on the arms of his chair.

"But you say he was conscious, sir. Didn't he speak?"

"I wasn't there, of course. I got the story from the rector, and from Payne, too; you remember Payne? Yes, he spoke. He not only spoke, but he seemed to be in a sort of ghoulish high spirits. Just at daybreak they knew he was dying. He had been writing, Dr. Markley said, on a board propped across him; they tried to prevent it, but he just showed his teeth. 'Instructions for my son,' he said—Martin was in America, as I told you—'there's the ordeal to be gone through, isn't there?' "

Dr. Fell stopped to light his pipe. He pulled the flame down fiercely into the bowl, as though it might give him clearer sight.

"They hesitated in calling Mr. Saunders, the rector, because Timothy was an old sinner and a furious hater of the Church. But he always said Saunders was an honest man, even if he didn't agree with him, so they brought him out at dawn to see whether the old man would agree to prayers for the dying. He went in to see old Timothy alone, and after a while he came out wiping the sweat off his forehead. 'My God!' says the rector, as though he were praying, 'the man's not in his right mind. Somebody go in there with me.' 'Will he hear the commitment?' says Timothy's nephew, who was looking queer. 'Yes, yes,' says the rector, 'but it isn't that. It's the way he's talking.' 'What did he say?' asks the nephew. 'I'm not allowed to tell you that,' says the rector, 'but I wish I could.'

"In the bedroom they could hear Timothy croaking gleefully, though he couldn't move for the splints. He called out to see Dorothy next, alone, and after that Payne, his lawyer. It was Payne who called out that he was going fast. So just as daylight was growing outside the windows, they all went into the big oak room with the canopied bedstead. Timothy was nearly speechless now, but he said one clear word, which was, 'Handkerchief,' and he seemed to be grinning. The rest of them knelt down while the rector said the prayers, and just as Saunders was making the sign of the cross, some froth came out of Timothy's mouth, and he jerked once and died."

During a long silence, Rampole could hear the blackbirds piping outside. The sun was growing long and wan in the branches of the yew.

"It's odd enough," the American assented at length. "But if he said nothing, you've hardly any grounds to suspect murder."

"Haven't I?" said Dr. Fell, musingly. "Well, maybe not. ... The same night—of the day he died, I mean—the same night there was a light in the window of the Governor's Room."

"Did anybody investigate?"

"No. You couldn't get any of the villagers near there after dark for a hundred pounds."

"Oh, well! A superstitious imagination—"

"It wasn't a superstitious imagination," the doctor affirmed, shaking his head. "At least, I don't think so. I saw the light myself."

Rampole said, slowly, "And tonight your Martin Starberth spends an hour in the Governor's Room."

"Yes. If he doesn't funk it. He's always been a nervous chap, one of the dreamy kind, and he was always a little ticklish about the prison. The last time he was in Chatterham was about a year ago, when he came home for the reading of Timothy's will. One of the specifications of the inheritance, of course, was that he should pass the customary 'ordeal.' Then he left his sister and his cousin Herbert in charge of the Hall, and returned to America. He's in England only for the—the merry festivities."

Rampole shook his head.

"You've told me a lot about it," he said; "all but the origin. What I don't see is the reason behind these traditions."

Dr. Fell took off his eyeglasses and put on a pair of owlish reading-spectacles. For a moment he bent over the sheets of paper on his desk, his hands at his temples.

"I have here copies of the official journals, made from day to day like a ship's log, of Anthony Starberth, Esquire, Governor of Chatterham Prison 1797-1820, and of Martin

Starberth, Esquire, Governor 1821-1837. The originals are kept at the Hall; old Timothy gave me permission to copy them. They ought to be published in book form, one day, as a sidelight on the penal methods of that day." He remained for a time with his head down, drawing slowly on his pipe and staring with brooding eyes at the inkwell. "Previous to the latter part of the eighteenth century, you see, there were very few *detention* prisons in Europe. Criminals were either hanged outright, or branded and mutilated and turned loose, or deported to the colonies. There were exceptions, like the debtors, but in general no distinction was made between those who had been tried and those who were awaiting trial; they were flung in willy-nilly, under a vicious system.

"A man named John Howard started an agitation for detention prisons. Chatterham prison was begun even before Milbank, which is generally supposed to be the oldest. It was built by the convicts who were to occupy it, of stone quarried from the Starberth lands, under the muskets of a redcoat troop commissioned by George III for that purpose. The cat was freely used, and sluggards were hung up by their thumbs or otherwise tortured. Every stone, you see, has meant blood."

As he paused, old words came unbidden to Rampole's mind, and he repeated them: " 'There was a great crying in the land . . .' "

"Yes. A great and bitter one. The governorship, of course, was given to Anthony Starberth. His family had been active in such interests for a long time; Anthony's father, I believe, had been deputy sheriff of Lincoln Bourough. It has been recorded," said Dr. Fell, a long sniff rumbling up in his nose, "that every day during the building, light or dark, sun or sleet, Anthony would come riding out on a dappled mare to oversee the work. The convicts grew to know him, and to hate him. They would always see him sitting on his horse, up against the sky and the black line of the marshes, in his three-cornered hat and his blue camlet cloak.

"Anthony had one eye put out in a duel. He was a bit of a dandy, though very miserly except where his person was concerned; he was stingy and cruel; he wrote bad verses by the hour, and hated his family for ridiculing them. I believe he used to say they would pay for making fun of his verses.

"They finished the prison in 1797, and Anthony moved in. He was the one who instituted the rule that the eldest son must look at what he'd left in the safe of the Governor's Room. His governorship, I needn't tell you, was a trifle worse than hellish; I'm deliberately toning down the whole recital. His one eye and his grin . . . it was a good job," Dr. Fell said, putting his palm down flat on the papers as though he were trying to blot out the writing—"it was a good job, my boy, that he made his arrangements for death when he did."

"What happened to him?"

"*Gideon!*" cried a reproachful voice, followed by a fusillade of knocks on the study door which made Rampole jump. "Gideon! *Tea!*"

"Eh?" said Dr. Fell, looking up blankly.

Mrs. Fell stated a grievance. "Tea, Gideon! And I wish you'd let that horrible beer alone, though goodness knows the butter-cakes are bad enough, and it's so stuffy in there, and I see the rector and Miss Starberth coming up the road as it is." There was the sound of a deep breath being drawn, whereupon Mrs. Fell summed it up saying, "Tea!"

The doctor rose with a sigh, and they heard her fluttering down the passage, repeating, "Bother, bother, bother!" like the exhaust of an automobile.

"We'll save it," said Dr. Fell.

Dorothy Starberth was coming up the lane, moving with her free stride beside a large and bald-headed man who was fanning himself with his hat. Rampole felt a momentary qualm. Easy!— Don't act like a kid, now! He could hear her light, mocking voice. She was wearing a yellow jumper with a high neck, and some sort of brown skirt and coat into whose pockets her hands were thrust. The sun glimmered on her rich black hair, caught carelessly round her head; and as she turned her head from side to side you could see a clear profile, somehow as poised as a bird's wing. Then they were coming across the lawn, and the dark-blue eyes were fixed on him under long lashes. . . .

"I think you know Miss Starberth," Dr. Fell was saying. "Mr. Saunders, this is Mr. Rampole, from America. He's staying with us."

Rampole found his hand grasped with the vigour of muscular Christianity by the large and bald-headed man. Mr. Thomas Saunders was smiling professionally, his shaven jowls gleaming; he was one of those clergymen whom people praise by saying that they are not at all like clergymen. His forehead was steaming, but his bland blue eyes were as alert as a scoutmaster's. Mr. Saunders was forty years old, and looked much younger. He served his creed, you felt, as clearly and unthinkingly as he had served Eton (or Harrow, or Winchester, or whatever it was) on the playing-fields. Round his pink skull a fringe of fair hair fluffed like a tonsure, and he wore an enormous watch-chain.

"I am delighted to make your acquaintance, sir," the rector boomed, heartily. "I—ah—was pleased to know many of your countrymen during the war. Cousins over the sea, you know; cousins over the sea!"

He laughed, lightly and professionally. This air of professional smoothness and ease irritated the American; he murmured something and turned towards Dorothy Starberth. . . .

"How do you do?" she said, extending a cool hand. "It's jolly seeing you again!— How did you leave our mutual friends, the Harrises?"

Rampole was about to demand, *"Who?"* when he caught the expectant innocence of her glance and the half-smile which animated it.

"Ah, the Harrises," he said. "Splendid, thank you, splendid." With a startling burst of inspiration he added. "Muriel is cutting a tooth."

As nobody seemed impressed by this intelligence, and he was a trifle nervous about the ring of authenticity he had put into it, he was about to add further intimate details of the Harris household when Mrs. Fell suddenly shot out of the front door in another of her cuckoo-like appearances, to take charge of them all. She made a variety of unintelligible remarks which seemed to be chiefly concerned with beer, butter-cakes, and the dear thoughtfulness of the rector; and had he quite recovered from being drenched by that horrible water-sprinkler; and was he *sure* he hadn't got pneumonia? Mr. Saunders coughed experimentally, and said he hadn't.

"Dear me . . . bother!" said Mrs. Fell, walking into some plants. "So near-sighted, blind as a bat, dear Mr. Saunders. . . . And my dear," whirling on the girl, "where is your brother? You said he'd be here."

Momentarily the shade was back on Dorothy Starberth's face, as Rampole had seen it last night. She hesitated, putting a hand to her wrist as though she would like to look at her watch; but taking it away instantly.

"Oh, he'll be here," she said. "He's in the village—buying some things. He'll be along directly."

The tea table was set out in the garden behind the house; it was shaded by a large lime tree, and a singing stream ran a few yards away. Rampole and the girl lagged behind the other three on the way.

"Baby Eadwig," said Rampole, "is down with mumps—"

"Smallpox. Ugh, you beast! I thought you were going to give me away. And in a community like this—I say, how did they know we'd met?"

"Some old fool of a lawyer saw us talking on the platform. But I thought you were going to give *me* away."

At this extraordinary coincidence they both turned to look at each other, and he saw her eyes shining again. He felt exhilarated, but prickly. He said, "Ha!" rather like Dr. Fell, and noticed the dappling of shadows that trembled on the grass, and they both laughed. She went on in a low voice:

"I can't tell you—I was feeling desperately low last night, what with one thing and another. And London is so big, and everything was wrong. I wanted to talk to somebody. And then you bumped into me and you looked nice, so I did."

Rampole felt a desire to give somebody a joyous poke in the jaw. In imagination he lashed out triumphantly. He had a sensation as though somebody were pumping air into his chest.

He said, not wittily, but—be honest with yourself, sneering peruser!—very naturally:

"I'm glad you did."

"So am I."

"Glad?"

"Glad."

"HAH!" said Rampole, exhaling the air in triumph.

From ahead of them rose Mrs. Fell's thin voice. "— Azaleas, petunias, geraniums, hollyhocks, honeysuckle, and eglantine!" she shrilled, as though she were calling trains. "I can't see 'em, on account of being so near-sighted, but I know they're there." With a beaming if somewhat vague smile she grasped the newcomers and urged them into chairs. "Oh, Gideon, my love, you're not going after that horrible beer, are you?"

Dr. Fell was already bending over the stream. Puffing laboriously, he extracted several beaded bottles and hauled himself up on one cane.

"Notice, Mr. Rampole," said the rector, with an air of comfortable tolerance. "I often think," he continued, as though he were launching a terrible accusation but slyly smiling to mitigate it—"I often think that the good doctor can't be English at all. This barbarous habit of drinking beer at tea-time—my dear sir! It isn't—well, it isn't English, you know!"

Dr. Fell raised a fiery face.

"Sir," he said, "it's tea that isn't English, let me inform you. I want you to look at the appendix of my book, Note 86, Chapter 9, devoted to such things as tea, cocoa, and that unmentionably awful beverage known as the ice-cream soda. Tea, you will find, came into England from Holland in 1666. From Holland, her bitter enemy; and in Holland they contemptuously called it hay-water. Even the French couldn't stand it. Patin calls tea *'l'impertinente nouveauté du siècle,'* and Dr. Duncan, in his *Treatise on Hot Liquors*—"

"And in front of the rector, too!" said Mrs. Fell, wailing.

"Eh?" said the doctor, breaking off with some vague

idea that she thought he was swearing. "What, my dear?"

"Beer," said Mrs. Fell.

"Oh, hell!" said the doctor, violently. "Excuse me, excuse me." He turned to Rampole. "Will *you* have some beer with me, my boy?"

"Why, yes," the other answered, with gratitude. "Thanks, I will."

"—and coming out of that cold water, it'll probably give you both pneumonia," Mrs. Fell said, darkly. She seemed to have an *idée fixe* on the subject of pneumonia. "What it's coming to I don't know—more tea, Mr. Saunders, and there are the cakes beside you—with everybody catching pneumonia the way they are, and that poor young man having to sit up in that draughty governor's place tonight; *he'll* probably have pneu—"

There was an abrupt silence. Then Saunders began talking very smoothly and easily about the flowers, pointing to a bed of geraniums; he seemed to be trying to alter their minds by altering the direction of their gaze. Dr. Fell joined in the discussion, glowering at his wife. She was quite unconscious of having opened that forbidden subject. But constraint had come upon the party under the lime tree, and would not go away.

A soft pink afterglow had crept across the garden, though it would be yet light for several hours. In silver flakes through the tree branches the west glowed clear and warm. All of them, even Mrs. Fell, were silent, staring at the tea-service. A wicker chair creaked. Distantly they could hear the clank and jangle of bells; and Rampole pictured the cows, somehow lonely in a vast meadow, being driven home through mysterious dusk. A deeper hum pulsed in the air.

Dorothy Starberth rose suddenly.

"Stupid of me!" she said. "I'd almost forgot. I must go in to the village and get some cigarettes before the tobacconist closes." She smiled at them, with an affected ease which deceived nobody; the smile was like a mask. She glanced with elaborate carelessness at her watch. "It's been divine being here, Mrs. Fell. You must come over to the Hall soon. I say," with an air of inspiration, to Rampole, "wouldn't you like to walk along with me? You haven't seen our village yet, have you? We've rather a good early Gothic church, as Mr. Saunders would tell you."

"Yes, indeed." The rector seemed to hesitate, looked at them in a heavily paternal way, and waved his hand. "Go along, do. I'll have another cup of tea, if Mrs. Fell doesn't mind. It's so comfortable here," he beamed on his hostess; "makes one ashamed of being lazy."

He sat back with a smug air, as of one who murmurs, "Ah, I was young once!" but Rampole had the impression that he didn't like it at all. It suddenly struck the American that this patronizing old bald-head (sic, in Rampole's inflamed thoughts) had a more than clerical interest in Dorothy Starberth. Why, damn the man—! Come to think of it, the way he had hung over her shoulder, smoothly, as they walked down the lane. . . .

"I had to get out of there," the girl said, half breathlessly. Their quick footsteps rustled in the grass. "I wanted to walk, fast."

"I know."

"When you're walking," she explained, in that same breathless voice, "you feel free; you don't feel you have to keep things in the air, like a juggler, and strain yourself not to drop one. . . . Oh!"

They were going down the shadowed lane, where the grass muffled their footsteps. Its junction with the road was hidden by the hedgerows, but they became aware of feet scuffling in the dust out there, and a murmur of conversation. Abruptly one voice rose. It came twitching through the soft air, alive and ugly.

"You know the word for it right enough," the voice said. "The word is *Gallows*. Yes, and you know it as well as I do."

The voice laughed. Dorothy Starberth stopped, and her face—sharp against the dark-green hedge—was a face of fear.

Chapter 4

"I SHALL have to hurry to catch that tobacconist," the girl declared, instantly. Her small voice was raised, insistent to be heard. "Good Lord! it's past six o'clock!—But then he always reserves a box of my special brand, every day, and if I'm not there . . . I say! Hullo, Martin!"

She stepped out into the road, motioning Rampole to follow. The murmur of voices had frozen. Standing in the middle of the road, still with his hand half lifted, a slightly built young man had twisted round to face her. He had the spoiled, selfconscious face of one who generally gets his way with women, with dark hair and a contemptuous mouth; and he was a little drunk. He swayed a little now. Behind him Rampole could see a crooked track in the white dust to show his progress.

"Hello, Dot!" he said, abruptly. "You can certainly sneak up on a fellow. What's the idea?"

He spoke with a strong attempt at an American accent. Laying a hand on the arm of the person with him, he assumed dignity. This latter was obviously a relation; his features were blunt where the other's were delicate, his clothes rode high on him, and his hat did not have the same careless curve as Martin Starberth's, but there was an undeniable resemblance. He looked embarrassed, and his hands seemed too big.

"Been—been in to tea, Dorothy?" he asked, fumbling. "Sorry we're late. We—we were detained."

"Of course," the girl said, impassively. "May I present: Mr. Rampole, Mr. Martin Starberth, Mr. Herbert Starberth. Mr. Rampole's a countryman of yours, Martin."

"You an American?" demanded Martin, in a brisk manner. "That's good. Whereya from? New York? That's good. I just left there. I'm in the publishing business. Whereya staying?—Fell's? *That* old codger. Look here, come on up to the house and I'll give you a little drink."

"We're going to tea, Martin," Herbert said, with a sort of stolid patience.

"Ah, t'ell with that tea stuff. Listen, you come up to the house—"

"You'd best not go to tea, Martin," said his sister; "and, please, no more to drink. I wouldn't care, but you know why."

Martin looked at her. "I'm going to tea," he said, sticking out his neck, "and, what's more, I'm going to have another little drink. Come on, Bert."

He had forgotten Rampole, for which the American was grateful. He adjusted his hat. He brushed his arms and shoulders, though there was no dust on him, and straightened up, clearing his throat. As the stolid Herbert guided him on, Dorothy whispered: "Don't let him go there, and see that he's all right by dinner-time. Do you hear?"

Martin heard it, too. He turned, put his head on one side, and folded his arms.

"You think I'm drunk, don't you?" he demanded, studying her.

"Please, Martin!"

"Well, I'll show you whether I'm drunk or not! Come on, Bert."

Rampole quickened his step beside the girl as they moved off the other way. As they turned a bend in the road he could hear the cousins arguing, Herbert in a low voice, and Martin vociferously, his hat pulled down on his eyebrows.

For a time they walked in silence. That momentary encounter had jarred against the fragrance of the hedgerows, but it was swept away by the wind over the grass in the meadows that surrounded them. The sky was watery yellow, luminous as glass, along the west; firs stood up black against it, and even the low bog water had lights of gold. Here were the lowlands, sloping up into wolds; and from a distance the flocks of white-faced sheep looked like toys out of a child's Noah's ark.

"You mustn't think," the girl said, looking straight ahead of her and speaking very low—"you mustn't think he's always like that. He isn't. But just now there's so much on his mind, and he tries to conceal it by drinking, and it comes out in bravado."

"I knew there was a lot on his mind. You can't blame him."

"Dr. Fell told you?"

"A little. He said it was no secret."

She clenched her hands. "Oh no. That's the worst of it. It's no secret. Everybody knows, and they all turn their heads away. You're *alone* with it, do you see? They can't talk about it in public; it isn't done. They can't talk about it to me. And *I* can't mention it either. . . ."

A pause. Then she turned to him almost fiercely.

"You say you understand, and it's nice of you; but you don't! Growing up with the thing. . . . I remember, when Martin and I were tiny children, mother holding us each up to the window so that we could see the prison. She's dead now, you know. And father."

He said, gently, "Don't you think you're making too much of a legend?"

"I told you—you wouldn't understand."

Her voice was dry and monotonous, and he felt a stab. He was conscious of searching desperately for words, feeling his inadequacy every time he found one; yet groping after a common point with her, as he might have groped after a lamp in a haunted room.

"I'm not intelligent about practical things," he said, blankly. "When I get away from books or football, and up against the world, I'm just mixed up. But I think that, whatever you told me, I would understand it, provided it concerned you."

Across the lowlands drifted a clangor of bells. A slow, sad, ancient clangor, which swung in the air and was a part of it. Far ahead, the church-spire among the oaks caught the last light. Birds twittered into flight from its belfry as the bell notes clashed with iron weariness, and a rook was cawing. . . . They had stopped by a stone bridge over a broad stream. Dorothy Starberth turned and looked at him.

"If you can say that," she said, "it's all I could ask."

Her lips moved slowly, with a faint smile, and the breeze was smoothing her dark hair.

"I hate practicality," she went on, with sudden vehemence. "I've had to be practical ever since father died. Herbert's a good old dependable horse, with about as much imagination as that hayrick over there. And there's Mrs. Colonel Granby, and Leutitia Markley, and Mrs. Payne who uses the ouija board, and Miss Porterson who almost gets round to reading the new books. There's Wilfrid Denim, who comes to pay me attentions every Thursday night at nine P.M. precisely, runs out of new conversational matter at nine five, and continues to talk about a play he saw in London three years ago, or else illustrates tennis strokes till you think he's jolly well got St. Vitus' dance. Oh yes—and Mr. Saunders. St. George for merrie England, and if Harrow beats Eton this year the country's in the hands of the Socialists. *Woof!*"

She wound up breathlessly, again shaking her head with vehemence until she had to smooth back the cloudy hair. Then she smiled, rather shame-facedly. "I don't know what you'll think of me for talking like this—"

"I think you're absolutely right!" Rampole returned, enthusiastically. He had particularly relished that crack about Mr. Saunders. "Down with ouija boards. *À bas le* tennis. I hope Harrow knocks Eton for a row of brick—ahem! What I mean to say is, you're absolutely right and long live Socialism."

"I didn't say anything about Socialism."

"Well, say something about it, then," he offered, magnanimously. "Go on, say something about it. Hurrah for Norman Thomas! God bless—"

"But *why,* silly? Why?"

"Because Mr. Saunders wouldn't like it," explained Rampole. The thesis seemed to him a good one, if vague. But another idea struck him, and he inquired, suspiciously: "Who is this Wilfrid person who comes round to see you every Thursday night? 'Wilfrid' is a lousy name, anyway. It sounds like somebody with marcelled hair."

She slid off the coping of the bridge, and she seemed somehow set free in the strength of her small body. Her laughter—real and swashbuckling, as he had heard it the night before—had got out of its prison, too.

"I say! We'll *never* get those cigarettes if we don't hurry. . . . I feel the way you talk. D'you want to run for it? But take it easy; it's a quarter of a mile."

Rampole said, "What ho!" and they clipped out past the hayricks with the wind in their faces, and Dorothy Starberth was still laughing.

"I hope I meet Mrs. Colonel Granby," she said, breathlessly. She seemed to think this a wicked idea, and turned a flushed face over her shoulder, eyes dancing. "It's nice, it's nice.—Ugh! I'm glad I have on low-heeled shoes."

"Want to speed it up?"

"Beast! I'm warm already. I say, are you a track man?"

"Hmf. A little."

A little. Through his brain ran white letters on black boards, in a dusky room off the campus, where there were silver cups in glass cases and embalmed footballs with dates painted on them. Then, with the road flying past, he remembered another scene of just such an exhilaration as he felt now. November, with a surf of sound beating, the rasp of breathing, and the quarterback declaiming signals like a ham actor. Thick headache. Little wires in his legs drawn tight, and cold fingers without feeling in them. Then the wheeze and buckle of the line, and thuds. Suddenly the cold air streaming in his face, a sensation of flying over white lines on legs wired like a puppet's, and a muddy object he plucked out of the air just under the goal-posts. . . . He heard again that stupefying roar, and felt his stomach opening and shutting as the roar lifted the dusky air like a lid off a kettle. That had been only last autumn, and it seemed a thousand years ago. Here he was on a weirder adventure in the twilight, with a girl whose very presence was like the tingle of those lost, roaring thousand years.

"A little," he repeated, suddenly, drawing a deep breath.

They were into the outskirts of the village, where thick-waisted trees shaded white shop-fronts, and the bricks of the sidewalks ran in crooked patterns like a child's writing-exercise. A woman stopped to look at them. A man on a bicycle goggled so much that he ran into the ditch and swore.

Leaning up against a tree, flushed and panting, Dorothy laughed.

"I've had enough of your silly game," she said, her eyes very bright. "But, O Lord! I feel better!"

From the furious excitement which had possessed them, neither knowing why, they passed to deep contentment and became carefully decorous. They got the cigarettes, the tobacconist explaining as 'ow he had stopped there after hours, and Rampole gratified a long-cherished wish to buy a church-warden pipe. He was intrigued by the chemist's shop; with its large glass vats of red and green and its impressive array of drugs, it was like something out of a mediæval tale. There was an inn, called The Friar Tuck, and a public-house called The Goat and Bunch of Grapes. Rampole was steered away from the latter only by the girl's (to him) inexplicable refusal to accompany him into the bar. All in all, he was much impressed.

"You can get a shave and a hair-cut in the cigar store," he continued to muse. "It isn't so different from America, after all."

He felt so fine that even the trials were nothing. They ran into Mrs. Theodosia Payne, the lawyer's wife, who was stalking grimly along the High Street with her ouija board under her arm. Mrs. Payne had a formidable hat. She moved her jaws like a ventriloquist's dummy, but spoke like a sergeant-major. Nevertheless, Rampole listened with Chesterfieldian politeness while she explained the vagaries of Lucius, her "control"—apparently an erratic and dissipated member of the spirit world, who skidded all over the board and spelled with a strong cockney accent. Dorothy saw her companion's face looking dangerously apoplectic, and got him away from Mrs. Payne before they both exploded into mirth.

It was nearly eight o'clock before they started back. Everything pleased these two, from the street lamps (which resembled glass coffins, and burnt a very consumptive sort of gas) to a tiny shop with a bell over the door, where you could get gilt-covered gingerbread animals and the sheets of long-forgotten comic songs. Rampole had always had a passion for buying useless junk, on the two sound principles that he didn't need it and that he had money to spend; so, finding a kindred spirit who didn't think it was childish, he indulged. They went back through a luminous dusk, the song-sheets held between them like a hymnal, earnestly singing a lament called, "Where Was You, 'Arry, on the Last Bank 'Oliday?"— and Dorothy was sternly ordered to repress her hilarity in the pathetic parts.

"It's been glorious," the girl said when they had almost reached the lane leading to Dr. Fell's. "It never occurred to me that there was anything interesting in Chatterham. I'm sorry to go home."

"It never occurred to me, either," he said, blankly. "It just seemed that way this afternoon."

They meditated this a moment, looking at each other.

"We've got time for one more," he suggested, as though that were the most important thing in the world. "Do you want to try 'The Rose of Bloomsbury Square'?"

"Oh no! Dr. Fell's an old dear, but I've got to preserve some dignity. I saw Mrs. Colonel Granby peeping through the curtains all the time we were in the village. Besides, it's getting late. . . ."

"Well—"

"And so—"

They both hesitated. Rampole felt a little unreal, and his heart was pounding with enormous rhythm. All about them the yellow sky had changed to a darkling light edged with purple. The fragrance of the hedgerows had become almost overpowering. Her eyes were very strong, very living, and yet veiled as though with pain; they went over his face with desperate seeking. Though he was looking only there, he somehow felt that her hands were extending. . . .

He caught her hands. "Let me walk home with you," he said, heavily; "let me—"

"Ahoy there!" boomed a voice from up the lane. "Hold on! Wait a minute."

Rampole felt something at his heart that was like a

physical jerk. He was trembling, and he felt through her warm hands that she was trembling, too. The voice broke such an emotional tensity that they both felt bewildered; and then the girl began to laugh.

Dr. Fell loomed up, puffing, out of the lane. Behind him Rampole saw a figure that looked familiar; yes, it was Payne, with the curved pipe in his mouth. He seemed to be chewing it.

Dread, coming back again after a few brief hours. . . .

The doctor looked very grave. He stopped to get his breath, leaning one cane up against his leg.

"I don't want to alarm you, Dorothy," he began, "and I know the subject is taboo; all the same, this is a time for speaking straight out—"

"Er!" said Payne, warningly, making a rasp in his throat. "The—er—guest?"

"He knows all about it. Now, girl, it's none of my business, I know—"

"Please tell me!" She clenched her hands.

"Your brother was here. We were a bit worried about the state he's in. I don't mean the drinking. That'll pass off; anyway, he was sick, and he was almost cold sober when he left. But it's the fright he's in; you could see it in the wild and defiant way he acted. We don't want him to get wrought up and do himself an injury over this silly business. Do you see?"

"Well? Go on!"

"The rector and your cousin took him home. Saunders is very much upset about this thing. Look here, I'll be absolutely frank. You know, of course, that before your father died he told Saunders something under a sort of seal of confession; and Saunders just thought he was out of his head at the time? But he's beginning to wonder. *Now there may not be anything in this,* but—just in case —we're going to keep guard. The window of the Governor's Room is plainly visible from here, and this house isn't much over three hundred yards from the prison itself. Do you see?"

"Yes!"

"Saunders and I, and Mr. Rampole, if he will, are

going to be on the watch all the time. There'll be a moon, and we can see Martin when he goes in. All you have to do is walk to the front of the lawn, and you have a good view of the front gates. Any noise, any disturbance, anything at all suspicious—Saunders and the young un here will be across that meadow before a ghost could vanish." He smiled, putting his hand on her shoulder. "This is all moonshine, I know, and I'm just a crazy old man. But I've known your people a long time—you see? Now, then, what time does the vigil commence?"

"At eleven o'clock."

"Ah, I thought so. Now, then, just after he's left the Hall, *telephone us.* We'll be watching. Naturally, you're not to mention this to him; it isn't supposed to be done, and if he knew it he might be in just such a state of nervous bravado to go the other way and block our plans. But you might suggest to him that he sit somewhere near the window with his light."

Dorothy drew a deep breath. "I knew there was something in it," she said, dully. "I knew you were all keeping something from me. . . . O my God! why does he have to go, anyway? Why can't we break a silly custom, and—"

"Not unless you want to lose the estate," Payne said, gruffly. "Sorry. But that's the way it's arranged. And I have to administer it. I have to deliver several keys—there's more than one door to be got through—to the heir. When he returns them to me, he must show me a certain thing from inside that vault, never mind what, to show me he's really opened it."

Again the lawyer's teeth gripped his pipe hard. The whites of his eyes looked luminous in the dusk.

"Miss Starberth knew all that, gentlemen, whether the rest of you did or not," he snapped. "We grow frank. Very well. Permit me to shout *my* affairs from the church spire. My father held this trust from the Starberths before me. So did my grandfather, and his grandfather. I state these details, gentlemen, so as not to seem a fool for technicalities. Even if I wanted to break the law, I tell you frankly I wouldn't break the trust."

"Well, let him forfeit the estate, then! Do you think any of us would care a snap of our fingers—"

Payne cut her short, testily: "Well, *he* isn't such a fool, however you and Bert feel about it. Good Lord! girl, do you want to be a pauper as well as a laughingstock? This procedure may be foolish. Very well. But it's the law and it's a trust." He brought the palms of his hands together with a sort of hollow *thock*. "I'll tell you what is more foolish. Your fears. No Starberth has suffered harm like that since 1837. Just because your father happened to be near the Hag's Nook when his horse threw him—"

"Don't!" the girl said, wretchedly.

Her hand quivered, and Rampole took a step forward. He did not speak; his throat felt hot and sanded with fury. But he thought, If I hear that man's voice a minute longer, by God! I'll break his jaw.

"You've said enough, Payne, don't you think?" grunted Dr. Fell.

"Ah," said Payne. "Just so."

Anger was in the air. They heard a small noise of Payne sucking his leathery jaws in against his teeth. He repeated, "Just so!" in his low, dry voice, but you knew that he felt the licking flames.

"If you will excuse me, gentlemen," he continued, very impassive, "I shall accompany Miss Starberth. . . . No, sir," as Rampole made a movement, "on this occasion, no. There are confidential matters I must express. Without interference, I hope. I have already discharged a part of my duty in handing over the keys to Mr. Martin Starberth. The rest remains. As—ah—possibly an older friend than the rest of you," his thin voice went high and rasping, and he almost snarled, "I may possibly be permitted to keep *some* matters confidential."

Rampole was so mad that he came close to an absurd gulp. "Did you say 'manners'?" he asked.

"Steady," said Dr. Fell.

"Come along, Miss Starberth," said the lawyer.

They saw him shoot in his cuffs and hobble forward, and the white flash of his eyes as he glanced back over his shoulder. Rampole pressed the girl's hand; then both of them were gone. . . .

"Tut, tut!" complained the doctor, after a pause. "Don't swear. He's only jealous of his position as family adviser. I'm much too worried to swear. I had a theory, but . . . I don't know. It's going all wrong. All wrong. . . . Come along to dinner."

Mumbling to himself, he led the way up the lane. Something cried aloud in Rampole's heart, and the dusk was full of phantoms. For a moment the released, laughing creature with the wind in her hair as she raced; the wistfulness of the square sombre face, wry-smiling on a bridge; the practicality, the mockery, the little Puckish humours; then suddenly the pallor by the hedge, and the small gasp when these terrors crept back. Don't let anything happen to her. Keep good watch, that no harm may touch her. Keep good watch, for this is her brother. . . .

Their footfalls rustled in the grass, and the insect-hum pulsed in shrill droning. Distantly, in the thick air to the west, there was a mutter of thunder.

Chapter 5

HEAT. Heat thick and sickly, with breezes that came as puffs out of an oven, made a gust in the trees, and then died. If this cottage had really been a Swiss barometer, the little figures would have been wildly swinging in their châlet now.

They dined by candlelight, in the little oak room with the pewter dishes round the walls. The room was as warm as the dinner, and the wine warmer than both; Dr. Fell's face grew redder as he kept filling and refilling his glass. But his blowings and easy oratory were gone now. Even Mrs. Fell was quiet, though jumpy. She kept passing the wrong things, and nobody noticed it.

Nor did they linger over coffee, cigars, and port, as was the doctor's custom. Afterwards Rampole went up to his room. He lighted the oil-lamp and began to change his clothes. Old soiled tennis-flannels, a comfortable shirt, and tennis shoes. His room was a small one with a sloping roof, under the eaves, its one window looking out towards the side of Chatterham prison and the Hag's Nook. Some sort of flying beetle banged against the window-screen with a thump that made him start, and a moth was already fluttering round the lamp.

It was a relief to be doing something. He finished dressing and took a few restless strides about. Up here the heat was thick with a smell of dry timber, like an attic; even the paste behind the flowered wall-paper seemed to give out a stifling odour; and the lamp was worst of all. Putting his head against the screen, he peered out. The moon was rising, unhealthy and yellow-ringed; it was past ten o'clock. Damn the uncertainty!— A travelling-clock ticked with irritating nonchalance on the table at the head of his four-poster bed. The calendar in the lower part of the clock-case showed a staring figure where he had been last July 12th, and couldn't remember. Another gust of wind swished in the trees. Heat, prickling out damply on him and flowing over the brain in dizzy waves; *heat*. . . . He blew out the lamp.

Stuffing pipe and oilskin pouch into his pocket, he went downstairs. A rocking-chair squeaked tirelessly in the parlour, where Mrs. Fell was reading a paper with large pictures. Rampole groped out across the lawn. The doctor had drawn two wicker chairs round to the side of the house looking towards the prison, where it was very dark and considerably cooler. Glowing red, the bowl of the doctor's pipe moved there; Rampole found a cold glass put into his hand as he sat down.

"Nothing now," said Dr. Fell, "but to wait."

That very distant thunder moved in the west, with a noise which was really like a bowling-ball curving down the alley, never to hit any pins. Rampole took a deep drink of the cold beer. That was better!—The moon was far from strong, but already the cup of the meadow lay washed in a light like skimmed-milk, which was creeping up the walls.

"Which is the window of the Governor's Room?" he asked, in a low voice.

The red bowl gestured. "That large one—the only large one. It's in an almost direct line from here. Do you see it? Just beside it there's an iron door opening on a small stone balcony. That's where the governor stepped out to oversee the hangings."

Rampole nodded. The whole side was covered with ivy, bulging in places where the weight of the masonry had made it sink into the crest of the hill. In the skimmed-milk light he could see tendrils hanging from the heavy bars in the window. Immediately beneath the balcony, but very far down, was another iron door. In front of this door, the limestone hill tumbled down sheer into the pointed fir trees of the Hag's Nook.

"And the door below," he said, "is where they took the condemned out, I suppose?"

"Yes. You can still see the three blocks of stone, with the holes in them, that held the framework of the gallows. . . . The stone coping of the well is hidden in those trees. They weren't there, of course, when the well was in use."

"All the dead were dumped into it?"

"Oh yes. You wonder the whole countryside isn't polluted, even after a hundred years. As it is, the well is a rare place for bugs and vermin. Dr. Markley had been agitating about it for the last fifteen years; but he can't get the borough or council to do anything about it, because it's Starberth land. Hmf."

"And they won't let it be filled in?"

"No. That's a part of the old mumbo-jumbo, too; a relic of the eighteenth-century Anthony. I've been going over Anthony's journal again. And when I think of the way he died, and certain puzzling references in the journal, I sometimes think . . ."

"You haven't yet told me how he died," Rampole said, quietly.

As he said it he wondered whether he wanted to know. Last night he thought, he was certain, that something wet had been looking down from the prison wall. In daytime he had not noticed it, but now he was aware of a distinct marshy smell, which seemed to be blowing across the meadow from the Hag's Nook.

"I forgot," muttered the old lexicographer. "I was going to read it to you this afternoon when Mrs. F. interrupted us. Here." There was a rustle of paper, and a thick bundle of sheets was put into his hand. "Take it upstairs later; I want you to read it and form your own opinions."

Were those frogs croaking? He could hear it plainly above the twitching and pulsing of insects. By God! that marshy odour *was* stronger; it was no illusion. There must be some natural explanation of it—the heat of the day released from the ground, or something. He wished he knew more about nature. The trees had begun to whisper uneasily again. Inside the house, a clock bonged out a single note.

"Half-past ten," grunted his host. "And I think that's the rector's car coming up the lane."

Unsteady headlights were gleaming there. Bumping and rattling, a high old Model T Ford—the kind they used to tell the jokes about—swung round to a stop, the rector looking huge on his perch. He hurried over in the moonlight, catching up a chair from the front of the lawn. His bluff and easy airs were not so much in evidence now; Rampole had a sudden feeling that they were assumed, for social purposes, to cover an intense self-consciousness. They could not see his face well in the gloom, but they knew he was perspiring. He panted as he sat down.

"I snatched a quick meal," he said, "and came straightway. Did you arrange everything?"

"Everything. She'll telephone when he leaves. Here, have a cigar and a glass of beer. How was he when you saw him last?"

A bottle jittered and clicked against the side of a glass. "Sober enough to be frightened," the rector answered. "He went for the sideboard as soon as we reached the Hall. I was of two minds as to whether to stop his drinking. Herbert's got him in hand, though. When I left the Hall he was sitting up in his room lighting one cigarette from the end of the last; he must have smoked a whole box just while I was there. I—er—I pointed out the deleterious effect of so much tobacco— No, thanks; I won't smoke— on his system, and he flew at me."

They all fell silent. Rampole found himself listening for the clock. Martin Starberth would be watching it, too, in another house.

Inside the house, the telephone rang stridently.

"There it is. Will you get the message, my boy?" asked Dr. Fell, breathing a little faster. "You're more spry than I am."

Rampole almost fell over the front steps in his hurry. The telephone was of the ancient type you crank up, and Mrs. Fell was already holding out the receiver to him.

"He's on his way," the voice of Dorothy Starberth told him. It was admirably calm now. "Watch the road for him. He's carrying a big bicycle lamp."

"How is he?"

"A little thick-spoken, but sober enough." She added, rather wildly, *"You're* all right, aren't you?"

"Yes. Now don't worry, please! We'll take care of it. He's in no danger, dear."

It was not until he was on his way out of the house that he remembered the last word he had quite unconsciously used over the phone. Even in the turmoil it startled him. He had no recollection whatever of using it at the time.

"Well, Mr. Rampole?" the rector boomed out of the dark.

"He's started. How far is the Hall from the prison?"

"A quarter of a mile beyond, in the direction of the railway station. You must have passed it last night." Saunders spoke absently, but he seemed more at his ease now that the thing was begun. He and the doctor had both come round to the front of the house. He turned, big and bold-shining in the moonlight. "I've been imagining—dreadful things—all day. When this business was far off, I laughed at it. Now that it's here . . . well, old Mr. Timothy Starberth . . ."

Something was worrying the good rector's Eton conscience. He mopped his forehead with a handkerchief. He added:

"I say, Mr. Rampole, was Herbert there?"

"Why Herbert?" the doctor asked, sharply.

"It's—ah—it's only that I wish he were here. That young man is dependable. Solid and dependable. No nerves. Admirable; very English, and admirable."

Again the rumble of thunder, prowling stealthily and low down along the sky. A fresh breeze went swishing through the garden, and white blossoms danced. There was a flicker of lightning, so very brief that it was like an electrician flashing on footlights momentarily to test them before the beginning of a play.

"We'd better watch to see that he gets in safely," the doctor suggested, gruffly. "If he's drunk, he may get a bad fall. Did she say he was drunk?"

"Not very."

They tramped up along the lane. The prison lay in its own shadow on that side, but Dr. Fell pointed out the approximate position of the gateway. "No door on it, of course," he explained. But the rocky hill leading up to it was fairly well lighted by the moon; a cow-path meandered almost into the shadow of the prison. For what seemed nearly ten minutes nobody spoke. Rampole kept trying to time the pulse of a cricket, counting between rasps, and got lost in a maze of numbers. The breeze belled out his shirt with grateful coolness.

"There it is," Saunders said, abruptly.

A beam of white light struck up over the hill. Then a figure, moving slowly but steadily, appeared on the crest with such weird effect that it seemed to be rising from the ground. It tried to move with a jaunty swing, but the light kept flickering and darting—as though at every slight noise Martin Starberth were flashing it in that direction. Watching it, Rampole felt the terror which must be running in the slight, contemptuous, tipsy figure. Very tiny at that distance, it hesitated at the gates. The light stood motionless, playing on a gaping archway. Then it was swallowed inside.

The watchers went back and sank heavily into their chairs.

Inside the house, the clock began to strike eleven.

"—if she only told him," the rector had been running on for some time, but Rampole only heard him now, "to sit near that window!" He threw out his hands. "But, after all, we must be sensi—we must— What *can* happen to him? You know as well as I do, gentlemen. . . ."

—*Bong,* hammered the clock slowly. *Bong,* three, four, five—

"Have some more beer," said Dr. Fell. The rector's smooth, unctuous voice, now raised shrilly, seemed to irritate him.

Again they waited. An echo of footfalls in the prison, a scurry of rats and lizards as the light probed; in Rampole's taut fancy he could almost hear them. Some lines in Dickens came back to him, a sketch of prowling past Newgate on a drizzly night and seeing through a barred window the turn-keys sitting over their fire, and their shadows on the whitewashed wall.

A gleam sprang up now in the Governor's Room. It did not waver. The bicycle lamp was very powerful, cutting a straight horizontal band against which the bars of the window leapt out. Evidently it had been put down on a table, where it remained, sending its beam into one corner of the room without further movement. That was all— the tiny shaft of brightness behind ivy-fouled bars, lonely against the great ivy-fouled hulk of the prison. The shadow of a man hovered there, and then vanished.

It seemed to have an incredibly long neck, that shadow.

To his surprise, Rampole discovered that his heart was bumping. You had to do something; you had to concentrate. . . .

"If you don't mind, sir," he said to his host, "I'd like to go up to my room and look at these journals of the two governors. I can keep my eye on the window from there. And I want to *know.*"

It suddenly seemed vitally important to know how these men had come to death. He fingered the sheets, which were damp from his hand. They had been there, he remembered, even when he held the receiver of the telephone in the same hand. Dr. Fell grunted, without seeming to hear him.

The thunder went rattling, with a suggestion of heavy carts shaking the window panes, when he ascended the stairs. His room was now swept by a thick breeze, but still exhaling heat. Lighting the lamp, he drew the table before the window and put down the manuscript sheets. He glanced round once before he sat down. There were the copies of those comic songs, lying scattered on the bed, which he had bought this afternoon; and there was the church-warden pipe.

He had a queer, vague idea that if he were to smoke that pipe, the relic of lightheartedness, it might bring him closer to Dorothy Starberth. But he felt foolish, and cursed himself, the moment he picked it up. When he was about to replace it there was some noise; the brittle clay slipped through his fingers and smashed on the floor.

It shocked him, like breaking a living thing. He stared at it for a moment, and then hurried over to sit down facing the windows. Bugs were beginning to tick and swarm against the screen. Far across the meadow was that tiny, steady lamp in the window of the prison, and he could hear the voices of the rector and Dr. Fell mumbling in conversation just below.

A. Starberth, Esquire, His Journal.

PRIVATE.

(Eighth September, 1797. This being the First Year in the Good Works of Chatterham Gaol, in the Shire of Lincoln; like-wise the Thirty-Seventh in the Reign of His Sovereign Majesty, George III).
Quae Infra Nos Nihil Ad Nos.

These typewriter sheets carried a more vivid suggestion, Rampole felt, than would have the yellowed originals. You imagined the handwriting to have been small, sharp, and precise, like the tight-lipped writer. There followed some fancy composition, in the best literary style of the day, on the majesty of justice and the nobility of punishing evil-doers. Suddenly it became business-like:

TO BE HANGED, Thursday, the tenth inst., the following, viz.:

John Hepditch. For Highway Robbery.
Lewis Martens. For Uttering Forged Notes, the amt. £2.

Cost of timber for erecting gallows, 2s 4d. Parson's fee 10d, which I would readily do away with but that it is subscribed by law, these being men of low birth and with small need of ghostly consolation.

This day I have overseen the digging of the well to a commodious depth, viz., 25 feet, and 18 feet across at the wide lip—it being rather a moat than a well proper, and being designed to hold the bones of evil-doers, thus saving any unnecessary cost of burial, as well as a most praiseworthy safeguard for that side. Its edge has been buttressed by a row of sharpened iron spikes, by order of me.

I am much vexed, in that my new suit of scarlet, together with the laced hat, which I ordered these six weeks ago, did not arrive by the mail-coach. I had resolved to present a good appearance—scarlet, like a judge, would (I am convinced) make an imposing figure—at the hangings, and have prepared words to speak from my balcony. This John Hepditch (I have heard) has a pretty talent for the making of speeches, though of low birth, and I must take care he doth not outshine me.

I am informed by the chief turnkey that there is some discontent, and a striking upon cell-doors, in the underground corridors, due to a species of large grey field-rat which eats the bread of those confined, and is not easily frightened away; these men further complain that, due to natural darkness, they are unable to see such rats until the rats are upon their arms and snatch at food. Master Nick. Threnlow asked me, What he should do? To which I replied, That it was through the instigation of their own wicked habits that they had come to such a pass, and must endure it; and I further counselled that any unwarranted noises should be met by such Floggings as would induce the malefactors to preserve their proper chastened demeanour.

This evening I began writing a new ballade, in the French manner. I think it very good.

Rampole moved in his chair, and looked up uneasily, to be met by the staring light across the meadow. Below him on the lawn he heard Dr. Fell expounding some point in connection with the drinking customs of England, and the protesting rumble of the rector. Then he continued reading, skimming the pages. They were far from complete. A number of entire years were omitted altogether, and in others there were merely some jottings. But the parade of horror, cruelty, high-sounding preachments, and miserly chucklings over twopence saved, while old Anthony scribbled away at his verses . . . these were only a prelude.

A change was coming over the writer. He began to scream to his journal.

They call me a "limping Herrick," do they? [he writes in 1812]. A "Dryden in falsetto." But I begin to think of a plan. I do heartily abhor and curse each of those to which I have the misfortune to be bound by ties of blood. There are things one can buy and things one can do to defeat them. *By which I am reminded that the rats are growing thicker lately.* They come into my room, and I can see them beyond the circle of my lamp as I write.

He has grown a new literary style with the passing years, but his rage grows like a mania. Under the year 1814 there is only one entry:

I must go slowly with the buying. Each year, each year. The rats seem to know me now.

Out of all the rest of them, one passage brought Rampole up with a shock.

June 23. I am wasting, and I find it difficult to sleep. Several times I have believed to hear a knocking on the outside of the iron door which leads to my balcony. But there is no person there when I open it. My lamp smokes worse, and I believe to feel things in my bed. *But I have the beauties safe.* It is good that I am strong in the arms.

Now the wind rushed fully in at the window, almost blowing the sheets from Rampole's hands. He had a sudden horrible feeling as though they had been jerked away from him; and the ticking and scrambling of the bugs outside did not add to his easiness. The lamp flame jumped slightly, but resumed its steady yellow glow. Lightning illuminated the prison, followed in an instant by a full crash of thunder. . . .

Not yet through with Anthony's journal, and the diary of another Starberth still to come. But he was too fascinated to read faster; he had watched the one-eyed old governor shrivel up with the years, wearing now his tall hat and tight-waisted coat, and carrying the gold-headed cane he mentioned frequently. All of a sudden, the dogged quiet of the diary was broken!

July 9. Oh Lord Jesus, sweet dispenser of mercy to the helpless, look upon me and aid me! I do not know why, but my sleep is gone, and I can thrust a finger between the bones of these ribs. Will they eat my pets?

Yesterday we hanged a man for murder, as already noticed. He wore a blue-and-white striped waistcoat to the gallows. The crowd booed me.

I sleep now with two rush-lights burning. There is a soldier on guard at my door. But last night, the while I was making out my report upon this execution, I heard patterings in my room, to the which I tried to pay no heed. I had trimmed my bedside candle, put on my nightcap, and prepared to read in bed, when I noted a movement among the bedclothes. Whereupon I took my loaded pistol from the table and called to the soldier to throw back the clothes. And when he had done it, doubtless thinking me mad, I saw in the bed a large grey rat looking up at me with his eyes. He was wet, and there was a large pool of black water there; and the rat was gorged fat, and seemed to be trying to shake loose from his sharp teeth a flimsy of blue-and-white striped cloth.

This rat the soldier killed with the butt of his musket, the rat being not well able to run across the floor. Nor would I sleep in the bed that night. I had them kindle a great fire, and dozed before it in a chair with warm rum. I thought that I was just falling asleep when I heard a murmur as of many voices on the balcony outside my iron door—though this is impossible, so many feet from the ground—and a low voice whispered at the key-hole, *"Sir, will you come out and speak with us?"* And, as I looked, methought there was water running under the door.

Rampole sat back with a constriction at his throat and the palms of his hands damp. He was not even startled when the storm broke, the rain sheeting down into the dark lawn and hissing among the trees. He heard Dr. Fell cry: "Get those chairs in! We can watch from the dining-room!"—and the rector replying with something unintelligible. His eyes were fixed on the pencilled note at the end of the journal; Dr. Fell's handwriting, for it bore the initials G.F.

He was found dead on the morning of Sept. 10, 1820. The night before had been stormy, with a high wind, and it is improbable that the turnkeys or soldiers would have heard any cry had he made one. He was found lying with his neck broken across the stone coping around the well. Two of the spikes on this coping had been driven entirely through his body and impaled him with his head pointing down into the well.

There was some suggestion of foul play. No signs of any struggle were visible, however; and it was pointed out that, had he been attacked, even several assailants would have had their hands full. Despite his age, he was widely celebrated for the almost incredible strength of his arms and shoulders. This is a curious fact, since he seemed to develop it after he had taken over the governorship of the prison, and it steadily increased with the years. Latterly he remained always at the prison, rarely visiting his family at the Hall. The eccentric behavior of his later life influenced the findings of the coroner's jury, which were: "Death by misadventure while of unsound mind."

—G.F., Yew Cottage, 1923.

Putting his tobacco-pouch on the loose sheets to keep them from blowing, Rampole sat back again. He was staring out at the drive of the rain, visualizing that scene. Automatically he lifted his eyes to the window of the Governor's Room. Then he sat for an instant motionless. . . .

The light in the Governor's Room was out.

Only a sheet of rain flickering in darkness before him. He got up spasmodically, feeling so weak that he could not push the chair away, and glanced over his shoulder at the travelling-clock.

It was not yet ten minutes to twelve. A horrible sensation of unreality, and a feeling as though the chair were entangled in his legs. Then he heard Dr. Fell's shout from downstairs somewhere. They had seen it, too. It couldn't have been out more than a second. The face of the clock swam; he couldn't take his eyes from those placid small hands, or hear anything but the casual ticking in a great silence. . . .

Then he was wrenching at the knob of the door, throwing it open, and stumbling downstairs, in a physical nausea which made him dizzy. Dimly he could see Dr. Fell and the rector standing bareheaded in the rain, staring towards the prison, and the doctor still was carrying a chair under his arm. The doctor caught his arm.

"Wait a minute! What's the matter, boy?" he demanded. "You're as white as a ghost. What—"

"We've got to get over there! The light's out! The—"

They were all panting a little, heedless of the rain splashing into their faces. It got into Rampole's eyes, and for a moment he could not see.

"I shouldn't go so fast," Saunders said. "It's that beastly business you've been reading; don't believe in it. He may have miscalculated the time. . . . Wait! You don't know the way!"

Rampole had torn from the doctor's grasp and was running through the soggy grass towards the meadow. They heard Rampole say, "I promised her!"—and then the rector was pounding after him. Despite his bulk, Saunders was a runner. Together they slithered down a muddy bank; Rampole felt water gushing into his tennis shoes as he bumped against a rail fence. He vaulted it, plunged down a slope and up again through the long grass of the meadow. He could see little through the blinding cataract of rain, but he realized that unconsciously he was bearing to the left, toward the Hag's Nook. That wasn't right; that wasn't the way in; but the memory of Anthony's journal burned too vividly in his brain. Saunders cried out something behind him, which was lost under the crackle and boom of thunder. In the ensuing flash of lightning he saw a gesticulating Saunders running away from him to the right, towards the gate of the prison, but he still kept on his way.

How he reached the heart of the Hag's Nook he could never afterwards remember. A steep slippery meadow, grass that twisted the feet like wires, then brambles and underbrush tearing through his shirt; he could see nothing except that he was bumping into fir trees with a gutted precipice looming up ahead. Breath hurt his lungs, and he stumbled against sodden bark to clear the water from his eyes. But he knew he was *there*. All around in the dark was a sort of unholy stirring and buzzing, muffled splashes, a sense of things that crawled or crept, but, worst of all, an odour.

Things were flicking against his face, too. Throwing out his hand, he encountered a low wall of rough stone, and felt the rust of a spike. There must be something in the feel of this place that made your head pound, and your blood turn thin, and your legs feel weak. Then the lightning came with broken illumination through the trees. . . . He was staring across the wide well, on a level with his chest, and hearing water splash below.

Nothing there.

Nothing hanging head down across the edge of the well, impaled on a spike. In the dark he began groping his way round the side of the well, holding to the spikes, in a frenzy to know. It was not until he was just beneath the edge of the cliff, and beginning to gasp with relief, that his foot kicked something soft.

He started groping in the dark, so numb that he groped with hideous care. He felt a chilly face, open eyes, and wet hair, but the neck seemed as loose as rubber, because it was broken. It did not need the lightning-flare immediately afterwards to tell him it was Martin Starberth.

His legs gave, and he stumbled back against the cliff— fifty feet below the governor's balcony, which had stood out black against the lightning a moment before. He shuddered, feeling drenched and lost, with only one sick thought—that he had failed Dorothy Starberth. Everywhere the rain ran down him, the mud thickened under his hands, and the roar of the shower deepened. When he lifted stupid eyes, he suddenly saw far across the meadow, at Dr. Fell's cottage, the yellow lamp in the window of his room. There it was, plain through a gap in the fir trees; and the only images that stuck in his mind, wildly enough, were the scattered music sheets across the bed—and the fragments of a brittle clay pipe, lying broken on the floor.

Chapter 6

MR. BUDGE, the butler, was making his customary rounds at the Hall to see that all the windows were fastened before he retired to his respectable bachelor bed. Mr. Budge was aware that all the windows were fastened, had been fastened every night during the fifteen years of his officiation, and would continue so until the great red-brick house should fall or Get Took By Americans—which latter fate Mrs. Bundle, the housekeeper, always uttered in a direful voice, as though she were telling a terrible ghost story. None the less, Mr. Budge was darkly suspicious of housemaids. He felt that, when his back was turned, every housemaid had an overpowering desire to sneak about, opening windows, so that tramps could get in. His imagination never got so far as burglars, which was just as well.

Traversing the long upstairs gallery with a lamp in his hand, he was especially careful. There would be rain before long, and much weighed on his mind. He was not worried about the young master's vigil in the Governor's Room. That was a tradition, a foregone conclusion, like serving your country in time of war, which you accepted stoically; like war, it had its dangers, but there it was. Mr. Budge was a reasonable man. He knew that there were such things as evil spirits, just as he knew there were toads, bats, and other unpleasant things. But he suspected that even spooks were growing mild and weak-voiced in these degenerate days when housemaids had so much time off. It wasn't like the old times of his father's service. His chief concern now was to see to it that there was a good fire in the library, against the young master's return; a plate of sandwiches, and a decanter of whisky.

No, there were more serious concerns on his mind. When he reached the middle of the oaken gallery, where the portraits hung, he paused as usual to hold up his lamp briefly before the picture of old Anthony. An eighteenth-century artist had depicted Anthony all in black, and the decorations on his chest, sitting at a table with a skull under his hand. Budge had kept his hair and was a fine figure of a man. He liked to imagine a resemblance to himself in the pale, reserved, clerical countenance of the first governor, despite Anthony's history; and Budge always walked with even a more dignified gait when he left off looking at the portrait. Nobody would have suspected his guilty secret—that he wept during the sad parts at the motion pictures, to which he was addicted; and that he had once tossed sleepless for many nights in the horrible fear that Mrs. Tarpon, the chemist's wife, had seen him in this condition during a performance of an American film called "Way Down East" at Lincoln.

Which reminded him. Having finished with the upstairs, he went in his dignified Guardsman's walk down the great staircase. Gas burning properly in the front hall—bit of a sputter in that third mantle to the left, though; they'd be having in electricity one of these days, he shouldn't wonder! Another American thing. Here was Mr. Martin already corrupted by the Yankees; always a wild one, but a real gentleman until he began talking in this loud gibberish you couldn't understand, nothing but bars and drinks named after pirates—made with gin, too, which was fit for nobody but old women and drunkards; yes, and carrying a revolver, for all *he* knew! "Tom Collins"; that was the pirate one, wasn't it, or was the pirate called John Silver? And something called a "sidecar." . . .

Sidecar. That suggested Mr. Herbert's motorbike. Budge felt uneasy.

"Budge!" a voice said from the library.

Habit cleared Budge's mind as it cleared his face. Setting down his lamp carefully on the table in the hall, he went into the library with just the proper expression of being uncertain he had heard.

"You called, Miss Dorothy?" said the public face of Mr. Budge.

Even though his mind was a sponged slate, he could not help noticing a startling (almost shocking) fact. The wall safe was open. He knew its position, behind the portrait of Mr. Timothy, his late master; but in fifteen years he had never seen it indecently naked and open. This he observed even before his automatic glance at the fireplace, to see that the wood was drawing well. Miss Dorothy sat in one of the big hard chairs, with a paper in her hands.

"Budge," she said, "will you ask Mr. Herbert to step downstairs?"

A hesitation. "Mr. Herbert is not in his room, Miss Dorothy."

"Will you find him, then, please?"

"I believe Mr. Herbert is not in the house," said Budge, as though he had given some problem deep consideration and were arriving at a decision.

She dropped the paper into her lap. "Budge, what on earth do you mean?"

"He—er—mentioned no prospective departure, Miss Dorothy? Thank you."

"Good Heavens, no! Where would he be going?"

"I mentioned the matter, Miss Dorothy, because I had occasion to go to his room shortly after dinner on an errand. He appeared to be packing a small bag."

Again Budge hesitated. He felt uneasy, because her face had assumed an odd expression. She got up.

"When did he leave the house?"

Budge glanced at the clock on the mantel-shelf. Its hands pointed to eleven-forty-five. "I am not certain, Miss Dorothy," he replied. "Quite soon after dinner, I think. He went away on his motor-bicycle. Mr. Martin had asked me to get him an electric bicycle-lamp as being—ah—more convenient for his sojourn across the way. That is how I happened to notice Mr. Herbert's departure. I went out to the stable to detach a lamp from one of the machines, and —ah—he drove past me. . . ."

(Odd how Miss Dorothy was taking this! Of course, she had a right to be upset, what with Mr. Herbert's unheard-of departure without a word to anybody, and the safe standing open for the first time in fifteen years; but he did not like to see her show it. He felt as he had once felt when he peeked through a keyhole and saw— Budge hastily averted his thoughts, embarrassed at remembering his younger days.)

"It's strange I didn't see him," she was saying, looking at Budge steadily. "I sat on the lawn for at least an hour after dinner."

Budge coughed. "I was about to say, Miss Dorothy, that he didn't go by the drive. He went out over the pasture, towards Shooter's Lane. I noticed it because I was some time in finding a proper lamp to take to Mr. Martin, and I saw him turning down the lane then."

"Did you tell Mr. Martin of this?"

Budge permitted himself to look slightly shocked. "No, Miss Dorothy," he answered, in a tone of reproof. "I gave him the lamp, as you know, but I did not think it within my province to explain—"

"Thank you, Budge. You needn't wait up for Mr. Martin."

He inclined his head, noting from a corner of his eye that the sandwiches and whisky were in the proper place, and withdrew. He could loosen his grammar now, like a tight belt; he was Mr. Budge again. A queer one, the young mistress was. He had almost thought, "pert little piece," but that it would be disrespectful. All stiffness and high varnish, with her straight back and her coolish eyes. No sentiment. No 'eart. He had watched her growing up—let's see; she was twenty-one last April—since she was six. A child not condescending or sure of getting her way, like Mr. Martin, or quietly thankful for attention, like Mr. Herbert, but odd. . . .

It was thundering more frequently now, he noted, and little streaks of lightning penetrated dark places of the house. Ah, a good job he'd lit that fire! The grandfather clock in the hall wanted winding. Performing that office, he kept thinking of what a hodd child Miss Dorothy had been. A scene came back: the dinner table, with himself in the background, when the master and the mistress were alive. Master Martin and Master Herbert had been playing war in Oldham orchard, with some other boys; in talking of it at dinner, Master Martin had twitted his cousin about not climbing into the branches of the highest maple as a look-out. Master Martin was always the leader, and Master Herbert trotted after him humbly; but this time he refused to obey orders. "I wouldn't!" he repeated at the table. "Those branches are rotten." "That's right, Bert," said the mistress, in her gentle way. "Remember, even in war one must be cautious." And then little Miss Dorothy had astonished them all by suddenly saying, very violent-like, though she hadn't spoken all evening: "When I grow up, *I'm* going to marry a man without any caution at all." And looked very fierce. The mistress had reproved her, and the master had just chuckled in his dry, ugly way; queer to remember that now. . . .

It was raining now. As he finished winding the clock, it began to strike. Budge, staring at it vacantly, found himself surprised, and wondered why. Midnight, the clock was striking. Well, that was all right, surely. . . .

No. Something was wrong. Something jarred at the back of his small, automatic brain. Troubled, he frowned at the landscape painted on the clock-face. Ah, he had it now! Just a few minutes ago he had been talking to Miss Dorothy, and the library clock had said eleven forty-five. The library clock must be wrong.

He drew out his gold watch, which had not erred in many years, and opened it. Ten minutes to twelve. No, the library clock had been right; this old grandfather, by which the housemaids set the other time-pieces in the house, was precisely ten and a half minutes fast. Budge permitted a groan to go backwards down his windpipe, and thus remain unheard. Now, before he could retire with an undisturbed conscience, he must go about and inspect the other clocks.

The clock struck twelve.

And then, presently, the telephone rang. Budge saw Dorothy Starberth's white face in the library door as he went to answer it. . . .

Chapter 7

SIR BENJAMIN ARNOLD, the chief constable, sat behind the writing-table in Dr. Fell's study, his bony hands folded on it like a schoolmaster. He looked a little like a schoolmaster also, but for the burnt color and horsiness of his face. His thick greyish hair was combed pompadour; his eyes looked sharp behind a pince-nez.

"—I thought it best," he was saying, "to take personal charge. It was suggested that an inspector be sent down

from Lincoln. However, I have known the Starberths, and
Dr. Fell in particular, for such a long time that I thought it
best to drive over and superintend the Chatterham police
myself. In that way we may save any scandal, or as much
beyond what the inquest is bound to bring out."

He hesitated, clearing his throat.

"You, Doctor—and you, Mr. Saunders—are aware that
I have never had occasion to handle a murder case. I am
almost certain to being out of my depth. If everything fails,
we shall have to call in Scotland Yard. But among us we
may be able to straighten this unfortunate business out."

The sun was high in a clear, warm morning, but the
study still held little light. During a long silence they could
hear a police constable walking up and down the hall outside. Saunders nodded ponderously. Dr. Fell remained
frowning and glum. Rampole was too tired and muddled to
pay much attention.

"You—ah—said 'murder case,' Sir Benjamin?" the rector inquired.

"I know the Starberth legend, of course," answered the
chief constable, nodding. "And I confess I have a theory
about it. Perhaps I should not have said 'murder case' in
the properest sense. Accident we may put out of the question. But I will come to that presently. . . . Now, Doctor."

He squared himself, drawing in his lips and tightening
fingers round his bony knuckles; shifting a little, like a lec-
turer about to commence on an important subject.

"Now, Doctor. You have told everything up to the time
the light went out in the Governor's Room. What happened
when you went up to investigate?"

Moodily Dr. Fell poked at the edge of the writing-table
with his cane. He rumbled and bit at his moustache.

"I didn't go. Thanks for the compliment, but I couldn't
move like these other two. H'mf, no. Better let them tell
you."

"Quite. . . . I believe, Mr. Rampole, that you discovered the body?"

The clipped, official lines of this procedure made Rampole feel uneasy. He couldn't talk naturally, and felt that
anything he said might be used against him. Justice!—it

was a big, unnerving thing. He felt guilty of something without knowing what.

"I did."

"Tell me, then: Why did it occur to you to go directly to the well, instead of through the gate and up to the Governor's Room? Had you reason to suspect what had happened?"

"I—I don't know. I've been trying to figure it out all day. It was just automatic. I'd been reading those journals—the history of the legend, and all that—so . . ." He gestured, helplessly.

"I see. What did you do afterwards?"

"Well, I was so stunned that I sort of fell back against the hill and sat there. Then I remembered where I was and called for Mr. Saunders."

"And you, Mr. Saunders?"

"For for myself, Sir Benjamin," the rector said, giving the title its full value, "I was almost to the gate of the prison when I—ah—heard Mr. Rampole's summons. I thought it somewhat odd that he should go directly towards the Hag's Nook, and tried to beckon him. But there was scarcely time to—think much." He frowned judicially.

"Quite. When you stumbled on the body, Mr. Rampole, it was lying at the edge of the well, directly beneath the balcony?"

"Yes."

"How lying?—I mean, on its back or face?"

Rampole reflected, closing his eyes. All he could think of was the wetness of the face. "On his side, I think. Yes, I'm certain."

"Left or right?"

"I don't know . . . wait a minute! Yes, I do. It was the right."

Doctor Fell bent forward unexpectedly, poking the table sharply with his cane. "You're sure of that?" he demanded. "You're sure of it, now, boy? Remember, it's easy to be confused."

The other nodded. Yes—feeling that dead man's neck, bending over and finding it all squashed into his right shoulder; he nodded fiercely, to drive away the image. "It was the right," he answered. "I'll swear to it."

"That is quite correct, Sir Benjamin," the rector affirmed, putting his finger tips together.

"Very well. What did you do next, Mr. Rampole?"

"Why, Mr. Saunders got there, and we weren't certain what to do. All we could think of was getting him out of the wet. So first we thought we'd carry him down to the cottage here, and then we didn't want to frighten Mrs. Fell; so we took him up and put him in a room just inside the prison. Oh, yes—and we found the bicycle lamp he'd been using for a light. I tried to work it so as to give us some light, but it had been smashed by the fall."

"Where was this lamp? In his hand?"

"No. It was some distance away from him. It looked as though it had been pitched over the balcony; I mean, it was too far away for *him* to have been carrying it."

The chief constable tapped his fingers on the table. A spiral of wrinkles ascended his leathery neck as he kept his head sideways, staring at Rampole.

"That point," he said, "may be of the utmost importance in the coroner's verdict between accident, suicide, or murder. . . . According to Dr. Markley, young Starberth's skull was fractured, either by the fall or by a heavy blow with what we generally term a blunt instrument; his neck was broken, and there were other contusions of a heavy fall. But we can go into that later. . . . What next, Mr. Rampole?"

"I stayed with him while Mr. Saunders went down to tell Dr. Fell and drive to Chatterham after Dr. Markley. I just waited, striking matches and—I mean, I just waited."

He shuddered.

"Thank you. Mr. Saunders?"

"There is little more to add, Sir Benjamin," Saunders returned, his mind on details. "I drove to Chatterham, after instructing Dr. Fell to telephone to the Hall, speak to Budge, the butler, and inform him what had happened. . . ."

"That fool—" Dr. Fell began explosively. As the rector glanced at him in shocked surprise he added: "Budge, I mean. Budge isn't worth a two-ounce bottle in a crisis. He repeated what I said over the phone, and I heard somebody scream; and, instead of keeping it from Miss Starberth until somebody could tell her gently, she knew it that minute."

"As I was saying, Sir Benjamin—of course you're right, Doctor; it was most inopportune—as I was saying," the rector went on, with the air of a man trying to please several people at once, "I drove to get Dr. Markley, stopping only at the rectory to procure myself a raincoat; then we returned, taking Dr. Fell to the prison with us. After a brief examination, Dr. Markley said there was nothing to do but notify the police. We took the—the body to the Hall in my car."

He seemed about to say more, but he shut his lips suddenly. There was an enormous pressure of silence, as though everyone had checked himself in the act of speaking, too. The chief constable had opened a large claspknife and begun to sharpen a pencil; the small quick rasps of the knife against lead were so loud that Sir Benjamin glanced up sharply.

"You questioned the people at the Hall?" he asked.

"We did," said Dr. Fell. *"She* was bearing up admirably. We got a clear, concise account of everything that had happened that evening, both from her and from Budge. The other servants we did not disturb."

"Never mind. I had better get it first hand from them.— Did you speak to young Herbert?"

"We did not," the doctor responded, after a pause. "Just after dinner last night, according to Budge, he packed a bag and left the Hall on his motor-cycle. He has not returned."

Sir Benjamin laid down knife and pencil on the table. He sat rigid, staring at the other. Then he took off his pince-nez, polished it on an old handkerchief; his eyes, from being sharp, suddenly looked weak and sunken.

"Your implication," he said at length, "is absurd."

"Quite," echoed the rector, looking straight ahead of him.

"It's not any implication. Good God!" Dr. Fell rumbled, and slapped the ferrule of his cane against the floor. "You said you wanted facts. But you don't want facts at all. You want me to say something like, 'Of course there is the little point that Herbert Starberth went to Lincoln to the cinema, taking some clothes to leave at the laundry, and that he left the theatre so late he undoubtedly decided to spend the night with a friend.' Those implications would be what you call the facts. But I give you the plain facts, and you call them implications."

"By Jove!" the rector said, thoughtfully, "he might have done just that, you know."

"Good," said Dr. Fell. "Now we can tell everybody just what he did. But don't call it a fact. That's the important thing."

The chief constable made an irritable gesture.

"He didn't tell anybody he was going?"

"Not unless he mentioned it to somebody other than Miss Starberth or Budge."

"Ah. Well, I'll talk to them. I don't want to hear anything more. . . . I say, there were no bad feelings between him and Martin, were there?"

"If there were, he concealed 'em admirably."

Saunders, stroking a plump pink chin, offered: "He may have come back by this time, you know. We haven't been at the Hall since last night."

Dr. Fell grunted. Rising with obvious reluctance, Sir Benjamin stood and worked with the point of his knife at the table blotter. Then he made a schoolmaster's gesture, compressing his lips again.

"If you gentlemen don't mind, we'll go and have a look at the Governor's Room. I take it none of you went up there last night? . . . Good. Then we shall begin with unprejudiced minds."

"I wonder," said Dr. Fell.

Something said, "Oooo-o!" and gave a fluttering jump as they left the study, and Mrs. Fell went scuttling down the hall. They could see by the police constable's distracted expression that she had been talking to him; and the constable was holding, with obvious embarrassment, a large doughnut.

"Put that thing down, Withers," the chief constable rasped, "and come with us. You've posted a man at the prison? . . . Good. Come along."

They went out into the highroad, Sir Benjamin in the lead with his old Norfolk jacket flying and a battered hat stuck on the side of his head. Nobody spoke until they had climbed the hill to the great gate of the prison. The iron grating which had once barred it sagged open in rusty drunkenness; Rampole remembered how it had jarred and squeaked when they had carried Martin Starberth's body inside. A dark passage, cold and alive with gnats, ran straight back. Coming in here out of the sunlight was like entering a spring-house.

"I've been in here once or twice," the chief constable said, peering round curiously, "but I don't remember the arrangement of the rooms. Doctor, will you lead the way? . . . I say! The Governor's Room part of the place is kept locked, isn't it? Suppose young Starberth locked the outer door of the room when he went in; how do we manage it? I should have got the keys from his clothes."

"If somebody chucked him over that balcony," Dr. Fell grunted, "you can rest assured the murderer had to get out of the Governor's Room afterwards. He didn't try to make a fifty-foot jump from the window, either. Oh, we shall find the door open, right enough."

"It's confoundedly dark in here," said Sir Benjamin. Craning his long neck, he pointed to a door at the right. "Is that where you carried young Starberth last night?"

Rampole nodded, and the chief constable pushed a rotting oak door a little way open to peer inside.

"Not much in there," he announced. "Ugh! Damn the cobwebs. Stone floor, grated window, fireplace, what I can see of it. Not much light." He slapped at some invisible bugs before his face.

"That was the turnkeys' waiting-room, and the prison office beyond it," Dr. Fell amplified. "There was where the governor interviewed his guests and recorded 'em before they were assigned their quarters."

"It's full of rats, anyway," Rampole said, so suddenly that they all glanced at him.

The earthy, cellary smell of the place still seemed to be about him as it had been last night. "It's full of rats," he repeated.

"Oh, ah—undoubtedly," said the rector. "Well, gentlemen?"

They pushed forward along the passage. These walls were uneven with ragged stones, and dark green moss patched the cracks; a rare place, Rampole thought, for typhoid fever. Now scarcely anything could be seen, and they blundered forward by holding to one another's shoulders.

"We should have brought a flashlight," growled Sir Benjamin. "There's an obstruction—"

Something struck the weedy stone floor with a dull crash, and they jumped involuntarily.

"Manacles," said Dr. Fell from the gloom ahead. "Leg irons and such. They're still hanging from the wall along here. That means we're entering the wards. Look sharp for the door."

It was impossible, Rampole thought, to straighten out the tangle of passages; though some small light filtered in once they had passed the first of the inner doors. At one point a heavily grated window, sunk in the five-foot thickness of the wall, looked out upon a dank, shaded yard. It had once been paved, but it was now choked in weeds and nettles. Along one side a line of broken cell-doors hung like decayed teeth. Weirdly, just in the centre of this desolate yard grew a large apple tree in white bloom.

"The condemned ward," said Dr. Fell.

Nobody spoke after that. They did not explore, nor did they ask their conductor to explain the meaning of certain things they saw. But, in one airless room just before they came to the staircase for the second floor, they saw the Iron Maiden by the light of matches; and they saw the furnaces for certain charcoal fires. The Iron Maiden's face wore a drowsy, glutted smile, and spiders swung in webs from her mouth. There were bats flopping around in that room also, so that they did not linger.

Rampole kept his hands clenched tightly; he did not mind anything but the things that flicked against his face, briefly, or the feeling that something was crawling up the back of his neck. And you could hear the rats. When they stopped at last before a great door, bound in iron, along a gallery on the second floor, he felt that he was out of it; he felt as though he had just plunged into clear cool water after sitting on an anthill.

"Is it—is it open?" asked the rector, his voice startlingly loud.

The door rasped and squealed as Dr. Fell pushed it back, the chief constable lending him a hand; it was warped, and difficult to jar backwards along the stone floor. A sifting of dust shook round them.

Then they stood on the threshold of the Governor's Room, looking round.

"I dare say we shouldn't be going in here," Sir Benjamin muttered, after a silence. "All the same!— Any of you ever seen the room before? . . . No? I didn't expect so. H'm. They can't have changed the furniture much, can they?"

"Most of the furniture was old Anthony's," said Dr. Fell. "The rest of it belonged to his son Martin, who was governor here until he—well, died—in 1837. They both gave instructions that the room wasn't to be altered."

It was a comparatively large room, though with rather a low ceiling. Directly opposite the door in which they stood was the window. That side of the prison was in shadow, and the ivy twined round the window's heavy grating did not admit much light; puddles of rain water still lay under it on the uneven stone floor. Some six feet to the left of the window was the door giving on the balcony. It was open, standing out almost at right-angles to the wall; and trailing strands of vine, ripped apart when the door had been opened, drooped across the entrance; so that it allowed but little more light than the window.

There had evidently been an effort, once upon a time, to lend a semblance of comfort to this gloomy place. Black-walnut panelling, now rotting away, had been superimposed on the stone walls. In the wall towards the left of the watchers, just between a tall wardrobe and a bookcase full of big discoloured volumes in calfskin, was a stone chimneypiece with a couple of empty candlesticks on its ledge. A mildewed wing-chair had been drawn up before the fireplace. There (Rampole remembered) would be where old Anthony sat in his nightcap before the blaze, when he heard a knocking at the balcony door and a whispered invitation to come out and join dead men. . . .

In the centre of the room was an old flat desk, thick with dust and debris, and a straight wooden chair drawn up beside it. Rampole stared. Yes, in the dust he could see a narrow rectangular space where the bicycle-lamp had stood last night; there, in that wooden chair facing the right-hand wall, was where Martin Starberth had sat with the ray of his lamp directed towards . . .

So. In the middle of the right-hand wall, set flush with it, was the door to the vault or the safe or whatever it was called. A plain iron door, six feet high and half as wide, now dull with rust. Just under its iron handle was a curious arrangement like a flattened box, with a large keyhole in one end, and in the other what resembled a metal flap above a small knob.

"The reports were correct, then," Dr. Fell said, abruptly. "I thought so. Otherwise it would have been too easy."

"What?" asked the chief constable, rather irritably.

The doctor pointed with his cane. "Suppose a burglar wanted to key into that thing. Why, with only a keyhole in plain sight, he might get an impression of the lock and have a skeleton key made; though it would be an infernally big key. . . . But with *this* arrangement, he couldn't have got in short of blowing the whole wall out with dynamite."

"With what arrangement?"

"A letter combination. I'd heard there was one. It isn't a new idea, you know. Metternich had one; and Talleyrand speaks of, *'Ma porte qu'on peut ouvrir avec un mot, comme les quarante voleurs de Scheherazade.'* You see that knob, with the sliding metal thing above it? The metal piece covers a dial, like a modern safe, except that there are the twenty-six letters of the alphabet instead of numbers. You must turn that knob and spell a word—the word arranged on—before the door can be opened; without that word, a mere key is useless."

"Provided anybody wanted to open the dashed thing," said Sir Benjamin.

They were silent again, all uncomfortable. The rector was mopping his forehead with a handkerchief, a sure sign, and regarding a large canopied bed against the right-hand wall. It was still laid with moth-eaten, decaying clothes and bolster; and fragments of the curtains hung on black brass rings about the tester. There was a night table beside it, with a candlestick. Rampole found himself thinking of lines out of Anthony's manuscript: "I had trimmed my bedside candle, put on my nightcap, and prepared to read in bed, when I saw a movement among the bedclothes. . . ."

The American removed his eyes quickly. Well, one more person had lived and died in this room since Anthony. Over beyond the safe there was a desk-secretary with glass doors; on top of it he could see a bust of Minerva and a huge Bible. None of them, with the exception of Dr. Fell, could quite shake off a sense that they were in a dangerous place where they must walk lightly and not touch. The chief constable shook himself.

"Well," Sir Benjamin began, grimly, "we're here. I'm hanged if I see what we do now. There's where the poor chap sat. There's where he put his lamp. No sign of a struggle—nothing broken—"

"By the way," interposed Dr. Fell, thoughtfully, "I wonder if the safe is still open."

Rampole felt a constriction in his throat.

"My dear Doctor," said Saunders, "do you think the Starberths would quite approve. . . . Oh, I say!"

Dr. Fell was already lumbering past him, the ferrules of his canes ringing on the floor. Turning sharply to Saunders, Sir Benjamin drew himself up.

"This is murder, you know. We've got to see. But wait!—Wait a minute, Doctor!" He strode over, earnest and horsy, with his long head poked forward. In a lower voice he added, "Do you think it's wise?"

"I'm also curious," the doctor was ruminating, without seeming to hear him, "as to what letter they have the combination on now. Will you stand aside a moment, old man? Here. . . . By Jove! the thing's *oiled!*"

He was working the metal flap up and down as they crowded about him.

"It's set on the letter 'S.' Maybe that's the last letter of the word, and maybe it isn't. Anyhow, here goes."

He turned, with a sleepy grin among his chins, peering at them mockingly over his glasses, as he seized the handle of the safe.

"Everybody ready? Look sharp, now!"

He twisted the handle, and slowly the door creaked on its hinges. One of his canes fell down with a sharp clatter.

Nothing came out. . . .

Chapter 8

RAMPOLE did not know what to expect. He held his ground at the doctor's elbow, though the others had instinctively backed away. During an instant of silence they heard rats stirring behind the wainscot.

"Well?" demanded the rector, his voice high.

"I don't see anything," said Dr. Fell. "Here, young fellow—strike a match, will you?"

Rampole cursed himself when he broke off the head of the first match. He struck another, but the dead air of the vault extinguished it the moment he put it inside. Stepping inside, he tried another. Mould and damp, and a strand of cobweb brushing his neck. Now a tiny blue flame burnt in the cup of his hand. . . .

A stone enclosure, six feet high and three or four feet deep. Shelves at the back, and what looked like rotting books. That was all. A sort of dizziness went from him, and he steadied his hand.

"Nothing," he said.

"Unless," said Dr. Fell, chuckling, *"unless it got out."*

"Cheerful blighter, aren't you?" demanded Sir Benjamin. "Look here—we've been wandering about in a nightmare, you know. I'm a business man, a practical man, a sensible man. But I give you my word, gentlemen, that damned place put the wind up me for a moment. It did for a fact."

Saunders ran his handkerchief round under his chin. He had suddenly become pink and beaming, drawing a gusty lungful of air and making a broad unctuous gesture.

"My dear Sir Benjamin," he protested, boomingly, "nothing of the kind! As you say—practical men. As a servant of the Church, you know, I must be the most practical person of all in regard to—ah—matters of this kind. Nonsense! Nonsense!"

He was altogether so pleased that he seemed about to shake Sir Benjamin's hand. The latter was frowning over Rampole's shoulder.

"Anything else?" he asked.

The American nodded. He was holding the flame of the match down against the door, and moving it about. Clearly something had been there, by the outline in the heavy dust: a rectangular outline about eighteen by ten inches. Whatever it was, it had been removed. But he hardly heard the chief constable's request to close the vault again. The last letter of the combination was "S." Something was coming back to him, significant and ugly. Words spoken over a hedge at twilight, words flung at Herbert Starberth by a drunken, contemptuous Martin when the two were coming home from Chatterham yesterday afternoon. "You know the word for it right enough," Martin had said. "The word is *Gallows*." . . .

Rising and slapping dust from his knees, he pushed the door shut. Something had been in that vault—a box, in all likelihood—and the person who killed Martin Starberth had stolen it.

"Somebody took—" he said, involuntarily.

"Yes," said Sir Benjamin. "That seems fairly clear. They wouldn't hand down such a piece of elaborate mummery all these years without any secret at all. But there may be something else. Has it occurred to you, Doctor?"

Dr. Fell was already lumbering round the centre table, as though he were smelling it. He poked at the chair with his cane; he bent down, his big mop of hair flying, to peer under it; and then he looked up vacantly.

"Eh?" he muttered. "I beg your pardon. I was thinking of something else. What did you say?"

The chief constable assumed his schoolmaster's air again, drawing in his chin and compressing his lips to indicate that a deep subject was coming. "Look here," he said, "look here. Don't you think it's more than a coincidence that so many of the Starberth family have died in this particular way?"

Dr. Fell looked up with the expression of a man who has just been hit on the head with a club in a movie comedy.

"Brilliant!" he said. "Brilliant, my boy!—Well, yes. Dense as I am, the coincidence gradually begins to obtrude itself. What then?"

Sir Benjamin was not amused. He folded his arms.

"I think, gentlemen," he announced, seeming to address everybody, "that we shall get forrader in this investigation if we acknowledge that I am, after all, the chief constable, and that I have been at considerable trouble to take over—"

"Tut! I know it. I didn't mean anything." Dr. Fell chewed his moustache to keep back a grin. "It was your infernally solemn way of saying the obvious, that's all. You'll be a statesman yet, son. Pray go on."

"With your permission," conceded the chief constable. He tried to retain his schoolmaster's air; but a smile crept up his speckled face. He rubbed his nose amiably, and then went on with earnestness: "No, see here now. You were all sitting on the lawn watching this window, weren't you? You'd have seen anything untoward that happened up here, certainly—a struggle, or the light knock over, or something. Eh? You'd certainly have heard a cry."

"Very probably."

"And there wasn't any struggle. Look where young Starberth was sitting. He could see the only door in the room; it's exceedingly likely he had it locked, too, if he was as nervous as you say. Even if a murderer could have got into the room first, there was no place for him to hide—unless — Hold on! That wardrobe. . . ."

He strode across and opened the doors, disturbing thick dust.

"That's no good, either. Nothing but dust, mouldy clothes . . . I say, here's one of your frogged greatcoats with the beaver collars; George IV style—spiders!" Closing the doors with a slam, he turned back. "Nobody hid there, I'll swear. And there was no place else. In other words, young Starberth couldn't have been taken by surprise, without fight or at least outcry. . . . Now, then, how do you know the murderer didn't come in here *after* young Starberth had fallen from the balcony?"

"What the devil are you talking about?"

Sir Benjamin's mouth assumed a tight mysterious smile.

"Put it this way," he urged. "Did you actually see this murderer throw him over? Did you see him fall?"

"No, as a matter of fact, we didn't, Sir Benjamin," put in the rector, who evidently felt he had been neglected long enough. He looked thoughtful. "But then we wouldn't have, you know. It was very dark and raining hard, and the light was out. I am of the opinion that he could have been thrown over even while the light was on. You see . . . here's where the light was, on the table. The broad end of the lamp is here, meaning that the beam was directed on the safe. Six feet to the other side, where the balcony door is, and a person would have been in complete darkness."

The chief constable drew up his shoulders and stabbed one long finger into the palm of his head.

"What I am trying to establish, gentlemen, is this: There may have been a murderer. But that murderer did not necessarily creep in here, smash him over the head, and pitch him down to his death; I mean, there may not have been *two* people on the balcony at all. . . . What about a death-trap?"

"Ah!" muttered Dr. Fell, hunching his shoulders. "Well—"

"You see, gentlemen," Sir Benjamin went on, turning to the others in an agony of verbal precision, "I mean . . . At least two Starberths have met their deaths off that balcony before this one. Now suppose there were something about that balcony—a mechanism—eh?"

Rampole turned his eyes towards the balcony door. Beyond the torn ivy he could see a low stone wall, balustraded, suggestive. The very room seemed to grow darker and more sinister.

"I know," he nodded. "Like the stories. I remember one I read when I was a kid, and it made a powerful impression on me. Something about a chair bolted to the floor in an old house, and a weight that swung down out of the ceiling and killed whoever sat under it. But, look here! That sort of thing doesn't happen. Besides, you'd have to have somebody to work a thing like that. . . ."

"Not necessarily. There may have been a murderer; but the 'murderer' may have been dead two hundred years." Sir Benjamin's eyes opened wide, and then narrowed. "By George! I'm getting rather good at this sort of thing!—It just occurred to me: Suppose young Martin opens the safe, finds a box there, and in it directions to do something *on the balcony?* Well, something happens; the box flies out of his hand, down into the well—the lamp goes in another direction, where you find it later—eh?"

Any enthusiastic theory could generally carry Rampole with it. Again he found himself thinking of lines out of Anthony's manuscript: "But I begin to think of a plan. I do heartily abhor and curse each of those to whom I have the misfortune to be bound by ties of blood. . . . By which I am reminded that the rats are growing thicker lately."

And yet—no. Even in his excitement, doubts rattled round inside this smooth hypothesis.

"But look here, sir," he protested, "you can't seriously mean that Anthony wanted to plan a death-trap for all his descendants! Even if he did, it wouldn't be very practical. He would just have got one person with it. The victim takes the box out, reads the paper or whatever it is, gets pitched off the balcony. All right. But the next day they discover the secret, don't they?"

"On the contrary. That's exactly what they haven't discovered. Suppose the instructions were like this: Read this paper, put it back in the box, close the safe again, and then do as directed therein. . . . But this time," said Sir Benjamin, growing so excited that he began to poke Rampole in the chest with a long forefinger—"this time the victim, from whatever cause, takes box and paper along—and down they go into the well."

"Well, then, what about the other Starberths who haven't died in that way? There have been several between Martin in 1837 and Martin in 1930. Timothy got his neck broken in the Hag's Nook, but there's no means of knowing . . ."

The chief constable settled his pince-nez more firmly, even benignantly. He was the professor aiding a favourite pupil.

"My dear Mr. Rampole," he said, with a class-room clearing of his throat, "surely you expect too much of the man's mechanical devices to think it will catch *all* his descendants? No, no. It wouldn't always work, of course, from one cause or another. Anthony may have died in testing it out. . . . Of course, you can take the first theory I outlined, if you prefer it. I confess I'd forgotten that, momentarily. I mean a murderer who wants to steal something from that safe. He has prepared this death-trap on the balcony, using old Anthony's for his own modern use. He waits until young Martin had opened the safe. Then—by some means—he sees to it that Martin is lured out in the balcony, where the mechanism tips him over. The light is thrown and broken. The murderer (who has never actually touched his victim) takes his booty and departs. There, I submit, are two theories, both revolving round a death-mechanism created in the past by Anthony Starberth."

"HEY!" boomed a thunderous voice.

By this time the two parties to the argument had become so engrossed with tapping each other on the shoulder or squaring away to emphasize a point that they had entirely forgotten the others. The violent exclamation from Dr. Fell brought them up with a start. It was followed by heavy rappings of a cane on the floor. Rampole turned to see Dr. Fell's great bulk spread out on the chair beside the table; he was glowering at them and shaking the other cane in the air.

"You two," said the doctor, "have the most brilliantly logical minds I ever listened to. You're not trying to solve anything. You're simply arguing about what would make the best story."

He made a tremendous challenging sound in his nose, like a battle-cry. Then he went on more mildly:

"Now, I'm very fond of such stories, myself. I have been improving my mind with fiction of the Bloody Hand variety for the last forty years. So I know all the conventional death-traps: the staircase that sends you down a chute in

the dark, the bed with the descending canopy, the piece of
furniture with the poisoned needle in it, the clock that fires
a bullet or sticks you with a knife, the gun inside the safe,
the weight in the ceiling, the bed that exhales the deadly
gas when the heat of your body warms it, and all the rest
of 'em . . . probable or improbable. And I confess," said
Dr. Fell, with relish, "that the more improbable they are,
the better I like 'em. I have a simple melodramatic mind,
gentlemen, and I would dearly love to believe you. Have
you ever seen 'Sweeney Todd, the Demon Barber of Fleet
Street'? You should. It was one of the original thriller
plays, well known in the early eighteen-hundreds; all about
a devilish barber's chair which dropped you into the cellar
so that the barber could cut your throat at his leisure.
But—"

"Hold on!" said Sir Benjamin irritably. "All this just
means, then, that you think the notion is too far-fetched?"

"The Gothic romance in particular," pursued Dr. Fell,
"is full of such—eh?" he broke off, lifting his eyes. "Far-
fetched? God bless my soul, no! Some of the most far-
fetched of the death-traps have been real ones, like Nero's
collapsing ship, or the poisoned gloves that killed Charles
VII. No, no. I don't mind your being improbable. The
point is that you haven't any grounds to be improbable *on.*
That's where you're far behind the detective stories. They
may reach an improbable conclusion, but they get there on
the strength of good, sound, improbable evidence that's in
plain sight.— How do you know there was any 'box' inside
that safe?"

"Well, we don't, of course; but—"

"Exactly. And you no sooner have the box, than you get
an inspiration of a 'paper' inside it. Then you get the paper,
and you put 'instructions' on it. Then young Starberth goes
over the balcony; the box becomes inconvenient, so you
drop it after him. Splendid! Now you've not only created
the box and the paper, but you've made them disappear
again, and the case is complete. As our American friends
say, Horse-blinders! It won't do."

"Very well, then," the chief constable said, stiffly. "You

can examine that balcony, if you like. I'm jolly certain *I* won't."

Dr. Fell hoisted himself to his feet. "Oh, I'm going to examine it. Mind, I don't say there wasn't any death-trap; you may be right," he added. He stared straight ahead of him, his big red face very intent. "But I want to remind you that there's only one thing we're absolutely sure of—that Starberth was lying under that balcony with his neck broken. That's *all*."

Sir Benjamin smiled in that tight way of his which seemed to pull the corners of his mouth down rather than up. He said, ironically:

"I'm glad you see at least a little virtue in the notion. I have advanced two perfectly good theories of the death, based on a trap—"

"They're rubbish," said Dr. Fell. He was already staring across at the door to the balcony, and he seemed preoccupied.

"Thank you."

"Oh, all right," the doctor murmured, wearily. "I'll show you, if you like. Both of your ideas, then, are based on young Starberth's being lured out on that balcony, either (A) by instructions he found in the safe, or (B) by the stratagem of some person who wanted to rob the safe, and so got him out there to let the balcony do its villainous job. EH?"

"Quite right."

"Now, then, put yourself in young Starberth's place. You're sitting at this table, where he sat, with your bicycle-lamp beside you; as nervous as he was, or as cool as you might be—either way? Got it? Got the scene?"

"Perfectly, thank you."

"For whatever purpose, you get up to go over to that door, which hasn't been opened in God knows how many years; you're not only trying to open a sealed door, but you're going out on a balcony that's blacker than pitch. . . . What do you do?"

"Why, I pick up the lamp and I—"

"Precisely. That's it. That's the whole story. You hold your lamp while you're opening the door, and flash it out on the balcony to see where you're going, before you've even set foot out there. . . . Well, that's precisely what our victim didn't do. If so much as a crack of light had shown through this door anywhere, we should have seen it from my garden. But we didn't."

There was a silence. Sir Benjamin pushed his hat over to one side of his head and scowled.

"By Jove!" he muttered, "that sounds reasonable, you know. Still— Oh, look here! There's something wrong. I don't see any earthly way a murderer could have come in this room without an outcry on Starbeth's part."

"Neither do I," said Dr. Fell. "If that encourages you any. I . . ." He broke off, a startled expression coming into his eyes as he stared at the iron door to the balcony. "O Lord! O Bacchus. O my ancient hat. This won't do."

He went stumping over to the door. First he knelt down and examined the dusty, gritty floor, where bits of dirt and stone had fallen when the door was opened. He ran his hand along them. Rising, he examined the outer face of the door; then he pushed it partly shut and looked at the keyhole.

"Opened with a key, right enough," he mumbled. "Here's a fresh scratch in the rust where it slipped . . ."

"Then," snapped the chief constable, "Martin Starberth did open that door, after all?"

"No. No, I don't think so. That was the murderer." Dr. Fell said something else, but it was inaudible because he had stepped through the sheathing ivy out upon the balcony.

The rest of them looked at one another uneasily. Rampole found himself more afraid of that balcony than he had even been of the safe. But he found himself moving forward, with Sir Benjamin at his elbow. The rector, he discovered as he glanced over his shoulder, was intently examining the titles of the calf-bound books in the shelves to the right of the fireplace; he seemed reluctant to drag himself away, though his feet appeared to be moving in the direction of the balcony.

Pushing aside the vines, Rampole stepped out. The balcony was not large; hardly more than a stone shelf about the base of the door, with stone balustrades built waist-high. There was little more room than would comfortably accommodate the three of them as he and Sir Benjamin stepped to either side of the doctor.

Nobody spoke. Over the top of the prison the morning sun had not yet struck; these walls, the hill, and the Hag's Nook below were still in shadow. Some twenty feet down, Rampole could see the edge of the cliff jutting out in mud and weeds, and the triangle of stone blocks which had once supported the gallows. Through the little door down there they had brought out the condemned from the pressroom, where the smith had struck off their irons before the last jump. From up here Anthony had watched it, in his "new suit of scarlet and laced hat." Bending over, Rampole could see the well gaping among the firs; he thought he could discern the green scum upon its water many feet farther down, but it was in heavy shadow.

Only that gaping pit, ringed in spikes, fifty feet below the balcony. Beyond it the northern meadows were sunlit, and starred with white flowers. You could see across the low-lands, cut with hedgerows like a rolling checkerboard; the white road, the stream glimmering, the white houses among trees, and the church spire. Peace. The meadows were not now black with faces to watch a hanging. Rampole could see a hay-wagon dawdling along the road.

"—it seems solid enough," Rampole heard Sir Benjamin saying, "and we've quite a lot of weight on it. I don't like messing about with it, though. Steady! What are you doing?"

Dr. Fell was grubbing among the ivy over the black balustrades.

"I've always wanted to examine this," he said, "but I never thought I should have the opportunity. H'm. It wouldn't wear, or would it?" he added to himself. There followed a sound of ripping ivy.

"I should be careful, if I were you. Even if—"

"Ha!" cried the doctor, loosing his breath in a gust. "What ho! *'Drinc heil!'*—as the Saxon toast was. Mud in your eye! I never thought I should find it, but here it is. Heh. Heh-heh-heh-heh." He turned a beaming face. "Look here, on the outer edge of the balustrade. There's a worn place I can put my thumb in. And another, not so worn, on the side towards us."

"Well, what about it?" demanded Sir Benjamin. "Look here, I shouldn't mess about with that. You never know."

"Antiquarian research. We must celebrate this. Come along, gentlemen. I don't think there's anything more out here."

Sir Benjamin looked at him suspiciously as they reëntered the Governor's Room. He demanded:

"If you saw anything, I'm hanged if I did. What has it got to do with the murder, anyhow?"

"Nothing whatever, man! That is," said Dr. Fell, "only indirectly. Of course, if it weren't for those two worn places in the stone . . . Still, I don't know." He rubbed his hands together. "I say, do you remember what old Anthony's motto was? He had it stamped on his books, and his rings, and Lord knows what all. Did you ever see it?"

"So," the chief constable said, narrowing his eyes, "we come back to Anthony again, do we? No. I never saw his motto.— But unless you have anything more to suggest, we'd better get out of here and pay a visit to the Hall. Come, now! What's this all about?"

Dr. Fell took a last glance about the gloomy room.

"The motto," he said, "was '*Omnia mea mecum porto*' —'All that belongs to me I carry with me.' Eh? Think it over. Look here, what about a bottle of beer?"

Chapter 9

A GRAVEL walk, winding. Grey pigeons that waddled suspiciously under elms. Shaven lawns, and the shadows of birds under the sun. The tall, bluff house of mellowed red brick, with white facings and a white cupola surmounted by a gilt weather-vane, growing old gracefully since the days when Anne was queen. Bees somewhere, droning, and a sweet smell of hay in the air.

Rampole had not seen it thus the night before. It had been raining when the rector's Ford drew up here then, and he and Saunders had carried the light, stiffening body up those steps. Before him had opened the mellow hallway, as though he had been suddenly thrust on a lighted stage with that dripping burden, before a thousand people. As he walked up the drive with his companions now, he shrank from meeting Her again. That was how it had been: thrust upon a stage, without lines, dazed and futile; unclothed, the way you feel in dreams sometimes. She hadn't been in the hall then. There had been only that butler—what was his name?—stooping slightly forward, his hands clasped together. He had prepared a couch in the drawing-room.

She had come out of the library, presently. Her red eyes showed that she had been crying desperately, in one of those horrible paroxysms; but she was steady and blank-faced then, squeezing a handkerchief. He hadn't said anything. What the devil was there to say? A word, a motion, anything would have seemed crude and clumsy; he didn't know why; it just would have seemed so. He had merely stood wretchedly by the door, in his soaked flannels and tennis shoes, and left as soon as he could. He remembered leaving: it had just stopped raining a moment before, and the grandfather clock was striking one. Through his wretchedness he remembered fastening foolishly on a small point: the rain stopped at one o'clock. The rain stopped at one o'clock. Got to remember that. Why? well, anyway—

It wasn't as though he could feel any sorrow at the death of Martin Starberth. He hadn't even liked Martin Starberth. It was something he stood for; something lost and damned in the girl's face when she walked in to look at her dead; a squeeze of a flimsy handkerchief, a brief contortion of a face, as at pain too great to be borne. The immaculate Martin looked queer in death: he wore an ancient pair of grey flannels and a torn tweed coat. . . . And how would Dorothy feel now? He saw the closed shutters and the crape on the door, and winced.

Budge opened the door to them now, looking relieved when he saw the chief constable.

"Yes, sir," he said. "Shall I call Miss Dorothy?"

Sir Benjamin pulled at his lower lip. He was uneasy.

"No. Not for the moment, anyhow. Where is she?"

"Upstairs, sir."

"And Mr. Starberth?"

"Upstairs also, sir. The undertaking people are here."

"Anybody else here?"

"I believe Mr. Payne is on his way, sir. Dr. Markley was to call; he told me that he wished to see you, sir, as soon as he had finished his morning round."

"Ah yes. I see. By the way, Budge . . . those undertakers: I shall want to see the clothes Mr. Starberth wore last night, and the contents of his pockets, you know."

Budge inclined his flattish head towards Dr. Fell. "Yes, sir. Dr. Fell mentioned that possibility last night. I took the liberty of preserving them without removing anything from the pockets."

"Good man. Get them and bring them to the library now. . . . And I say, Budge—!"

"Yes, sir?"

"If you should happen to see Miss Starberth," said Sir Benjamin, fidgeting, "just—er—convey my deepest . . . you know? Yes." He hesitated, this honest police official, growing slightly red in the face at what he apparently considered deception on friends. "And I should like to see Mr. Herbert Starberth as soon as is convenient."

Budge was impassive. "Mr. Herbert has not yet returned, sir."

"Oh, ah! I see. Well, get me those clothes."

They went into a darkened library. It is women who are most efficient in a house of death, where emotionalism runs high; men, like these four, are tongue-tied and helpless. Saunders was the only one who showed any degree of calmness; he was getting back his smooth manners, and seemed as unctuous as though he were opening a Prayer-book to read.

"If you'll excuse me, gentlemen," he said, "I think I had better see whether Miss Starberth will receive me. It's a trying time, you know; a trying time; and if I can be of any assistance. . . ."

"Quite," said the chief constable, gruffly. When the rector had gone, he began to pace up and down. "Of course it's a trying time. But why the devil talk about it? I don't like this."

Rampole thoroughly agreed with him. They all fidgeted in the big old room, and Sir Benjamin opened some shutters. Silver chimes rang with fluid grace from the great clock in the hall, sounding as though they were striking through the vault of a cathedral. In this library everything looked old and solid and conventional; there was a globe-map which nobody ever spun, rows of accepted authors which nobody ever read, and above the mantelpiece a large mounted swordfish which (you were convinced) nobody had ever caught. A glass ball was hung up in one window, as a charm against witches.

Budge returned presently, carrying a laundry-bag.

"Everything is here, sir," he announced, "with the exception of the underclothing. Nothing has been removed from the pockets."

"Thank you. Stay here, Budge; I shall want to ask you some questions."

Dr. Fell and Rampole came over to watch as Sir Benjamin put the bag on the centre table and began taking things out. A grey jacket, stiff with mud, the lining frayed and torn, and several buttons missing.

"Here we are," the chief constable muttered, feeling in the pockets. "Cigarette-case—handsome one, too. Full of . . . these look like American cigarettes. Yes. Lucky Strike. Box of matches. Pocket flask, brandy, a third gone. That's the lot."

He rummaged again.

"Old shirt, nothing in the pocket. Socks. Here are the trousers, also in disrepair. He knew it would be a dusty job, poking about that prison. Here's his wallet, in the hip pocket." Sir Benjamin paused. "I suppose I'd better look inside. H'm. Ten-shilling note, two pound notes, and a fiver. Letters, all sent to him in America, American postmark. 'Martin Starberth, Esq., 470 West 24th St., N. Y.' Look here, you don't suppose some enemy might have followed him from America . . . ?"

"I doubt it," said Dr. Fell. "But you might put them aside."

"Notebook of some sort, full of figures. 'A. & S.,' 25, 'Good Roysterers,' 10, 'Roaring Caravans,' 3, 'Oedipus Rises'; 'Bloomingdales,' 25 'Good—' What's all this?"

"Probably salesman's orders," said Rampole. "He told me he was in the publishing business. Anything else?"

"A number of cards. 'The Freedom Club, 65 West 51st St.' All clubs of some sort; dozens of them. 'Valhalla Cordial Shop, We Deliver, 342 Bleecker—' "

"That's all right," said Rampole. "I understand."

"That finishes the wallet, and the clothes, too. Wait! By Jove! here's his watch in his watch-pocket. And still running. His body broke the force of the fall, and the watch—"

"Let me look at that," Dr. Fell interposed, suddenly. He turned over the thin gold watch, whose ticking was loud in the quiet room. "In the stories," he added, "the dead man's watch is always very conveniently smashed, thus enabling the detectives to fix the wrong time of death because the murderer has set the hands at a different hour. Behold an exception from life."

"So I see," replied the chief constable. "But why are you so interested? In this case, the time of death isn't at all important."

"Oh, yes it is!" said Dr. Fell. "More important than you think. Er—at present this watch says five-and-twenty minutes past ten." He peered up at the clock on the mantelpiece. "That clock also says five-and-twenty minutes past ten, to the second. . . . Budge, do you happen to know whether that clock is right?"

Budge inclined his head. "Yes, sir. It is right. I can answer positively about that score, sir."

The doctor hesitated, peering sharply at the butler, and then put the watch down.

"You look confoundedly earnest, man," he said. "Why are you so positive?"

"Because an unusual thing happened last night, sir. The grandfather clock in the hall was ten minutes fast. I—er— happened to notice it by comparing it with the clock in here. Then I went round to look at all the other clocks in the house. We generally set our watches by the grandfather clock, sir, and I fancied—"

"You did?" demanded Dr. Fell. "You looked at the others, did you?"

"Why—yes, sir," said Budge, slightly shocked.

"Well? Were they all right?"

"That, if I may say so, sir, is the curious part of it. They were. All of them except the grandfather. I can't imagine how it came to be wrong, sir. Somebody must have set it that way. In the hurry and rush, I have not had an opportunity to enquire. . . ."

"What's this all about?" asked the chief constable. "According to what you've told me, young Starberth arrived at the Governor's Room on the tick of eleven—his watch is right—everything is right. . . ."

"Yes," said Dr. Fell. "Yes. That's what makes it wrong, you see. Just one more question, Budge. Is there a clock in Mr. Martin's room?"

"Yes, sir. A large one on the wall."

Dr. Fell nodded his head several times, in communication with himself. Then he went to a chair and lowered himself into it with a sigh.

"Carry on, old man. I may seem to ask a number of foolish questions at odd times, and I shall probably be doing it all day, to every one of your witnesses. Bear with me, will you?—But, Budge! When Sir Benjamin has finished talking to you, I wish you'd try to dig up the person who changed that clock in the hall. It's rather important."

The chief constable was tapping his fingers impatiently on the table. "You're sure you're quite through?" he asked. "If not—"

"Well, I might point out," said the doctor, raising one cane to point, "that the murderer has certainly pinched something out of those clothes. What?—Why, his keys, man! All the keys he had to have! You didn't find 'em, did you?"

Sir Benjamin remained silent, nodding to himself; then he made a gesture and turned resolutely to Budge. Again they were to go over the same bare ground as last night.

Rampole did not want to hear it. He already knew Budge's bare story, as the doctor had elicited it; and he wanted to see Dorothy Starbeth. The rector would be up there with her now, shovelling out platitudes like a pious stoker, with the idea that in quantity there was consolation. He could imagine Saunders saying the conventional things in just the smooth, unthinking fashion which makes women murmur, "Such a help, you know!"—and remarking how beautifully he behaved.

Why weren't people silent in the presence of death? Why, from everybody, this invariable ghoulish murmuring of, "So-natural-looking, isn't-he?" and all the comments which only started the women to weeping afresh? No matter. What he disliked was the idea of Saunders being so kind and big-brotherly (Saunders would enjoy that role, too) up there with Her. Budge's professionally serene visage was an annoyance, too; and Budge's carefully fashioned sentences where the h's were automatically clipped on, like caps upon bottles, as the words issued from the machine. Bad form or not, he couldn't sit here. Whatever the rest of them thought, he was somehow going to get closer to her. He slipped from the room.

But where would he go? Obviously not upstairs; that would be a little too much. But he couldn't prowl about the hall, as though he were looking for the gas-meter or something. Did they have gas-meters in England? Oh, well! Wandering towards the back of the dusky hall, he saw a door partly open near the stairs. A figure blocked the light and Dorothy Starberth was beckoning to him. . . .

He met her in the shadow of the stairs, clasping her hands hard, and he could feel her trembling. At first he was afraid to look at her face, because he was afraid, in the thickness of his throat, that he might blurt out, "I've failed you, and I shouldn't have failed you," and to say that —no! Or he might say, "I love you," here in the shadow, beneath the mellow ticking of the great clock; and the thought of what he might have said struck deep, with a barbed and shaking hurt.

But there were no words, and only the clock murmured in this quiet cathedral, and something sang within him, crying: Great God, why must there be all this nonsense about the glory of strength and self-reliance in such as she? I would not wish her so. This small body, which I might·hold in my arms now for a moment, I would shield and guard; and the whisper she might give me would be as a war-cry in the night; and against this shield, as I held her forever, even the gates of hell should not prevail. But he knew that this ache in the blood must be stifled now. He was only thinking crazy things; laugh-provoking things, so they said; and through the muddle of dreams he could be only his clumsy self, and say:

"I know. . . ."

A foolish whisper, as he patted her hand. Then somehow they were inside the door, in a small office with drawn blinds.

"I heard you come in," she said, in a low voice, "and I heard Mr. Saunders coming upstairs, and I couldn't talk to him; so I let Mrs. Bundle stop him—she'll talk his ears off—and came down the back stairs."

She sat down on an old horsehair sofa, her chin propped in the palm of her hand, her eyes heavy and dull. A silence. The closed, darkened room was thick with heat. When she started to speak again, with a little spasmodic movement of her hand, he touched her shoulder.

"If you'd rather not talk . . ."

"I've got to talk. It seems days since I've slept. And I must go in there, in a moment, and go over the whole thing again with Them."

His fingers tightened. She raised her head.

"You needn't look like that," she said, softly. "Would you—would you believe that I was never tremendously fond of Martin? It isn't that so much—his dying, I mean. He was never very close to any of us, you know. I ought to feel worse about it than I do."

"Well, then . . ."

"Either one of the two is just as bad!" she cried, her voice rising. "It's either—We can't help ourselves; we're haunted; we're damned, all of us, in the blood; retribution; I never believed it, I won't believe it; or else—"

"Steady! You've got to snap out of this."

"Or else—maybe it's both. How do we know what's in a person's blood? Yours or mine or anybody's? There may be a murderer's blood just as well as a ghost; more so. Is that door shut?"

"Yes."

"Any of us. Why"—her voice grew vague, and she put her hands together as though she were uncertain of their position, "I might—kill *you*. I might take the gun out of that desk drawer, just because I couldn't help myself, and all of a sudden . . ." She shuddered. "Why, if all those old people weren't damned to suicide, or being thrown off the balcony by destiny—ghosts—I don't know—then somebody was damned to kill them—in the family. . . ."

"You've got to stop this! Look here! Listen—!"

She nodded gently, touched her eyelids with her finger tips, and looked up. "Do you think Herbert killed Martin?"

"No! No, of course not. And it wasn't any foolery about ghosts, either. And—you know your cousin couldn't have killed Martin. He admired him; he was solid and dependable—"

"He talked to himself," the girl said, blankly. "I remember now; he talked to himself. It's the quiet people I'm afraid of. They're the ones who go mad, if it's tainted blood to begin with. . . . He had big red hands. His hair wouldn't stay down, no matter how much he slicked it. He was built delicately, like Martin, but his hands were too big. He tried to look like Martin. I wonder if he hated Martin?"

A pause, while she plucked at the edges of the sofa.

"And he was always trying to invent something that never worked. A new churn. He thought he was an inventor. Martin used to laugh at him. . . ."

The dim room was full of personalities. Rampole saw two figures standing in the middle of a white road at dusk, so like in appearance and yet so vitally unlike. Martin, drunk, a cigarette hanging from his lips. Herbert gawky and blunt-featured, with a badly fitting hat set exactly high and straight on his head. You felt that if Herbert smoked a cigarette, too, it would protrude from the exact centre of his mouth, and waggle awkwardly.

"Somebody opened the wall safe in the library last night," said Dorothy Starberth. "That was something I didn't tell Dr. Fell last night. I didn't tell him so much that was important. I didn't tell him that at dinner Herbert was more flustered than Martin. . . . It was Herbert who opened that library safe."

"But—"

"Martin didn't know the combination. He's been away two years, and he never had occasion to. The only ones who knew it were myself and Mr. Payne—and Herbert. I saw it standing open last night."

"Something was taken?"

"I don't think so. There was never anything valuable left in there. When father built this office here, he stopped using it. I'm sure he hadn't opened it for years, and none of the rest of us ever did. It was just full of some old papers for years back. . . . It wasn't that anything had been taken; at least, anything I know of. It was something I found."

He wondered whether she were becoming hysterical. She rose from the sofa, opened a secretary-desk with a key hung round her neck, and took out a yellowed piece of paper. As she handed it to him, he fought down a desire to take her in his arms.

"Read it!" she said, breathlessly. "I trust you. I won't tell the others. I must tell somebody. . . . Read it."

He glanced down, puzzled. It was headed, "Feb. 3, 1895. My copy of the verses—Timothy Starberth," in faded ink. It read:

> *How called the dwellers of Lyn-dun?*
> *Great Homer's tale of Troy,*
> *Or country of the midnight sun—*
> *What doth all men Destroy?*
>
> *Against it man hath dashed his foot;*
> *This angel bears a spear!*

> *In garden-glade where Lord Christ prayed*
> *What spawns dark stars and fear?*
>
> *This place the white Diana rose,*
>   *Of this, Dido bereft;*
> *Where on four leaves good fortune grows*
>   *East, west, south—what is left?*
>
> *The Corsican was vanquished there,*
>   *Oh, mother of all sin!*
> *Find green the same as shiretown's name,*
>   *Find Newgate Gaol, and win!*

"Well," said Rampole, muttering over the lines, "it's very bad doggerel, and it doesn't make the slightest sense so far as I can see; but that's true of a lot of verse I've read. . . . What is it?"

She looked at him steadily. "Do you see the date? February 3 was father's birthday. He was born in 1870, so in 1895 he would have been—"

"Twenty-five years old," interposed Rampole, suddenly.

They were both silent, Rampole staring at the enigmatic words with a slow comprehension. All the wild surmises which he and Sir Benjamin had been making, and which Dr. Fell had so violently ridiculed, seemed to grow substantial before him.

"Now let me lead *you* on," he suggested. "If that's true, then the original of this paper—it says 'my copy'—was in the vault in the Governor's Room. So?"

"It must be what the eldest sons were intended to see." She took the paper out of his hands as though she felt a rage against it, and would have crumpled it in her hand but that he shook his head. "I've thought about it, and thought about it, and that's the only explanation I can see. I hope it's true. I had fancied so many ghastly things that *might* be there. And yet this is just as bad. People still die."

He sat down on the sofa.

"If there was an original," he said, "it isn't there now."

Slowly, omitting nothing, he told her of their visit to the Governor's Room. "And that thing," he added, "is a cryptogram of some sort. It's got to be. Could anybody have killed Martin just to get at this?"

There was a discreet knock at the door, and they both started like conspirators. Putting her finger on her lips, Dorothy hastily locked the paper in the desk.

"Come in," she said.

Budge's smooth countenance floated in at the opening of the door. If he were surprised to find Rampole here, there was no sign of it.

"Excuse me, Miss Dorothy," he said. "Mr. Payne has just arrived. Sir Benjamin would like to see you in the library, if you please."

Chapter 10

THERE had been high words in the library a moment before; so much was plain from the constraint and tensity there, and the slight flush on Sir Benjamin's face. He stood with his back to the empty fireplace, his hands clasped behind him. In the middle of the room, Rampole saw, stood his own pet dislike—Payne, the lawyer.

"I'll tell you what you'll do, sir," said Sir Benjamin. "You'll sit down there like a sensible man, and you'll give your testimony when it's asked for. Not before."

Payne whirred in his throat. Rampole saw the short white hair bristle on the back of his head.

"Are you familiar with the law, sir?" he rasped.

"Yes, sir, I am," said Sir Benjamin. "I happen to be a magistrate myself, you know. Now will you obey my instructions, or shall I—"

Dr. Fell coughed. He inclined his head sleepily towards the door, hoisting himself up from his chair as Dorothy Starberth entered. Payne turned jerkily.

"Ah, come in, my dear," he said, pushing out a chair. "Sit down. Rest yourself. Sir Benjamin and I"—the whites of his eyes flashed over towards the chief constable, "will talk presently."

He folded his arms, but he did not move from the side of her chair, where he had taken up his stand like a guardian. Sir Benjamin was ill at ease.

"You know, of course, Miss Starberth," he began, "how we all feel about this tragic business. As long as I've known you and your family, I don't think I need say more." His sincere old face looked muddled and kindly. "I dislike intruding on you at this time. But if you feel up to answering a few questions . . ."

"You don't have to answer them," said Payne. "Remember that, my dear."

"You don't have to answer them," agreed Sir Benjamin, controlling his temper. "I only thought to save you trouble for the inquest."

"Of course," said the girl. She sat quietly, her hands in her lap, while she told the story she had told last night. They had finished dinner a little before nine o'clock. She had tried to entertain Martin and keep his mind off the forthcoming business; but he was moody and distraught, and had gone up to his room immediately. Where was Herbert? She did not know. She had gone out on the lawn, where it was cooler, and sat there for the better part of an hour. Then she had gone in to the office to look over the day's household accounts. In the hall she had met Budge, who informed her that he had taken a bicycle-lamp up to Martin's room, as Martin had asked. Several times, during the half-hour or three-quarters ensuing, she had been on the point of going up to Martin's room. But he had expressed a desire to be left alone; he was sullen, and had been bad-tempered at dinner; so she had refrained from doing so. He would feel better if nobody saw his state of nerves.

At about twenty minutes to eleven she had heard him leave his room, come downstairs, and go out the side door. She had run after him, reaching the side door as he was going down the drive, and called to him—afraid that he might have taken too much to drink. He had called back to her, snapping some words she did not catch; his speech was rather thick, but his step seemed fairly steady. Then she had gone to the telephone and communicated with Dr. Fell's house, telling them that he was on the way.

That was all. Her slow, throaty voice never faltered as she told it, and her eyes remained fixed on Sir Benjamin; the full pink lips, devoid of make-up, hardly seemed to move at all. At the conclusion, she sat back and looked at the sunlight in one unshuttered window.

"Miss Starberth," said Dr. Fell, after a pause, "I wonder if you'd mind my asking a question? . . . Thank you. Budge has told us that the clock in the hall out there was wrong last night, though none of the others were. When you say that he left the house at twenty minutes to eleven, do you mean the time by that clock, or the right time?"

"Why—" she looked at him blankly; then down at her wristwatch and up at the clock on the mantelpiece. "Why, the right time! I'm positive of it. I never even glanced at the clock in the hall. Yes, the right time."

Dr. Fell relapsed, while the girl regarded him with a slight frown. Evidently nettled at this irrelevancy being brought in again, Sir Benjamin began to pace up and down the hearth rug. You felt that he had been nerving himself up to ask certain questions, and the doctor's interruption had scattered his resolves. Finally he turned.

"Budge has already told us, Miss Starberth, about Herbert's entirely unexplained absence. . . ."

She inclined her head.

"Think, if you please! You are positive that he never mentioned the possibility of leaving suddenly—well, that is, you can think of no reason for his doing so?"

"None," she said, and added, in a lower voice: "You needn't be so formal, Sir Benjamin. I understand the implications as well as you do."

"Well, to be frank, then: the coroner's jury is likely to put an ugly interpretation on it, unless he returns immediately. Even so—you see? Has there been any ill-feeling between Herbert and Martin in the past?"

"Never."

"Or more recently?"

"We hadn't seen Martin," she answered, interlacing her fingers, "since about a month after father died, up until the time we met his boat at Southampton the day before yesterday. There has never been the slightest ill-feeling between them."

Sir Benjamin was plainly at a loss. He looked round at Dr. Fell, as though for prompting, but the doctor said nothing.

"At the moment," he went on, clearing his throat, "I can think of nothing else. It's—ah—very puzzling. Very puzzling indeed. Naturally, we don't want to subject you to any more of an ordeal than is necessary, my dear; and if you care to go back to your room . . ."

"Thanks. But if you don't mind," said the girl, "I should prefer to remain here. It's more—more . . . well, I should prefer to remain."

Payne patted her on the shoulder. "*I'll* attend to the rest of it," he told her, nodding towards the chief constable with dry, vicious satisfaction.

There was an interruption. They heard a nervous, whispering jabber in the hall outside, and a voice which suddenly croaked, "Nonsense!" with a shrillness so exactly like a talking crow that everybody started. Budge came sailing in.

"If you please, sir," he said to the chief constable, "Mrs. Bundle is bringing one of the housemaids who knows something about that clock."

"—now you march!" squawked the crow's voice. "You march right in there, young lady, and you speaks to 'em. It's a *nice* state of affairs, it's a *nice* state of affairs, I say, if we can't 'ave truth-telling people in the 'ouse, I say. . . . *Pop!*" concluded Mrs. Bundle, making a noise with her lips like a cork pulled out of a bottle.

Escorting a frightened housemaid, she came rolling through the door. Mrs. Bundle was a little lean woman with a sailor's walk, a lace cap coming down into her bright eyes, and a face of such extraordinary malevolence that Rampole stared. She glared upon everybody out of a dusty face, but she seemed less to be damning everybody than to be meditating some deep wrong. Then she assumed a wooden stare, which gave her a curious cross-eyed look.

" 'Ere she is," said Mrs. Bundle. "And what I say is

this: things being what they are, I say, we might as well all be murdered in our beds or Get Took By Americans. It's all the same. Many's the time I've said to Mr. Budge, I've said, 'Mr. Budge, you mark my words, there's no good a-going ter come of mucking about with them ghosters. 'Tain't in natur,' I've said, 'for this 'ere tenement of clay (which we all is) to be alwis a-trying to beard them ghosters by their beards,' I says. *Pop.* You'd think we was Americans. *Pop!* And them ghosters, now——"

"Of course, Mrs. Bundle, of course," the chief constable said, soothingly. He turned to the little housemaid, who trembled in Mrs. Bundle's grip like a virgin ensnared by a witch. "You know something about the clock——er——?"

"Martha, sir. Yes, sir. Truly."

"Tell us about it, Martha."

"They chews gum. Drat 'em!" cried Mrs. Bundle, with such ferocious malignancy that she gave a little hop.

"Eh?" said the chief constable. "Who?"

"They takes pies and hits people," said Mrs. Bundle. "Eee! Squee! Pop! Drat 'em! . . ."

The housekeeper showed a tendency to hold forth on this theme. She was not talking about the ghosters, it seemed, but about the Americans, whom she proceeded to describe as "nasty cowboy people with straw hats on." The ensuing monologue she delivered, shaking a bunch of keys in one hand and Martha in the other, was a trifle clouded in meaning, due to the listeners' inability to tell when she was referring to the Americans and when she was referring to the ghosters. She had concluded a lecture which seemed to deal with the ghosters' impolite habit of squirting one another in the face with soda-water from syphons, before Sir Benjamin summoned enough courage to interfere.

"Now, Martha, please go on. It was you who changed the clock?"

"Yes, sir. But he told me to do it, sir, and——"

"Who told you?"

"Mr. Herbert, sir. Truly. I was crossing the hall, and he comes out of the library a-looking at his watch. And he says to me, 'Martha, that clock's ten minutes slow; set it right,' he says. Sharp-like. You know. I was that astonished you could have knocked me over with a feather. Him speaking sharp-like, and all. Which he never does. And he says, 'See to the rest of the clocks, Martha; set 'em right if they're wrong. Mind!' "

Sir Benjamin looked over at Dr. Fell.

"It's your enquiry," said the chief constable. "Carry on."

"Hmf," said Dr. Fell. His rumbling from the corner startled Martha, whose pink face turned a trifle pinker. "When was this, did you say?"

"I didn't, sir, truly I didn't say, but I will, because I looked at the clock. Naturally. Changing it like he told me, and all. It was just before dinner, sir, and the rector had just went after bringing Mr. Martin home, and Mr. Martin was in the library, he was; and so I changed the clock, and it said five-and-twenty minutes past eight. Only it wasn't. Being ten minutes fast after I changed it. I mean—"

"Yes, of course. And why didn't you change the others?"

"I was a-going to, sir. But then I went into the library, and Mr. Martin was there. And he says, 'What are you doing?' and when I told him he says, 'You let them clocks alone,' he says. And of course I did. Him being the master, and all. And that's all I know, sir."

"Thank you, Martha. . . . Mrs. Bundle, did you or any of the housemaids see Mr. Herbert leaving the house last night?"

Mrs. Bundle thrust out her jaw. "When we went to the fair at Holdern," she replied, malignantly, "Annie Murphy's purse was stole by thiefpockets. And they put me on a thing what goes round and round, it did; round and round; and then I walks upon boards which shakes, and stairs which collapses, and in the dark, and me 'airpins comes loose, which is that the way to treat a lady? Eeee! Drat 'em!" squawked the housekeeper, shaking her keys ferociously. "It was a in-vention, that's what it was, a dratted in-ven-tion! All them inventions is like that, which I told Mr. Herbert about it many's the time, and when I see him going out to the stable last night—"

"You saw Mr. Herbert leave?" demanded the chief constable.

"—to the stable where he keeps them inventions which to be sure *I* don't look at stairs which shakes out me very 'airpins. Do I?"

"What inventions?" said the chief constable, rather helplessly.

"It's all right, Sir Benjamin," said Dorothy. "Herbert is always tinkering with something, without any success. He had a workshop out there."

Further than this no information could be elicited from Mrs. Bundle. All inventions, she was convinced, had to do with certain contraptions which threw one about in the dark at the Holdern fair. Apparently somebody with a primitive sense of humour had led the good lady into the Crazy House, where she had screamed until a crowd assembled, got caught in the machinery, hit somebody with an umbrella, and was finally escorted out by the police. Just as, after a tempestuous review of the matter without enlightenment for her hearers, she was led out by Budge.

"Waste of time," growled Sir Benjamin, when she had gone. "There's your question about the clock answered, Doctor. Now I think we can proceed."

"I think we can," Payne interposed, suddenly.

He had not moved from his position beside the girl's chair; small, his arms folded, ugly as a Chinese image.

"I think we can," he repeated. "Since you seem to get nowhere with this aimless questioning, I fancy that some explanations are due *me*. I hold a trust in this family. For a hundred years nobody except members of the Starberth family have been allowed in the Governor's Room on any pretext whatsoever. This morning, I am given to understand, you gentlemen—one of you a perfect stranger—violated that law. That in itself calls for an explanation."

Sir Benjamin shut his jaws firmly. "Excuse me, my friend," he said. "I don't think it does."

The lawyer was beginning, in a furious voice: "What you think, sir, is of minor—" when Dr. Fell cut him short. He spoke in a tired and indolent voice.

"Payne," said Dr. Fell, "you're an ass. You've made trouble at every turn, and I wish you wouldn't be such an old woman. . . . By the way, how did you know we were up there?"

The tone in which he spoke, one of mild expostulation, was worse than any contempt. Payne glared.

"I have eyes," he snarled. "I saw you leaving. I went up after you to be sure your meddling ways had interfered with nothing."

"Oh!" said Dr. Fell. "Then you violated the law too?"

"That is not the question, sir. I am privileged. I know what is in that vault. . . ." He was so angry that he grew indiscreet, and added, "It is not the first time I have been privileged to see it."

Dr. Fell had been staring blankly at the floor. Now he rolled up his big lionlike head, still with that vacant expression, to regard the other.

"That's interesting," he murmured. "I rather thought you had, too. H'mf. Yes."

"I must remind you again," said Payne, "that I hold a trust—"

"Not any longer," said Dr. Fell.

There was a pause, which somehow seemed to make the room cold. The lawyer opened his eyes wide, jerking his head towards Dr. Fell.

"I said, 'not any longer,'" the doctor repeated, raising his voice slightly. "Martin was the last of the direct line. It's all over. The trust, or the curse, or whatever you care to call it, is done with for ever; and for that part of it I can say, thank God. . . . Anyhow, it needn't be a mystery any longer. If you were up there this morning, you know that something has been taken from the safe. . . ."

"How do *you* know that?" demanded Payne, sticking out his neck.

"I'm not trying to be cute," the doctor responded, wearily. "And I wish you wouldn't try to be, either. In any case, if you want to help justice, you'd better tell us the whole story of your trust. We shall never know the truth about Martin's murder unless we know that. Go on, Sir Benjamin. I hate to keep butting in like this."

"That's the position exactly," said Sir Benjamin. "You'll

withhold no evidence, sir. That is, unless you want to be held as a material witness."

Payne looked from one to the other of them. He had had an easy time of it, you felt, up to now. Few people had crossed him or sat upon him. He was wildly trying to keep his cool dignity, like a man striving to manage a sailboat in a high wind.

"I will tell you as much as I think fit," he said with an effort, "and no more. What do you want to know?"

"Thank you," said the chief constable, drily. "First, you kept the keys to the Governor's Room, did you not?"

"I did."

"How many keys were there?"

"Four."

"Damn it, man," snapped Sir Benjamin, "you're not on the witness-stand! Please be more explicit."

"A key to the outer door of the room. A key to the iron door giving on the balcony. A key to the vault. And, since you have already looked inside that vault," said Payne, biting his words, "I can tell you the rest. A small key to a steel box which was inside the safe."

"A box—" Sir Benjamin repeated. He glanced over his shoulder at Dr. Fell; his eyes had verified a prediction, and there was a small, knowing, rather malicious smile in them. "A box. Which, we know, is gone. . . . What was inside the box?"

Payne debated something in his mind. He had not unfolded his arms, and the fingers of one hand began to tap on his biceps.

"All that it was my duty to know," he answered after a pause, "is that there are a number of cards inside, each with the eighteenth-century Anthony Starberth's signature on it. The heir was instructed to take out one of those cards and present it to the executor next day, as proof that he had actually opened the box. . . . Whatever else there may have been inside—" He shrugged.

"You mean you don't know?" asked Sir Benjamin.

"I mean that I prefer not to say."

"We will return to that in a moment," the chief constable said, slowly. "Four keys. Now, as to the word which opens the letter-lock . . . neither are we quite blind, Mr. Payne . . . as to the word: you are intrusted with that also?"

A hesitation. "In a manner of speaking, I am," the lawyer returned, after considering carefully. "The word is engraved on the handle of the key which opens the vault. Thus some burglar might get a duplicate key made for the lock; but without the original key he was powerless."

"Do you know this word?"

A longer hesitation. "Naturally," said Payne.

"Did anybody else know it?"

"I consider that question an impertinence, sir," the other told him. Small brown teeth showed under his upper lip. His face had become all wrinkles and ugliness, the grey cropped hair drawn down. He hesitated again, and then added, more mildly: "Unless the late Mr. Timothy Starberth communicated it to his son by word of mouth. He never took the tradition very seriously, I am bound to say."

For a moment Sir Benjamin went prowling up and down before the fireplace, flapping his hands behind his back. Then he turned.

"When did you deliver the keys to young Starberth?"

"At my office in Chatterham, late yesterday afternoon."

"Was anybody with him?"

"His cousin Herbert."

"Herbert was not present during the interview, I take it?"

"Naturally not. . . . I delivered the keys, and gave the only instructions left me: that he open the safe and the box, examine what was inside, and bring me one of the cards inscribed with Anthony Starberth's name. That was all."

Rampole, sitting far back in the shadow, remembered those figures in the white road. Martin and Herbert had been coming from the lawyer's office when he saw them, and Martin had uttered that inexplicable taunt, "The word is *Gallows*." And he thought of that paper, written over with the queer meaningless verses, which Dorothy had shown him; it was fairly clear, now, what had been inside the box, despite Dr. Fell's ridicule of a "paper." Dorothy Starberth sat motionless, her hands folded; but she seemed to be breathing more rapidly. . . . Why?

"You refuse to tell us, Mr. Payne," the chief constable pursued, "what was inside that box in the vault?"

Payne's hand fluttered up to stroke his chin; that gesture, Rampole remembered, he always used when he was nervous.

"It was a document," he responded at length. "I cannot say more, because, gentlemen, I do not know."

Dr. Fell got to his feet, a bulky walrus coming to the surface.

"Ah," he said, blowing out his breath and hitting one stick sharply on the floor, "that's what I thought. That's what I wanted to know. The document was never allowed to leave that iron box, was it, Payne? . . . Good! Very good! Then I can go on."

"I thought you didn't believe in any document," said the chief constable, turning with a still more satiric expression.

"Oh, I never said that," the other protested, mildly. "I only protested at your guessing, without any logical reasons, that there was a box and a document. I never said you were wrong. On the contrary, I had already arrived at your own conclusions, with good and logical evidence to support them. That's the difference, you see."

He lifted his head to look at Payne. He did not raise his voice.

"I'll not trouble you about the document that Anthony Starberth left for his heirs in the early nineteenth century," he said. "But, Payne, what about the *other* document?"

"Other—?"

"I mean the one that Timothy Starberth, Martin's father, left in the steel box, in that same vault, less than two years ago."

Payne made a small motion of his lips, as though he were blowing out tobacco smoke slowly. He shifted his position, so that the floor creaked, and you could hear it plainly in the great stillness of the room.

"What's this? What's this?" gabbled Sir Benjamin.

"Go on," said Payne, softly.

"I've heard the story a dozen times," Dr. Fell went on, nodding his head in a detached, meditative fashion. "About old Timothy's lying there writing, just before he died. Sheets upon sheets he was writing—though his body was so smashed he could scarcely hold a pen. Propped up with a writing-board, cackling and howling with glee, determined to go on . . ."

"Well?" demanded Sir Benjamin.

"Well, what was he writing? 'Instructions for my son,' he said, but that was a lie. That was to throw some of you off the track. His son, by the nature of the so-called 'ordeal,' didn't need any instructions—he only needed to get the keys from Payne. In any event, he didn't need page after page of closely written script. Old Timothy wasn't copying anything, because he didn't need to do that, either . . . this 'document' of Anthony's, Payne says, never left the safe. So what was he writing?"

Nobody spoke. Rampole found himself moving out towards the edge of the chair. From where he sat he could see Dorothy Starberth's eyes, unwinking, fixed on the doctor. Sir Benjamin spoke, loudly:

"Very well, then. What *was* he writing?"

"The story of his own murder," said Dr. Fell.

Chapter 11

"IT ISN'T every day, you know," the doctor explained, apologetically, "that a man gets the opportunity to write the story of his own murder."

He looked round the circle, leaning heavily on one cane, his big left shoulder hunched high. The broad ribbon on his eyeglasses hung almost perpendicular to the floor. A wheezing pause. . . .

"I don't need to tell you that Timothy Starberth was a strange man. But I wonder if any of you appreciate just how strange? You knew his bitterness, his rather satanic humours, his exquisite appreciation of this sort of jest; in many respects—you'll agree—he was a throwback to old Anthony himself. But you possibly didn't think he would conceive of a thing like this."

"Like what?" asked the chief constable, in a curious voice.

Dr. Fell raised his cane to point.

"Somebody murdered him," he answered. "Somebody killed him and left him in the Hag's Nook. In the Hag's Nook—remember that! The murderer thought he was dead. But he lived a good many hours after that. And there you have the point of the joke.

"He could have denounced the man who killed him, of course. But that would have been too easy, don't you see? Timothy didn't want him to get off so lightly. So he wrote out the whole story of his own murder. He arranged that it should be sealed up and put—where? In the safest place of all. Behind key-locks, and letter-locks, and (best of all) in a place where nobody would suspect it—in the vault of the Governor's Room.

"For two whole years, you see—until Martin's opening of that vault on his birthday—everybody should still think he died by accident. *Everybody, that is, but the murderer.* He would take pains to get the knowledge conveyed to the murderer that this document was there! There was the joke. For two years the murderer would be safe, and suffering the tortures of the damned. Every year, every month, every day would narrow down the time when, inexorably, that story should come to light. Nothing could prevent it. It was like a death-sentence—slowly coming on. The murderer couldn't get at it. The only way he could have reached that damning paper would have been to blow the vault down with a charge of nitro-glycerin which would have taken the roof off the whole prison—not a very practical way out. It may sound feasible for a skilful cracksman, and in the city of Chicago; but it isn't very practical for an ordinary human being in an English village. Even in the doubtful event that you know something about cracking safes, you can't go playing about with burglar's tools and importing high explosives into Chatterham without

exciting considerable comment. In simple terms, the murderer was powerless. So can you conceive of the exquisite
agony he has undergone, as Anthony meant him to?"

Sir Benjamin, jarred thoroughly, shook his fist in the air.

"Man," he said, "you—you're—this is the insanest—!
You've no evidence he was murdered! You—"

"Oh, yes I have," said Dr. Fell.

Sir Benjamin stared at him. Dorothy Starberth had risen,
her hand making a gesture. . . .

"But, look here," the chief constable said, doggedly, "if
this crazy surmise is true—I say *if* it's true—why, then,
two years. . . . The murderer would just have run away,
wouldn't he, and be beyond pursuit?"

"Thereby," said Dr. Fell, "admitting his guilt beyond all
doubt, once the paper was found. . . . Confession! That's
what it would be. And wherever he went in the world,
wherever he hid himself, he would always have that hellish
thing hanging over him; and sooner or later they'd find him
out. No, no. His only safe way, the only thing he could
possibly do, was to stay here and try to lay hands on that
accusation. If the very worst came, he could always deny
it and try to fight it. In the meantime, there was always the
dogged hope that he could destroy it before they knew."
The doctor paused, and added in a lower voice:

"We know now that he has succeeded."

There were heavy footfalls on the polished floor. The
noise fell so eerily into the dusky room they all looked
up. . . .

"Dr. Fell is quite right, Sir Benjamin," said the voice of
the rector. "The late Mr. Starberth spoke to me before he
died. He told me about the person who murdered him."

Saunders paused by the table. His large pink face was a
blank. He spread out his hands and added, very slowly and
simply:

"God help me, gentlemen. I thought he was mad."

The silver chimes of the clock ran fluidly in the hall. . . .

"Ah," said Dr. Fell, nodding. "I rather thought he'd
told you. You were supposed to pass the information on to
the murderer. Did you?"

"He asked me to speak to his family, but to nobody else.

I did that much, as I'd promised," said Saunders, pressing a hand over his eyes.

From the shadow of the great chair, in which she had sat down again, Dorothy said:

"That was the other thing I was afraid of. Yes, he told us."

"And you never mentioned it?" cried the chief constable, with abrupt shrillness. "You knew a man was murdered, and none of you—?"

There was no heartiness or smooth bumptiousness about Saunders now. He seemed to be trying to apply the rules of English sports, suddenly, to a dark and terrible thing; and he could not find their application. His hand groped.

"They tell you things," he said, with an effort, "and you don't know—you can't judge. You— Well, I tell you, I simply thought he was out of his head. It was incredible, more than incredible. It was something nobody would ever *do,* don't you see?" His baffled blue eyes moved round the group, and he tried to catch at something in the air. "It just isn't so!" he went on desperately. "Up until last night I couldn't believe it. And then suddenly I thought—what if it were true, after all? And maybe there was a murderer. And so I arranged to watch, with Dr. Fell and Mr. Rampole here, and now I know . . . I know. But I don't know what to do about it."

"Well, the rest of us do," snapped the chief constable. "You mean he told you the name of the person who killed him?"

"No. He only said—it was a member of his family."

Rampole's heart was beating heavily. He found himself wiping the palms of his hands on the knees of his trousers, as though he were trying to dislodge something from them. He knew now what had been on the rector's mind last night; and he remembered that puzzling, quick question, "Where is Herbert?" which Saunders had asked when Dorothy Starberth had phoned to say Martin had left the house. Saunders had explained it, rather lamely, by saying Herbert was a good man to have around in a pinch. But he explained it much better now. . . .

And there was Dorothy, with her burnt-out eyes, and

her small, wry, vacant smile, as one who says, "Oh, well!" And Dr. Fell poking at the floor with his stick. And Saunders looking into the sun as though he were trying to do a penance by staring it out of the sky. And Payne humped, drawn into his little grey shell. And Sir Benjamin looking wry-necked at them all, like a horse round the corner of its stall.

"Well," said the chief constable, in a matter-of-fact voice, "I suppose we shall have to send out the drag-net for Herbert, after all. . . ."

Dr. Fell glanced up mildly.

"Isn't there something you've forgotten?" he enquired.

"Forgotten?"

"For instance," the doctor said, thoughtfully, "you were questioning Payne a moment ago. Why not ask him what he knows about it? Somebody had to take Timothy's statement over to the vault in the Governor's Room, you know. Does he know what was in it?"

"Ah," said Sir Benjamin, jerked out of his thoughts. "Ah yes. Of course." He adjusted his pince-nez. "Well, Mr. Payne?"

Payne's fingers flicked to his chin. He coughed.

"It may be so. Personally—I think you're talking nonsense. If Starberth had done any such thing, I think he ought to have told *me* about it. I was the logical one to tell. Not you, Mr. Saunders. Not you.—It is perfectly true, however, that he gave me a sealed envelope, inscribed with his son's name, to take to the vault."

"That's what you meant, is it, when you said you had been there before?" asked Dr. Fell.

"It is. The whole proceeding was most irregular. But"—the lawyer made gestures of discomfort, as though his cuffs were sliding down over his hands and impeding them—"but he was a dying man, and he said this envelope was vitally concerned with the ceremony the heir had to go through. Not knowing what was in the *other* document, I naturally could not judge. His death was sudden; there might have been things which he had left undone, and which must be done under the terms of my trust. So I accepted. I was the only one who could undertake the mission, of course; I had the keys."

"But he said no word about murder to you?"

"No. He only asked me to scribble a note testifying that he was in his right mind. He seemed so to me. The note he put into the envelope along with his manuscript, which I did not look at."

Dr. Fell brushed up the corners of his moustache, keeping on nodding in that monotonous toy-figure way.

"So this is the first time you have ever heard the suspicion mentioned?"

"It is."

"And when did you put the document in the steel box?"

"That night; the night of his death."

"Yes, yes," put in the chief constable, impatiently, "I can see all that. But we're off the subject. Hang it, look here! We've got a motive, right enough, as to why Herbert should have killed Martin. But why should Herbert have killed his uncle, at the start of the whole business? It's getting worse confused. . . . And if he killed Martin, why did he run away? When he'd had to keep his nerve for two years, and kept it successfully, why did he cut along just when he was safe? And what's more—look here!—where was he going on his bicycle, down a back lane and with a bag packed, several hours *before* the murder? It doesn't look right, somehow. . . ."

He drew a deep breath, scowling.

"In any case, I shall have to get busy. Dr. Markley wants to hold the inquest tomorrow, and we'll let them decide. . . . In the meantime, I had better have the number and description of that bicycle for a general alarm, Miss Starberth. I'm sorry. But it's necessary."

Sir Benjamin was clearly so bewildered that he wanted to break up the conference as soon as possible. You could see a whisky-and-soda in his eye even more clearly than any suspicions. They made their farewells rather awkwardly, with a tendency to bow to the wrong people. Rampole lagged behind at the door as Dorothy Starberth touched his sleeve.

If the questioning had strained her nerves, she did not

show it. She was only thoughtful, like a sombre child. She said in a low voice:

"That paper I showed you—the verses—we know now, don't we?"

"Yes. Directions of some kind. The heir was supposed to figure them out. . . ."

"But what for?" she asked, rather fiercely. "What for?"

One statement, made rather carelessly by the lawyer, had been at the back of Rampole's mind for some time. Something he had been groping for; it showed itself now, and asked a question.

"There were four keys—" he began, and glanced at her.

"Yes."

"To the door of the Governor's Room. That's reasonable. To the vault, and to the box inside it; those three are natural enough. But—why a key to the iron door going out on the balcony? What would anybody need that one for? Unless those directions, rightly interpreted, would lead the person out on the balcony. . . ."

Back again crept the formless surmises in which Sir Benjamin had been indulging. Every indication pointed to that balcony. He was thinking of the ivy, and the stone balustrade, and the two depressions in the stone which Dr. Fell had discovered. A deathtrap. . . .

Startled, he discovered that he had spoken aloud. He was aware of it by the quick look she turned on him, and he cursed himself for letting the words slip out. What he had said was:

"Herbert, they all say, was an inventor."

"You believe that he—?"

"No! I don't know what I meant!"

She turned a pale face in the dimness of the hall. "Whoever did this killed father, too. You all think so. And, listen! There was a reason. I *know* there was a reason now. And it's ghastly—and awful—and all that, but, O my God! I hope it's true! . . . Don't stare at me like that. I'm not mad. Really."

Her low voice was growing a trifle thick, and she spoke as one who begins to see shapes in a mist. The dark blue eyes were eerie now.

"Listen. That paper—it gives directions for something. What? If father was killed, murdered by somebody—no curse, but deliberately murdered—what then?"

"I don't know."

"But I think I do. If father was murdered, he wasn't murdered for following out directions in those verses. But maybe *somebody else* had fathomed the verses. Maybe there's something hidden—something those verses have a clue to—and the murderer killed father because father had surprised him at work . . . !"

Rampole stared at her tense face, and her hand groping before her as though she touched a secret, lightly. He said:

"You're—you're not talking about anything so wild as buried treasure?"

She nodded. "I don't care about that. . . . What I mean is, if that *is* true, don't you see, there isn't any curse—there isn't any madness—I'm not tainted, nor any of us. That's what I care about." In an even lower voice: "You've only got to wonder whether there's any horrible seed in your blood, and brood about it, to go through the worst hell—"

He touched her hand. There was a pent-up silence, a sense of fears pattering in a dark room, and windows that needed to be opened to daylight.

"—that's why I say I hope to God it's true. My father is dead, and so is my brother, and that can't be helped now. But at least it was something clean; it was something you could understand, like an auto wreck. Do you see?"

"Yes. And we've got to find the secret of that cryptogram, if there is a secret. Will you let me have a copy?"

"Come back and copy it now, before the rest of them get away. I mustn't see you for a while. . . ."

"But you can't—I mean, you've got to! We've got to see each other, if only for a few minutes—!"

She looked up slowly. "We can't. People would talk." Then, as he nodded blankly, she put out the palms of her hands as though she would put them against his breast, and went on in a strained voice: "Oh, do you think I don't want to as much as you? I do. More! But we can't. They'd talk. They'd say all sorts of horrible things, and that I was an unnatural sister, and—maybe I am." She shivered.

"They always said I was a strange one, and I'm beginning to think it's true. I shouldn't be talking like this, with my brother just dead, but I'm human—I— Never mind! Please go and copy out that paper. I'll get it for you."

They said no more as they went down to the little office, where Rampole scribbled down the verses on the back of an envelope. When they returned to the hall everybody had disappeared except a shocked and open-eyed Budge, who passed them with an air of not having seen them at all.

"You see?" she enquired, lifting her eyebrows.

"I know. I'll go, and I won't try to see you until you give the word. But—do you mind if I show this thing to Dr. Fell? He'll keep it a secret. And you know from today how good he is at this sort of thing."

"Yes, show it to Dr. Fell. Do! I hadn't thought of that. But not to anybody else—please. And now you must hurry along. . . ."

When she opened the great door for him, it seemed surprising to find the placid sunlight on the lawns as though this were only an English Sunday and no dead man lay upstairs. We are not touched so deeply by tragedy as we think. As he went down the drive to join his companions, he glanced back once over his shoulder. She was standing in the doorway, motionless, the breeze stirring her hair. He could hear doves in the tall elms, and sparrows bickering among the vines. Up on its white cupola, the gilt weather-vane had turned fiery against the noonday.

Chapter 12

"WE FIND," said the inquest, "that the deceased met his death as the result of—" The formal words had a habit of singing through Rampole's mind with thoughtless and irritating refrain. What they meant was that Herbert Starberth had killed his cousin Martin by throwing him from the balcony of the Governor's Room. Since the autopsy revealed blood in the nostrils and mouth, and a contusion at the base of the brain not explicable by the position in which he had fallen, it was pointed out by Dr. Markley that the deceased had in all likelihood been rendered insensible by a heavy blow before the actual murder took place. Martin's neck and right hip had been broken, and there were other pleasant details which had hung with cold ugliness in the stolid air of the inquest-room.

It was over now. In the London press Chatterham's wonder had not even lasted nine days; it blossomed into pictures, speculations, and hectic news stories, and then sank back among the advertisements. There remained only a man-hunt, baying after Herbert, and Herbert had not been found. That enigmatic figure on the green bicycle slid through England as through a mist. He was seen, of course, in a dozen places, but it never turned out to be Herbert Starberth. Assuming that he had ridden in the direction of Lincoln to take a train, it had been so far found impossible to trace his movements, nor was there any trace of the green motor-bike. Scotland Yard moved so quietly that it was as invisible as the fugitive, but there was no word of capture from the grim building above Westminster Pier.

A week after the inquest, and Chatterham slept again. All day the rain fell, sheeting these lowlands, droning on the eaves, and sputtering in chimneys where fires had been lighted against the damp. The ancient rain of England, which brought out old odours like ghosts, so that black-letter books, and engravings on the wall, seemed more alive than real people. Rampole sat before a coal fire in the grate of Dr. Fell's study. But for its creakings, Yew Cottage was quiet. Dr. and Mrs. Fell had gone to Chatterham for the afternoon; their guest, alone in an easy chair by firelight, wanted no lamps. He could see the rain thickening beyond grey windows, and he could see things in the fire.

The arch of the grate, black-shining; the flames, and Dorothy Starberth's face at the inquest—never turned towards him. There were too many rumours. Chairs rasping on the sanded floor; the voices that struck across the inquest-room sharply, like voices inside a stone jug. She had gone home, afterwards, in an old car driven by Payne, with its side curtains down. He had watched the dust that followed its jolting passage, and he had seen faces peering out slyly from the windows of houses along the way. Gossip had been a sly postman tapping at every door. The damned fools, he thought, and suddenly felt very miserable.

But the rustle of the shower deepened, a few drops hissing in the fire. He stared at the paper across his knee—those inane verses he had copied from the paper she had shown him. He had mentioned them to Dr. Fell, but the old lexicographer had not seen them yet. Decently, in view of the turmoil and later the funeral, they had been able to drop the puzzle for the time being. Yet now Martin Starberth was tucked away, out there under the rain. . . . Rampole shivered. Platitudes went through his brain; he knew them now to be terrifyingly true. And other words.

"Though worms destroy this body . . ." the strong, calm words uttered under an empty sky. Again in his memory the earth fell upon the coffin, thrown as with the motion of a sower of grain. He saw the sodden willows tossing against a grey horizon, and the sing-song intonation of the service was as weirdly moving as when once—long ago, as a child —he had heard at twilight distant voices singing "Auld Lang Syne."

What was that? He had been almost hearing again things lost far back in childhood, when he knew that there had been a real noise. Somebody was knocking at the outer door of Yew Cottage.

He got up, kindled the lamp on the table beside him, and carried it to light his way out into the hall. Raindrops blew into his face as he opened the door, and he held the lamp high.

"I came to see Mrs. Fell," said the girl's voice. "I wondered if she would offer me tea."

She looked up seriously from under her sodden hatbrim. The lamplight brought her close out of the rain. She spoke with an innocent, apologetic glance past him into the hall.

"They're out," he said. "But please don't let that stop you from coming in. I—I don't know whether I can manage making tea the right way. . . ."

"I can," she told him.

All the stiffness vanished. She smiled. So presently the wet hat and coat were hanging in the hall, and she was hurrying about the kitchen in a highly practical manner while he tried to give a decent appearance of being busy. There is never, he reflected, such a guilty feeling as standing in the middle of a kitchen during the preparation of food; it is like watching somebody change a tire. Whenever you try to move about, as though you were actually doing something, you run into the other person with a bump; and then you feel as though you had shoved the tire-changer over on his face for sheer devilment. They did not talk much, but Dorothy addressed the tea-things vigorously.

She laid the cloth on a small table before the fire in the doctor's study. The curtains were drawn, the blaze piled again with coal. Intent, her brows puckered, she was buttering toast; he could see the shadows under her eyes in the yellow lamplight. Hot muffins, marmalade, and strong tea; the rasp of the knife on toast, steadily, and the warm sweet odour of cinnamon spread on it. . . .

She looked up suddenly.

"I say, aren't you going to drink your tea?"

"No," he said flatly. "Tell me what's been happening."

The knife tinkled on the plate as she put it down, very quietly. She answered, looking away: "There isn't anything. Only, I had to get out of that house."

"*You* eat something. I'm not hungry."

"Oh, don't you see I'm not either?" she demanded. "It's so nice here; the rain, and the fire——" She flexed her muscles, like a cat, and stared at the edge of the mantelpiece. The teacups smoked between them. She was sitting on an old sagging sofa, whose cloth was of a dull red. Thrown down on the hearth, face upwards, lay the paper on which he had copied the verses. She nodded towards it.

"Have you told Dr. Fell about that?"

"I've mentioned it. But I haven't told him your idea that there is something hidden. . . ."

He realized that he had no idea what he was talking about. On an impulse that was as sudden as a blow in the chest, he rose to his feet. His legs felt light and shaky, and he could hear the teakettle singing loudly. He was conscious of her eyes, bright and steady in the firelight, as he went round to the sofa. For a moment she stared at the fire, and then turned towards him.

He found himself looking at the fire, its heat fierce on his eyes, listening vaguely to the singing kettle and the dim tumult of the rain. For a long time, when he had ceased to kiss her, she remained motionless against his shoulder, her eyes closed and waxen-lidded. Fear that he would be repulsed had lifted, and slowed the enormous pounding of his heart into a peace that was like a blanket drawn about them. He felt madly jubilant and, at the same time, stupid. Turning, he was startled to see her looking at the ceiling with a blank, wide-open stare.

His voice sounded loud in his own ears. "I—" he said, "I shouldn't have—"

The blank eyes moved over to his. They seemed to be looking up from some great depth. Slowly her arm moved up round his neck, and drew his face down again. A close, heart-pounding interval while the kettle ceased to sing and somebody seemed to be murmuring incoherently into his ear, through a warm mist. Then suddenly she broke away from him and got to her feet with a spasmodic motion. Walking back and forth in the lamplight, her cheeks flushed, she stopped before him.

"I know it," she said, breathlessly, in a hard voice. "I'm a callous little beast. I'm a rotter, that's all. To be doing that—with Martin . . ."

He got up sharply and took her by the shoulders.

"Don't think about that! Try to stop thinking about it," he said. "It's over and done with, don't you see? Dorothy, I love you."

"And do you think I don't love you?" she demanded. "I never will, I never could, love anybody as much as I do you. It scares me. It's the first thing I think of when I wake up in the morning, and I even dream about it at night. That's how bad it is. But it's horrible of me to be thinking about that now. . . ."

Her voice shook. He found that he had tightened his

grip on her shoulders, as though he were trying to hold her from a jump.

"We're both a little crazy," she went on. "I won't tell you I care for you. I *won't* admit it. We're both upset by this ghastly business. . . ."

"But it won't be for long, will it? My God! can't you stop brooding? You know what all these fears amount to. Nothing. You heard Dr. Fell say so."

"I can't explain it. I know what I'll do—go away. I'll go away now—tonight—tomorrow—and I'll forget you—"

"Could you forget? Because, if you could—"

He saw that her eyes were full of tears, and cursed himself. He tried to make his voice calm. "There isn't any need to forget. There's only one thing we've got to do. We've got to explain all this tommyrot, murders and curses and foolishness and everything, and then you'll be free. We'll both go away then, and—"

"Would you want me?"

"You little fool!"

"—Well," she said, plaintively, after a pause, "I only asked. . . . Oh, damn it, when I think of myself reading books a month ago, and wondering whether I might be in love with Wilfrid Denim and not know it, and wondering how they could make such a fuss about it; and then I think of myself now—I've played the silly fool, I'd have done anything—!" She shook her head fiercely and then smiled. The impish look came back; she spoke banteringly, yet it was as though she were pricking a knife-point against her flesh, half fearful that she might draw blood. "I hope you mean it, old boy. I rather think I should die if you didn't."

Rampole started in, oratorically, to tell how worthless he was; young men always feel impelled to do this, and Rampole even went so far as to mean it. The effect was somewhat marred by his putting his hand into the butter-dish at the height of the peroration, but she said she didn't care if he rolled in the butter, and laughed at his humiliation. So they decided they ought to eat something. She kept saying everything was "ridiculous," and Rampole seized recklessly on the idea.

"Have some of this damn silly tea," he suggested. "Take a little of this maundering, bughouse lemon and a *soupçon* of senile sugar. Go on, take it. It's a curious thing, but I feel like throwing the loony toast at you precisely because I love you so much. Marmalade? It has a very low I.Q. I recommend it. Besides—"

"Please! Dr. Fell will be in any moment. Do stop dancing about!—And would you mind opening a window? You beastly Americans like everything so stuffy. Please!"

He strode across to a window beside the fireplace and threw back the curtains, giving a very fair imitation of her accent as he continued his monologue. The rain had slackened. Throwing open the leaves of the window, he poked his head out, and instinctively looked towards Chatterham prison. What he saw caused him not a shock of surprise or fear, but a calm, cold jubilation. He spoke with pleasure and deliberateness.

"This time," he said, "I'm going to get the son—I'm going to get him."

He nodded as he spoke, and turned a queer face to the girl as he pointed out into the rain. Again there was a light in the Governor's Room of Chatterham prison.

It looked like a candle, small and flickering through the dusk. She took only one glance at it before she seized his shoulder.

"What are you going to do?"

"I've told you. Heaven willing," said Rampole, briskly, "I'm going to kick hell out of him."

"You're not going up there?"

"No? Watch me! That's all I ask, just watch me."

"I won't let you! No, I'm serious. I mean it! You can't—"

Rampole emitted a laugh modelled on the pattern of a stage villain. He took the lamp from the table and hurried out towards the hall, so that she was forced to follow. She seemed to be fluttering around him.

"I asked you not to!"

"So you did," replied the other, putting on his raincoat. "Just help me with the sleeve of this thing, will you? . . . Good girl! Now what I want," he added, inspecting the hatstand, "is a cane. A good heavy one. . . . Here we are. 'Are you armed, Lestrade?' 'I am armed.' Plenty."

"Then, I warn you, I'll go along!" she cried, accusingly.

"Well, get your coat on, then. I don't know how long that little joker will wait. Come to think of it, I'd better have a flashlight; the doctor left one here last night, as I remember. . . . Now."

"Darling!" said Dorothy Starbeth. "I was hoping you'd let me go. . . ."

Soaked, splattering through mud, they cut down across the lawn and into the meadow. She had some difficulty manœuvring the fence in her long raincoat; as he lifted her over it, he felt a kiss on his wet cheek, and the exultation of confronting that person in the Governor's Room began to leave him. This wasn't a joke. It was ugly, dangerous work. He turned in the dimness.

"Look here," he said, "seriously, you'd better go back. This isn't any lark, and I won't have you taking chances."

There was a silence while he heard the rain beating on his hat. Only that lonely light shone over the rain-sheets flickering white across the meadows. When she answered, her voice was small and cool and firm.

"I know it as well as you do. But I've got to know. And you've got to take me, because you don't know how to get to the Governor's Room unless I show you the way.— Checkmate, dear."

She began to splash ahead of him up the slope of the meadow. He followed, slashing at the soggy grass with his cane.

They were both silent, and the girl was panting, when they reached the gates of the prison. Away from firelight, you needed to deny to yourself several times that there could be nothing supernatural about this old house of whips and hangings. Rampole pressed the button of his flashlight. The white beam ran along that green-fouled tunnel; probed it, hesitated, and moved forward.

"Do you suppose," the girl whispered, "it's *really*—the man who—?"

"Better go back, I tell you!"

"It's worn off," she said in a small voice. "I'm afraid.

But I'd be more afraid to go back. Let me get a grip on your arm and I'll show you the way. Careful.—What do you suppose he's doing up there? He must be crazy to risk it."

"Do you suppose he can hear us coming?"

"Oh no. Not yet; it's miles and miles."

Their footfalls made sounds like the squish of oozing water. Rampole's light darted. Small eyes regarded them, scuttling away as the beam pried open dark corners. There were gnats flicking round their faces, and somewhere close there must have been water, for the croaking of frogs beat harshly in guttural chorus. Again that interminable journey wound Rampole through corridors, past rusty gates, down stone stairs and twisting up again. As the flashlight's beam found the face of the Iron Maiden, something whirred in the darkness. . . .

Bats. The girl ducked, and Rampole struck viciously with his stick. He had miscalculated, and the cane clanged against iron, sending a din of echoes along the roof. From a flapping cloud, the squeaks of the bats shrilled in reply. Rampole felt her hand shaking on his arm.

"We've warned him," she whispered. "I'm afraid. We've warned him. . . . No, no, don't leave me here! I've got to stay with you. If that light goes out. . . . Those ghastly things; I can almost feel them in my hair. . . ."

Though he reassured her, he felt the thick knocking of his own heart. If there were dead men walking in the stone house where they had died, he thought, they must have faces just like that big, empty, spider-hung countenance of the Iron Maiden. The sweat of the old torture-room seemed to linger. He tightened his jaws as though he were biting on a bullet, as soldiers did to stifle the pain of an amputation in Anthony's day.

Anthony. . . .

There was a light ahead. They could see it dimly, just at the top of a flight of stairs leading to the passage which ran outside the Governor's Room. Somebody was carrying a candle.

Rampole snapped off his light. He could feel Dorothy shaking in the dark as he put her behind him and began to edge up the stairs along the left-hand wall, the stick free in his right hand. He knew with cold clarity that he was not afraid of a murderer. He would even have liked to swing the heavy cane against a murderer's skull. But what made the small wires jerk and jump in his legs, what made his stomach feel cold as a squeezed rag, was the fear that this might be somebody else.

For a moment he was afraid the girl behind him was going to cry out. And he knew that he, too, would have cried out if there had been a shadow across that candle-light, and the shadow had worn a three-cornered hat. . . . Up there he heard footsteps. Evidently the other person had heard them coming, and then believed he must have been mistaken, for the sounds were going back in the direction of the Governor's Room.

Somewhere there was the tapping of a cane. . . .

Silence.

Slowly, during interminable minutes, Rampole moved up the staircase. A dim glow shone from the open door of the Governor's Room. Putting the electric torch in his pocket, he took Dorothy's cold and wet hand. His shoes squeaked a trifle, but the rats were squeaking, too. He moved down the corridor and peered round the edge of the door.

A candle in a holder was burning on the centre table. At the table, Dr. Fell sat motionless, his chin in his hand, his stick propped against his leg. On the wall behind him the candlelight reared a shadow which was curiously like that of the Rodin statue. And, sitting up on its haunches beneath the canopy of old Anthony's bed, a great grey rat was looking at Dr. Fell with shiny, sardonic eyes.

"Come in, children," Dr. Fell said, scarcely glancing at the door. "I confess I was reassured when I knew it was you."

Chapter 13

RAMPOLE let the stick slide through his hand until its ferrule clanged on the floor; then he leaned on it. He said, "Dr.—" and found that his voice had gone into a crazy key.

The girl was laughing, pressing her hand to her mouth.

"We thought—" Rampole said, swallowing.

"Yes," nodded the doctor, "you thought I was the murderer, or a ghost. I was afraid you might see my candle from Yew Cottage and come over to investigate, but there was no way to block the window. Look here, my dear girl, you'd better sit down. I admire your nerve in coming up here. As for me—"

From his pocket he took an old-style derringer revolver and weighed the heavy weapon in his palm reflectively. He wheezed, nodding again.

"Because, children, I rather think we're up against a very dangerous man. Here, sit down."

"But what are *you* doing here, sir?" Rampole asked.

Dr. Fell laid the pistol on the table beside the candle. He pointed to what looked like a stack of manuscript ledgers, rotten and mildewed, and to a bundle of brown dry letters; with a large handkerchief he tried to mop the dust from his hands.

"Since you're here," he rumbled, "we might as well go into it. I was ransacking. . . . No, my lad, don't sit on the edge of that bed; it's full of unpleasant things. Here, on the edge of the table. You, my dear," to Dorothy, "may have the straight chair; the others are full of spiders.

"Anthony kept accounts, of course," he continued. "I fancied I should find 'em if I poked about. . . . The question is, what was Anthony hiding from his family. I must tell you, I think we're in for another old, old story about buried treasure."

130

Dorothy, sitting very quiet in her wet raincoat, turned slowly to look at Rampole. She only observed:

"I knew it. I said so. And after I found those verses—"

"Ah, the verses!" grunted Dr. Fell. "Yes. I shall want to look at those. My young friend mentioned 'em. But all you have to do is read Anthony's diary to get a hint about what he did. He hated his family; he said they'd suffer for ridiculing his verse. So he turned his verse into a means to taunt them. I'm no very good accountant, but I can see from these," he tapped the ledgers, "that he left 'em precious little cash out of a large fortune. He couldn't beggar them, of course, because the lands—the biggest source of revenue—were entailed. But I rather think he put a gigantic sum beyond their reach. Bullion? Plate? Jewels? I don't know. You'll remember, he keeps referring in the diary to *the things one can buy to defeat them,* meaning his relatives; and again he says, 'I have the beauties safe.' Have you forgotten his signet, 'All that I have I carry with me?'—'Omnia mea mecum porto.'"

"And left the clue in the verses?" asked Rampole. "Telling where the hiding-place is?"

Dr. Fell threw back his ancient box-pleated cape and drew out pipe and tobacco-pouch. Reeling out the black ribbon, he adjusted his glasses more firmly.

"There are other clues," he said, meditatively.

"In the diary?"

"Partly. 'M. For instance, why was Anthony so strong in the arms? He was rather puny when he became governor; nothing about him developed except his arms and shoulders. We know that. . . . Eh?"

"Yes, of course,"

The doctor nodded his big head. "Then again, you saw that deeply worn groove in the stone railing of the balcony over there. Eh? It was about of a size to contain a man's thumb," added the doctor, examining his own thumb reflectively.

"You mean a secret mechanism?" asked Rampole.

"Again," said the doctor, "again—and this is important —why did he leave behind him a key to the balcony door? Why the *balcony* door? If he left those instructions in the vault, all that his heirs would need to get at them would be three keys: one to the corridor door of this room, one to the vault, and one to the iron box inside the vault. Why, then, include that fourth key?"

"Well, clearly because his instructions entailed going out on the balcony," said Rampole. "That was what Sir Benjamin said when he was talking about a death-trap out there. . . . Look here, sir! By that groove the size of a man's thumb, do you mean a spring, a mechanism, to be pressed so that—"

"Oh, nonsense!" said the doctor. "I didn't say a man's thumb went there. A man's thumb, even in the course of thirty years, wouldn't have worn that groove. But I'll tell you what would have done it. A rope."

Rampole slid off the edge of the table. He glanced over at the balcony door, closed and sinister in the faint light of the candle.

"Why," he repeated aloud—"why was Anthony so strong in the arms?"—

"Or, if you want more questions," boomed the doctor, sitting up straight, "why is the destiny of everybody so intimately concerned with that well? Everything leads straight to the well.—There's Anthony's son, of course, the second Starberth who was a governor of this prison. He's the one who threw us all off the track. *He* died of a broken neck, like his father, and started the tradition. If he'd died in bed, there wouldn't have been any tradition, and we could examine the death of Anthony, his father, without any hocus-pocus. We could see it as the isolated problem it is. But it didn't happen that way. Anthony's son had to be governor of this prison when the cholera wiped out most of its inmates, and those poor devils went mad down in their airless cells. Well, the governor of the prison went mad from the same fever. He had it, too, and his delusions were too strong for him. You know what an effect that diary of his father's had on all of us? Then what sort of effect do you imagine it had on a nervous, bogey-ridden man who had been stricken with cholera in the bogey-ridden nineteenth century? What do you suppose is the effect on the brain of living just above the exhalations of a swamp where hanged men have been thrown to rot?—Anthony could hardly have hated his own son enough to want him to get up from his bed in delirium and throw himself from that balcony. But that's what the second governor did."

Rumbling, Dr. Fell exhaled his breath so hard that it almost blew out the candle, and Rampole jumped. For a moment the big room was quiet: dead men's books, dead men's chairs, and now the ancient sickness of their brains had become as terrible here as the face of the Iron Maiden. A rat scurried across the floor. Dorothy Starberth had put her hand on Rampole's sleeve; you would have said that she saw ghosts.

"And Anthony—?" Rampole put in, with an effort.

For a time Dr. Fell sat with his big shock of hair bowed.

"It must have taken him a long time," he remarked, vacantly, "to have worn so deep a groove in the stone. He had to do it all alone, and in the dead of night-time, when nobody could see him. Of course, there were no guards on that side of the prison, so he could escape unnoticed. . . . Still, I'm inclined to think he had a confederate for the first few years, until he could develop his own strength. His own terrific strength would come with patience, but until then he had to have a confederate up raise and lower him. . . . Probably, afterwards, he did away with the man. . . ."

"Wait, please!" said Rampole, hitting the table. "You say that the groove was worn by a rope because Anthony spent years . . ."

"Hauling himself up and down it."

"Into the well," the other observed, slowly. He had a sudden vision of a weird spiderish figure in black, swinging on a rope under the night sky. A lamp or two would be burning in the prison. The stars would be out. And Anthony would dangle by night where dead men dangled in daytime, working his way down to the well. . . .

Yes. Somewhere down in that broad well, God knew where, he had spent years in hollowing out a cache. Or possibly every night he had swung down to examine his treasures there. The reek from the well would dissolve his own sanity as it later dissolved his son's; but more subtly, for he was a harder man. He would see dead men climbing up from the well to knock at his balcony door. He would hear them whispering together at night, because he had decked their flesh with his wealth, and planted gold among their bones. Many nights he must have seen the rats eating in the well. It was only when he saw the rats in his own bed that he believed the dead men were coming to carry him down with them, soon.

Rampole's damp coat felt repulsive against him. The room was full of Anthony's presence.

Dorothy spoke in a clear voice. She did not look afraid now.

"And that," she said, "went on until—?"

"Until he grew careless," answered Dr. Fell.

The rain, which had almost died away, crept up on the prison once more; it rustled in the ivy at the window, splattering the floor; it danced through the prison, as though it were washing things away.

"Or perhaps," resumed the doctor, looking suddenly at the balcony door, "perhaps he didn't grow careless. Perhaps somebody knew of his visits, without knowing what they were about, and cut that rope. Anyway, the knot of his rope slipped, or was cut. It was a wild night, full of wind and rain. The rope, freed, went down with him. Since its edge was on the inside lip of the well, it slid over into the well; nobody would have cared to examine anything down there, so they didn't suspect a rope. But Anthony didn't fall into the well."

And Rampole thought: Yes, a rope that was cut. Much more probable than a noose that slipped. Perhaps there was a lamp burning in the Governor's Room, and the man with the knife was looking over the balcony rail, and saw Anthony's face momentarily as he went whirling down towards the spikes on the edge of the well. In Rampole's mind it was as horribly vivid as a Cruikshank print—the white, staring eyeballs, the outflung arms, the shadowy murderer.

A cry against the wind and rain; then the noise, however

it had sounded; and a lamp blown out. It was all as dead as one of those books in the shelves. Ainsworth might have imagined it, just as it took place, in the eighteen-twenties. . . .

Distantly he heard Dr. Fell say: "There, Miss Starberth. There's your damned curse. There's what's been worrying you all this time. Not very impressive, is it?"

She rose without speaking, and began to walk about the room, her hands thrust into her pockets, just as Rampole remembered her that first night at the train. Pausing in front of Dr. Fell, she took a folded paper from her pocket and held it out. The verses.

"Then," she asked, "this? What about this?"

"A cryptogram, undoubtedly. It will tell us the exact place. . . . But don't you see that a clever thief wouldn't have needed that paper, he wouldn't even need to have known of its existence, to know that there was something hidden in the well? He could have used just the evidence *I* used. It's all available."

The candle was getting low, and a broad sheet of flame curled about it, throwing momentary brightness. Dorothy went to where the rain was making splattered pools below the window, and stared blankly at the vines.

"I think I see," she said, "about my father. He was— wet, wet all over, when they found him."

"You mean," said Rampole, "that he caught the thief at work?"

"Well, is there any other explanation?" Dr. Fell growled. He had been making ineffectual efforts to light his pipe, and now he laid it down on the table. "He was out riding, you know. He saw the rope going down into the well. We can assume that the murderer didn't see him, because Timothy went down into the well. So—?" He glared ferociously.

"There's some sort of room, or hollowed-out place," Rampole nodded. "And the murderer didn't know he was there until he came down."

"Humph. Well. There's another deduction, but let it go. Excuse me, Miss Starberth: your father didn't fall. He was beaten, coldly and viciously, and then thrown into the bushes for dead."

The girl turned. *"Herbert?"* she demanded.

With his forefinger Dr. Fell was making a pattern in the dust of the table, like a child drawing, with the utmost absorption. He muttered:

"It can't be an amateur. The thing's too perfect. It can't be. But it's got to be, unless they tell me differently. And if he isn't, it must be a high stake."

Rampole somewhat irritably asked what he was talking about.

"I was talking," the doctor replied, "about a visit to London."

With an effort he hoisted himself to his feet on the two canes; he stood fiery and lowering, blinking about the room behind his glasses. Then he shook one stick at the walls like a schoolmaster.

"Your secret's out," he rumbled. "You can't scare anybody now."

"There's still a murderer," Rampole said.

"Yes. And, Miss Starberth, it's your father who has kept him here. Your father left that note in the vault, as I explained to you the other day. The murderer thinks he's safe. He has waited nearly three years to get that condemning paper back. Well, he isn't safe."

"You know who it is?"

"Come along," said the doctor, brusquely. "We've got to get home. I need a cup of tea or a bottle of beer, preferably the latter. And my wife will be returning from Mrs. Payne's before long. . . ."

"Look here, sir," Rampole persisted; "do you know who the murderer is?"

Dr. Fell pondered.

"It's still raining hard," he responded, at length, with the air of one meditating a move at chess. "Do you see how much water has accumulated under that window?"

"Yes, of course, but—"

"And do you see," he indicated the closed door to the balcony, "that none has got in through there?"

"Naturally."

"But if that door were open there would be much more water there than under the window, wouldn't there?"

If the doctor were doing all this merely for the purpose of mystification, Rampole could not tell it. The lexicographer was looking through his glasses in a rather cross-eyed fashion, and pinching at his moustache. Rampole grimly resolved to hang on to the coat-tails of the comet.

"Undoubtedly, sir," he agreed.

"Then," said the other, triumphantly, "why didn't we see his light?"

"O God!" said Rampole, with a faint groan.

"It's like a conjuring trick. Do you know," enquired Dr. Fell, pointing with one cane, "what Tennyson said of Browning's 'Sordello'?"

"No, sir."

"He said that the only things you could understand in the poem were the first line and the last—and that both of 'em were lies. Well, that's the key to this business. Come along, children, and have some tea."

There might still have been terror in the house of whips and hangings. But Rampole did not feel it when he led the way down again with his light.

Back in the lamplit warmth of Dr. Fell's house, they found Sir Benjamin Arnold waiting for them in the study.

Chapter 14

SIR BENJAMIN was moody. He had been cursing the rain, and, afterwards, the presence of strong language was still as palpable as a whisky breath. They found him looking hungrily at the cold tea-things before the study fire.

"Halloa!" said Dr. Fell. "My wife not back yet? How did you get in?"

"I walked in," the chief constable responded, with dignity. "The door was open. Somebody's been neglecting a jolly good tea. . . . I say, what about a drink?"

"*We*—ah—had tea," said Rampole.

The chief constable was aggrieved. "I want a brandy-and-soda. Everybody is pursuing me. First the rector. His uncle—New Zealander—old friend of mine; I got the rector the parish here—is making his first trip to England in ten years, and the rector wants me to meet him. How the devil can I go away? The rector's a New Zealander. Let *him* go to Southampton. Then Payne . . ."

"What's wrong with Payne?" asked Dr. Fell.

"He wants the door of the Governor's Room sealed up with bricks for good. Says its purpose is over now. Well, I only hope it is. But we can't do it yet. Payne always has a kind of mental toothache about something. Finally, since the last Starberth male heir is dead, Dr. Markley wants the well filled up."

Dr. Fell puffed out his cheeks. "We certainly can't do *that*," he agreed. "Sit down. There's something we've got to tell you."

While the doctor was pouring out stiff drinks at the sideboard, he told Sir Benjamin everything that had happened that afternoon. During the recital, Rampole was watching the girl's face. She had not spoken much since Dr. Fell had begun to explain what lay behind the Starberths; but she seemed to see peace.

Sir Benjamin was flapping his hands behind his back. His damp clothes exhaled a strong odour of tweed and tobacco.

"I don't doubt it, I don't doubt it," he grumbled. "But why did you have to be so confoundedly long about telling this? We've lost a lot of time.—Still, it doesn't alter what we've got to face—that Herbert's the only one who could be guilty. Inquest said so."

"Does that reassure you?"

"No. Damn it. I don't think the boy's guilty. But what else can we do?"

"No trace of him yet?"

"Oh, he's been reported everywhere; but they haven't found him. In the meantime, I repeat, what else can we do?"

"We can investigate the hiding-place Anthony made, for one thing."

"Yes. If this infernal cipher, or whatever it is . . . Let's have a look. I suppose we have your permission, Miss Starberth?"

She smiled faintly. "Of course—now. But I am inclined to think Dr. Fell has been overconfident. Here's my own copy."

Dr. Fell was seated spread out in his favourite arm-chair, his pipe glowing and a bottle of beer beside him. With white hair and whiskers, he could have made a passable double for Father Christmas. He watched be-nignly as Sir Benjamin studied the verses. Rampole's own pipe was drawing well, and he sat back comfortably on the red sofa where, in an unobtrusive way, he could touch Dorothy's hand. With his other hand he held a drink. Thus, he reflected, there were all the requisites of life.

The chief constable's horsy eyes squinted up. He read aloud:

> *"How called the dwellers of Lyn-dun;*
> *Great Homer's tale of Troy?*
> *Or country of the midnight sun—*
> *What doth all men destroy?"*

Slowly he read the lines again, in a lower voice. Then he said with heat:

"Look here, this is nonsense!"

"Ah!" said Dr. Fell, like one who savours a rare bouquet of wine.

"It's just a lot of crackbrain poetry—"

"Verse," corrected Dr. Fell.

"Well, it certainly isn't any cryptogram, whatever it is. Have you seen it?"

"No. But it's a cryptogram, all right."

The chief constable tossed the paper across to him. "Righto, then. Tell us what it means. 'How called the dwellers of Lyn-dun; Great Homer's tale of Troy?' It's a lot of rubbish. . . . Hold on, though!" muttered Sir Benjamin, rubbing his cheek. "I've seen those puzzles in the magazines. And I remember in the stories—you take every other word, or every second word, or something—don't you?"

"That won't work," said Rampole, gloomily. "I've tried all the combinations of first, second, and third words. I've tried it as an acrostic, down the whole four verses. The first letters give you 'Hgowatiwiowetgff.' With the last letters you produce 'Nynyfrdrefstenen.' The last one sounds like an Assyrian queen."

"Ah," said Dr. Fell, nodding again.

"In the magazines—" began Sir Benjamin.

Dr. Fell settled himself more deeply into his chair, blowing an enormous cloud of smoke.

"By the way," he observed, "I have a quarrel to pick with those puzzles in the magazines and illustrated papers. Now, I'm very fond of cryptograms myself. (Incidentally, you will find behind you one of the first books on cipher-writing: John Baptist Porta's *De Furtivis Literarum Notis*, published in 1563.) Now, the only point of a good cryptogram is that it should conceal something which somebody wanted to keep a secret in the first place. That is, it is really a piece of secret writing. Its message should be something like, 'The missing jewels are hidden in the archdeacon's pants,' or, 'Von Dinklespook will attack the Worcestershire Guards at midnight.'—But when these people in the illustrated papers try to invent a cryptogram which will baffle the reader, they don't try to baffle you by inventing a difficult cryptogram at all. They only try to baffle you by putting down a message which nobody would ever send in the first place. You puzzle and swear through a gigantic mass of symbols, only to produce the message: 'Pusillanimous pachyderms primarily procrastinate procreative prerogatives.' *Bah!*" stormed the doctor. "Can you imagine an operative of the German secret service risking his life to get a message like that through the British lines? I should think that General Von Googledorfer would be a trifle nettled when he got his dispatch decoded and found that cowardly elephants are in the habit of putting off any attempt to reproduce their species."

"That isn't true, is it?" inquired Sir Benjamin, with interest.

"I'm not concerned with the natural history of the statement," returned the doctor, testily; "I was talking about cryptograms." He took a long pull at his beer-glass, and went on in a more equable tone:

"It's a very old practice, of course. Plutarch and Gellius mention secret methods of correspondence used by the Spartans. But cryptography, in the stricter sense of substituting words, letters, or symbols, is of Semitic origin. At least, Jeremiah uses it. A variant of this same simple form is used in Cæsar's *'quarta elementorus littera,'* where—"

"But look at the blasted thing!" exploded Sir Benjamin, picking up Rampole's copy from the hearth and slapping it. "Look here, in the last verse. It doesn't make sense. *'The Corsican was vanquished here, Great mother of all sin.'* If that means what I think it does, it's a bit rough on Napoleon."

Dr. Fell took the pipe out of his mouth. "I wish you'd shut up," he said, plaintively. "I feel like lecturing, I do. I was going on from Trithemius to Francis Bacon, and then—"

"I don't want to hear any lecture," interposed the chief constable. "I wish you'd have a look at the thing. I don't ask you to solve it. But stop lecturing and just *look* at it."

Sighing, Dr. Fell came to the centre table, where he lighted another lamp and spread the paper out before him. The pipe smoke slowed down to thin, steady puffs between clenched teeth.

"H'm," he said. There was another silence.

"Wait a bit," urged Sir Benjamin, holding up his hand as the doctor seemed about to speak. "Don't begin talking like a damned dictionary, now. But do you see any lead there?"

"I was about to ask you," replied the other, mildly, "to pour me out another bottle of beer. However, since you mention it . . . the old-timers were children to our modern cryptographers; the war proved that. And this one, which was written in the late eighteenth or early nineteenth century, shouldn't be so difficult. The rebus was a favorite form then; it isn't that, I know. But it's a bit more difficult than the ordinary substitution cipher Poe was so fond of. It's something like a rebus, only . . ."

They had gathered round his chair and were bending over the paper. Again they all read the words:

> *How called the dwellers of Lyn-dun;*
> *Great Homer's tale of Troy?*
> *Or country of the midnight sun—*
> *What doth all men destroy?*

> *Against it man hath dashed his foot;*
> *This angel bears a spear!*
> *In garden glade where Lord Christ prayed*
> *What spawns dark stars and fear?*

> *In this the white Diana rose;*
> *Here was Dido bereft—*
> *Where on four leaves good fortune grows;*
> *East, south, west, what is left?*

> *The Corsican was vanquished here,*
> *Great mother of all sin;*
> *Find green the same as shiretown's name,*
> *Find Newgate Gaol, and win!*

Dr. Fell's pencil worked rapidly, making unintelligible symbols. He grunted, shook his head, and returned to the verses again. Reaching to a revolving bookshelf beside him, he took down a black-bound volume labelled, "L. Fleissner, *Handbuck der Kryptographik*," and glanced at the index, scowling again.

"Drafghk!" he snapped, like one who says "damn." "That works out to 'drafghk,' which is nonsense. I'll swear the thing isn't a substitution cipher at all. I'll try Latin as well as English on the tests. I'll get it. The classical background always triumphs. Never, young man," he said, fiercely, "forget that. . . . What's the matter, Miss Starberth?"

The girl was leaning both hands on the table, her dark hair gleaming under the light. She let out a small laugh as she glanced up.

"I was only thinking," she returned, in a puzzled way, "that, if you disregarded punctuation. . . ."

"What?"

"Well . . . look at the first verse. 'Homer's tale of Troy.' That's the Iliad, isn't it? 'Country of the midnight sun.' That's Norway. If you took each of the lines separately, and put down the definition for each—I hope I'm not being silly," she hesitated, "and put down the definition for each as a separate word. . . ."

"My God!" said Rampole, "it's a cross-word puzzle!"

"Nonsense!" shouted Dr. Fell, growing more red in the face.

"But look at it, sir," insisted Rampole, and bent over the paper suddenly. "Old Anthony didn't know he was doing a cross-word puzzle; but, in effect, that's what it is. You said it was a form of the rebus—"

"Come to think of it," rumbled Dr. Fell, clearing his throat, "the process was not unknown—"

"Well, work it!" said Sir Benjamin. "Try it that way. 'What called the dwellers of Lyn-dun?' I suposed that means, 'What were the dwellers of Lyn-dun called?' Does anybody know?"

Dr. Fell, who had been puffing out his moustache and acting like a sulky child, took up the pencil again. He answered, shortly:

" 'Fenmen,' of course. Very well, we'll try it. As Miss Starberth has suggested, our next two words are 'Iliad' and 'Norway.' 'What doth all men destroy?' I can't think of anything except Death. So there we are—FENMEN ILIAD NORWAY DEATH."

There was a silence.

"That doesn't seem to make much sense," muttered Sir Benjamin, dubiously.

"It makes the most sense of anything yet, at least," Rampole said. "Let's go on. 'Against it man hath dashed his foot . . .' That sounds familiar. 'Lest he dash his foot against a—' Got it! Try 'stone.' Now, what angel bears a spear?"

"That's Ithuriel," Dr. Fell pointed out, recovering his good humour. "The next line is obviously 'Gethsemane.' Let's see what we have now—FENMEN ILIAD NORWAY DEATH STONE ITHURIEL GETHSEMANE."

Then a broad grin creased up the folds of his many chins. He twisted his moustache like a pirate.

"It's all up now," he announced. "I've got it. Take the first letter of each word separately. . . ."

"F I N D—" Dorothy read, and then looked round, her eyes very bright. "That's it. S I G—What comes next?"

"We need an N. Yes. 'What spawns dark stars and fear?'" the doctor read. "The next word is 'Night.' Next, the place where the white Diana rose—Ephesus. The next line is bad, but Dido's city was Tyre. So we have FIND SIGNET. I told you it would be simple."

Sir Benjamin was repeating, "By Jove!" and slapping his fist into his palm. He had a burst of inspiration, and added:

"Good fortune growing on four leaves: that must mean a shamrock, or clover, or whatever they call the dashed things. Anyway, the answer is Ireland."

"And," Rampole put in, "after you've taken away east, west, and south, the only thing left is north. North. That adds an N. FIND SIGNET IN —"

Dr. Fell's pencil added four words and then four letters.

"Complete," he said. "In the last verse, the first word has to be 'Waterloo.' The second is 'Eve.' That line about a green the same as the shiretown's name—why, Lincoln, of course. Lincoln green. Finally, we find Newgate Gaol in London. The whole word is WELL." He threw down his pencil. "Crafty old devil! He kept his secret for over a hundred years."

Sir Benjamin, still muttering imprecations, sat down blankly. "And we solved it in half an hour. . . ."

"Let me remind you, sir," rumbled Dr. Fell, thoroughly roused, "that there is absolutely nothing in this cipher I couldn't have told you already. The explanation was all

made. This is only proof of the explanation. If this cryptogram had been solved without that previous knowledge,
it would have meant nothing. Now we know what it means,
thanks to—ah—that previous knowledge." He finished
his beer with a swashbuckling gesture, and glared.

"Of course, of course. But what does he mean by
signet?"

"It could be nothing but that motto of his, 'All that
I have I carry with me.' It's been helpful so far. And it'll
help us again. Somewhere down in that well it's carved on
the wall. . . ."

Again the chief constable was rubbing his cheek and
scowling.

"Yes. But we don't know where. And it's an unhealthy
place to go foraging, you know."

"Nonsense!" the doctor said, sharply. "Of course we
know where it is."

As the chief constable only looked sour, Dr. Fell settled
back again to a comfortable lighting of his pipe. He went
on in a thoughtful voice:

"If, for example, a heavy rope were to be run round
the balcony railing in the groove of old Anthony's rope,
and its end dropped into the well as Anthony's rope
was . . . well, we shouldn't be very far from the place,
should we? The well may be large, but a line dropped
from that groove would narrow our search down to a
matter of feet. And if a stout young fellow—such as our
young friend here—were to take hold of it at the mouth
of the well and swarm down . . ."

"That's sound enough," the chief constable acknowl-
edged. "But what good would it do? According to you,
the murderer has long ago cleaned out whatever might
have been in there. He killed old Timothy because Timothy
surprised him, and he killed Martin because Martin would
have learned his secret if he'd read the paper in the
vault. . . . What do you expect to find down there
now?"

Dr. Fell hesitated. "I'm not sure. But we should have
to do it, anyhow."

"I dare say." Sir Benjamin drew a long breath. "Well. Tomorrow morning I'll get a couple of constables—"

"We should have all Chatterham round us if we did it that way," said the doctor. "Don't you think this had better be kept among ourselves and done at night?"

The chief constable hesitated. "It's damned risky," he muttered. "A man could easily break his neck. What do you say, Mr. Rampole?"

It was an alluring prospect, and Rampole said so.

"I still don't like it," grunted the chief constable; "but it's the only way to avoid unpleasantness. We can do it tonight if the rain clears off. I'm not due back at Ashley Court until tomorrow, and I dare say I can put up at the Friar Tuck. . . . Look here. Won't lights in the prison, when we go up to attach that rope—well, won't they attract attention?"

"Possibly. But I'm pretty sure nobody will bother us. Anybody from the village would be too frightened."

Dorothy had been looking from one to the other, the lids tightening down over her eyes. There were small lines of anger round her nostrils.

"You're asking him to do this," she said, nodding at Rampole, "and I know him well enough to be sure he will. *You* can be cool. And you say none of the villagers will be there. Well, you may have forgotten somebody who *is* very apt to be there. The murderer."

Rampole had moved round to her side, and unconsciously he had taken her hand. She did not notice it; her fingers closed over his. But Sir Benjamin noticed it, with a startled expression which he tried to conceal by saying, "Hem!" and teetering on his heels. Dr. Fell looked up benevolently from his chair.

"The murderer," he repeated. "I know it, my dear. I know it."

There was a pause. Nobody seemed to know what to say. The expression of Sir Benjamin's eyes seemed to indicate that it wasn't British to back out now. In fact, he looked downright uncomfortable.

"Then I'll be on my way," he said at length. "I shall have to take the magistrate at Chatterham into my confi-

dence, by the way; we need ropes, spikes, hammers—
things like that. If the rain holds off, I can return here
about ten o'clock tonight."

He hesitated.

"But there's one thing I want to know. We've heard a
great deal of talk about that well. We've heard of drowned
men, and ghosts, and bullion and jewels and plate and
God knows what. Well, doctor, what are *you* looking for
down in that well?"

"A handkerchief," said Dr. Fell, taking another drink
of beer.

Chapter 15

MR. BUDGE had been spending an edifying evening. Three
nights a month he had to himself. Two of these he generally
contrived to spend at the motion pictures in Lincoln,
watching people being placed on the spot with gratifying
regularity, and refreshing his memory anew with such
terms as "scram," "screwey," and other expressions which
might be useful to him in his capacity as butler at the
Hall. His third evening out he invariably spent with his
good friends, Mr. and Mrs. Rankin, butler and housekeeper at the home of the Paynes in Chatterham.

In their snug rooms downstairs, the Rankins greeted
him with a hospitality whose nature rarely varied. Mr.
Budge had the best chair, a squeaky rush rocker whose
top towered far above the head of any sitter. Mr. Budge
was offered a drop of something—port from upstairs,
from the Paynes' own table, or a hot toddy in wet weather.
The gaslights would sing comfortably, and there would be
the usual indulgent baby-talk to the cat. Three rocking-
chairs would swing in their separate tempos—Mrs. Rankin's quick and sprightly, her husband's more judicially,
and that of Mr. Budge with a grave rolling motion, like
an emperor being carried in his litter.

The evening would be spent in a discussion of Chatter-

ham and the people of Chatterham. Particularly, when
the pretence of formality was dropped about nine o'clock,
the people of the big houses. At shortly after ten they
would break up. Mr. Rankin would recommend to Mr.
Budge's attention some worth-while book which his master had mentioned in the course of the week; Mr. Budge
would gravely make note of it, put on his hat with the
exactitude of a war helmet, button up his coat, and go
home.

This evening, he reflected as he started up the High
Street towards the Hall, had been unusually refreshing.
The sky had cleared, pale and polished and gleaming, and
there was a bright moon. Over the lowlands hung a faint
smokiness, and the moist air smelt of hay. On such a
night the soul of Mr. Budge became the soul of D'Artagnan
Robin Hood Fairbanks Budge, the warrior, the adventurer, the moustache-twister—even, in mad moments,
Budge the great lover. His soul was a balloon, a captive
balloon, but still a balloon. He liked these long walks,
where the stars were not merry at the antics of the other
Budge; where a man could take a savage pass at a hayrick
with an imaginary sword, and no housemaid the wiser.

But, while his footfalls were ringing on the hard white
road he was delaying these pleasant dreams as a luxury
for the last mile of his walk. He reflected on the evening.
He reflected particularly on the enormous news at the end
of it. . . .

There had been at first the usual talk. He himself had
discussed Mrs. Bundle's lumbago with affection. On the
other hand, there had been the news that Mr. Payne was
going on another of his trips to London for a legal conference. Mr. Rankin had dwelt upon this fact in the most
impressive terms, and mentioned mysterious brief-cases
which were as awesome as the wigs of judges. What impressed them all most about the legal profession was that
you had to read so many books in order to become a member of it. Mrs. Payne was in a rare bad temper, but what
could you expect, she being her?

Then, again, it had been bruited about the village that
the rector's uncle from Auckland was coming to visit him.

One of Sir Benjamin Arnold's oldest friends, he was; got the rector his appointment, he did; and he (the uncle) and Sir Benjamin had been with Cecil Rhodes in the Kimberley diamond-fields years ago. There was speculation about that. There was also a little speculation about the murder, but a very little, because the Rankins respected Mr. Budge's feelings. Budge felt grateful for that. He was morally certain Mr. Herbert had committed the murder, but he refused to think about it. Each time the ugly subject popped up in his mind, he closed it like the lid of a jack-in-the-box repressed, but it could be held down. . . .

No, what he was thinking about most concerned the rumour of an Affair. The capital letter was logical; it had a much more sinister sound, even in the imagination, and sounded almost French. An affair between Miss Dorothy and the young American who was stopping at Dr. Fell's.

At first Budge had been shocked. Not about the affair, but about the American. Odd—very odd, Budge reflected with a sudden start. Walking here, under the swishing tireless trees in the moonlight, things seemed different from their normal appearance at the Hall. Possibly it was Budge the swashbuckler, who could wink at an indiscretion as easily as (*"canaille!"*) he spitted a varlet on a rapier-point. The Hall was as stuffy and orderly as a game of whist. Here you wanted to kick over the table and sweep off the cards. It was only . . . well, these confounded Americans, and Miss Dorothy!

Good Lord! Miss Dorothy!

His earlier words came back to him, as they had formed in his mind that night Mr. Martin was murdered. Miss Dorothy: he had almost said a cold little piece. Dominating everything, what would Mrs. Bundle say? The idea would have turned him cold at the Hall. But here the beams of the silver screen made the soul of Mr. Budge gleam like armour.

He chuckled.

Now he was passing some hayricks, monstrous black shadows against the moon, and he wondered that he had come so far. His boots must be covered with dust, and his blood was heating from the rapid walk. After all, the young American had seemed a gentleman. There had been moments, certainly, when Budge had suspected him of the murder. He came from America; Mr. Martin had spent several years in America; there was an ominous inference. Even, for a delightful moment, there had been the suspicion that he might have been what Mrs. Bundle described as a gunster.

But the hayricks had turned to castles for the Duc de Guise's cannon, and the night as soft as the velvet a swordsman wore; and Mr. Budge grew sentimental. He remembered Tennyson. He could not at the moment think of anything Tennyson said, but he was sure Tennyson would have approved a love-affair between Miss Dorothy and the Yankee. Besides, Lord! what a secret satisfaction to see somebody bring her to life!—Ah! She had been absent from the Hall that afternoon, saying she wanted no tea. She had been absent from tea-time almost until the hour Budge had left for Chatterham. Ha! Budge was her protector by this time. (*Had she been absent,* demanded the police magistrate, deadly notebook at attention. And the dauntless Budge smiled at disaster, and replied, *No.*)

He stopped. He stopped exactly in the middle of the road, and a trembling quivered down one knee, and he was looking across the meadows to his left.

Ahead of him towards the left, clear against the moonlit sky, rose Chatterham prison. The light was so palesharp that he could even distinguish the trees of the Hag's Nook. A yellow gleam was moving among those trees.

For a long time Budge stood motionless in the middle of the white road. He had some vague idea that if there were dangers ahead, and you stood absolutely still, they could not hurt you—as, they said, a fierce dog would not attack a motionless man. Then, very meticulously, he moved his bowler hat and wiped his forehead with a clean pocket handkerchief. One queer little idea was twisting through his brain, almost pathetic in its intensity. Over there, where the goblin-light fluttered, was a test for the adventurer Budge. He had come home in the high night with the swagger within him. So, later on, the butler Budge must look at his white bed with a small shame, and realize that he was only the butler Budge, after all. . . .

Whereupon Mr. Budge did what, for his butler-self majestically moving in the Hall, would have seemed an insane thing. He climbed the stile, bending low, and began to move up across the slope of the meadow towards the Hag's Nook. And it is to be recorded that his heart suddenly sang.

It was still squashy from the recent rain. He had to climb the slope in full moonlight, and too late he remembered that he could have approached the Hag's Nook by a more circuitous route. Still, it was done now. He found himself puffing, with little saw-like cuts being drawn up and down in his throat; and he was hot and damp. Then, with an obedience which an eighteenth-century Budge would have accepted without thanks and even without comment, the moon slid behind a cloud.

He found himself on the edge of the Hag's Nook. There was a beech tree ahead, against which he leaned with a feeling as though his bowler were tightening against his brain, and a throat sore from running. He panted now.

This was mad.

Never mind the adventurer Budge. This was mad.

Ahead, the gleam showed again. He could see it near the well, some twenty or thirty feet ahead, through the twisted boles of trees. It flashed as though for a signal. Evidently in reply, another gleam winked out high above and away. Budge, craning his neck upwards, could have no doubt: it was from the balcony of the Governor's Room. Somebody had set down a light there. He saw the shadow of a very stout man bending over the railing, and this shadow seemed to be doing something to the rail.

A rope shot downwards, curling and darting with such suddenness that Budge jumped back. Hitting the side of the well with a dull *plop,* it straggled and then slid over the edge. Fascinated, Budge poked his head forward again. Now the light beside the well had turned into a steady beam; it seemed to be held by a small figure—almost, he thought, like a woman. A face moved into the beam; a face craning upwards, and a hand was waved towards the balcony far above.

The Yankee.

Even at that distance, there could be no doubt about it. The Yankee, with his strange, grinning, reckless face. His name was—Mr. Rampole. Yes. Mr. Rampole seemed to be testing the rope. He swung round on it, drawing up his legs. Climbing a few feet up the rope, he hung there with one hand and pulled at it with the other. Then he dropped to the ground and waved his hand again. Another light, like a bull's-eye lantern, flashed on. He hitched it to his belt, and into that belt he seemed to be thrusting other things—a hatchet and an instrument like a diminutive pick.

Sliding his body between two of the wide spikes on the edge of the well, he sat on the inner edge for a moment, holding the rope. He was grinning again, at the small figure which held the other light. Then he swung off the edge and down into the well; his lamp was swallowed. But not before the small figure had darted to the edge, and, as the beam of Rampole's lamp struck upwards for an instant, Budge saw that the face bending over the well was the face of Miss Dorothy. . . .

The watcher at the edge of the Hag's Nook was not now the adventurer Budge or even the butler Budge. He was simply a stooping, incredulous figure who tried to understand these amazing things. Frogs complained loudly, and there were bugs brushing about his face. Edging forward between the trees, he crept closer. Miss Dorothy's light went out. The thought went through his head that he would have a rare wild story to tell to the Rankins a month hence, over the port.

From the well a few broken reflections glimmered, as of a lamp sizzling out in water, but never quite extinguished. Momentarily the pointed leaves of a beech tree were outlined, and once (Budge thought) Miss Dorothy's face. But the cool moon had come out again, ghostly against the wall of the prison. Afraid of making a noise, tight-chested and sweating, Budge moved still closer. The chorus of frogs, crickets, God knew what!—this chorus was so loud that Budge wondered how any noise could be heard. It was cold here, too.

Now, it is to be urged that Budge was not, and never has been, an imaginative man. Circumstances do not permit it. But when he glanced away from the flickers of light dancing deep in the well, and saw a figure standing motionless in the moonlight, he knew it was an alien presence. Deep within him Budge knew that the presence of Miss Dorothy and the American was *right,* as right as gravy over roast beef, and that the other presence was wrong

It was—Budge tells it to this day—a small man. Standing some distance behind Miss Dorothy, a crooked shadow among the shadows of the trees against the moon, he seemed to grow into weird proportions, and he had something in his hand.

A muffled noise bubbled up from the well. There had been other noises, but this was definitely a cry or a groan or a strangling of breath. . . .

For a time Budge remembered nothing very clearly. Afterwards he tried to determine how long a time had elapsed between that booming echo and the time that a head appeared over the edge of the well once more, but he could never be sure. All he could be sure of was that Miss Dorothy, at some period or other, had snapped on her light. She did not point it down into the well. She kept it steady, across the mouth of the rusty spikes. . . . And up from the well, now, another lamp was strengthening as somebody climbed. . . .

A head appeared, framed between the spikes. At first Budge did not see it very clearly, because he was trying to peer into the darkness to find that alien figure on the outer edge; that motionless figure which somehow gave an impression of wire and hair and steel, like a monster. Failing to see it, Budge looked at the head framed between the spikes, coming higher and higher above the well.

It was not Mr. Rampole's face. It was the face of Mr. Herbert Starberth, rising up over the spikes of the well; and the jaw was fallen, and by this time Budge was so close he could see the bullet-hole between the eyes.

Not ten feet away from him he saw this head rising, horribly, as though Mr. Herbert were climbing out of the well. His sodden hair was plastered down over his forehead; the eyelids were down and the eyeballs showed white beneath; and the colour of the bullet-hole was blue. Budge staggered, literally staggered, for he felt one knee jerk sideways beneath him, and he thought he was going to be sick.

The head moved. It turned away from him, and a hand appeared over the edge of the well. Mr. Herbert was dead. But he seemed to be climbing out of the well.

Miss Dorothy screamed. Just before her lamp went out, Budge saw another thing which loosened his horror like a tight belt, and saved him from being sick. He saw the young American's head propped under Mr. Herbert's shoulder; and he saw that it was the Yankee's hand which had seized the wall, carrying a stiff corpse up out of the depths.

Silver-blue like the glow for a pantomime, the moonlight etched a Japanese tracery of trees. All of it had been done in pantomime. Budge never knew about the other figure, the *alien* figure he had seen standing beyond the well and peering towards the spikes. He never knew whether this man had seen the young American's head beneath Mr. Herbert's body at all. . . . But he did hear a flopping and stumbling among the brush, a wild rush as of a bat banging against walls to get out of a room. Somebody was running, with inarticulate cries, through the Hag's Nook.

The gauzy dimness of the pantomime was ripped apart. Far above, from the balcony of the Governor's Room, glared a bright light. It cut down through the trees, and the boom of a voice roared out from the balcony.

"There he goes! Grab him!"

Wheeling, the light made a green and black whirlpool among the trees. Saplings crackled, and feet sloshed on marshy ground. Budge's thoughts, in this moment, were as elementary as the thoughts of an animal. The only distinct impression in his mind was that here, crackling through these bushes, ran Guilt. He had a confused idea that there were several flash-lamps darting beams around the runner.

A head and shoulders were suddenly blocked out against the moon. Then Budge saw the runner sliding down a slippery bank, and the runner was coming straight for him.

Budge, fat and past fifty, felt the flesh shaking on his big body. He was neither Budge the swashbuckler nor Budge the butler; he was only an unnerved man leaning against a tree. Now, when the moonlight fell as with a shining of raindrops, he saw the other man's hand; it was encased in a big gardener's glove, and the forefinger was jammed through the trigger-guard of a long-barrelled pistol. Through Budge's mind went a vision of youth, of standing on a broad football field, wildly, and seeming to see figures coming at him from every direction. It was as though he were naked. The other man plunged.

Budge, fat and past fifty, felt a great pain in his lungs. He did not drop behind the tree. He knew what he had to do; he was solid, with a quiet brain and a very clear eye.

"All right," he said aloud. "All right!" and dived for the other man.

He heard the explosion. There was a yellowish spurt, like a bad gas-range when you apply a match to it. Something hit him in the chest, swirling him off balance as his fingers ripped down the other man's coat. He felt his finger nails tear in cloth, falling, and his hip was suddenly twisted into weakness. There was a sensation as though he were flying through the air. Then his face squashed into dead leaves, and he dimly heard a thud as of his own body hitting the ground.

That was how Budge the Englishman went down.

Chapter 16

"I DON'T think he's dead," said Rampole, going down on his knees beside the flattened figure of the butler. "Buck up, please! Hold your light down here while I roll him over. Where the devil is what's-his-name—Sir Benjamin?"

Budge was lying on his side, one hand still stretched out. His hat was crushed along one side with an almost rakish effect, and his respectable black coat had burst a button. Tugging at the dead weight, Rampole wrenched him over.

The face was like dough and the eyes were closed, but he was breathing. Since the wound was high along the left breast, blood had begun to soak through.

"Halloa!" Rampole shouted. "Halloa, there! Where are you?"

He lifted his head to glance at the girl. He could not see her distinctly; she was looking away, but the light did not waver much.

There was a crackling in the bushes. Sir Benjamin, his cap crushed down like a gangster in a motion picture, pushed through. His long arms dangled out of his sleeves, and you could see the freckles against the muddy pallor of his face.

"He—he got away," the chief constable said rather hoarsely. "I don't know who he was. I don't even know what happened. Who's this?"

"Look at him," said Rampole. "He must have tried to stop . . . the other one. Didn't you hear the shot? For God's sake let's get him to your car and down to the village. Take his feet, will you?—I'll get his head. Try not to jolt him."

It was a heavy weight. It had a habit of sagging between them, as when two people try to move a large mattress. Rampole found his chest tight and his muscles aching. They staggered through the scratching arms of bushes, and out across the long slope to where Sir Benjamin's Daimler was parked in the road.

"You'd better stay here on guard," the chief constable said, when they had steadied Budge in the tonneau. "Miss Starberth, will you ride in to Dr. Markley's with me and hold him on the rear seat? Thank you. Steady, now, while I turn round."

The last sight Rampole had was of her holding Budge's head in her lap as the motor churned into life, and the big headlamps swung. When he turned to go back towards the prison, he found he was so weak that he had to lean against the fence. His brain, tired and stupid, moved round like a creaky wheel. So there he was, clinging to the fence in the clear moonlight, and still holding Budge's crushed hat in one hand.

He glanced at it, dully, and let it fall. Herbert Star-berth—

A light was coming closer. Dr. Fell's bulk waddled above the grey meadow.

"Halloa there!" the doctor called, poking his chins forward. He came up and put his hand on Rampole's shoulder. "Good man," he said after a pause. "Well? What happened? Who was hurt?"

The doctor tried to speak levelly, but his voice grew high. He went on:

"I saw most of it from the balcony. I saw him run, and called out, and then I thought he fired at somebody. . . ."

Rampole put a hand to his head. "That butler fellow—what's his name—Budge. He must have been watching us from the wood. God knows why. I'd just hoisted *him*—you know, the dead one—over the edge of the well, and I heard you call, and somebody start to run. Budge got in his way, and took it in the chest."

"He isn't—?"

"I don't know," the American answered, despairingly. "He wasn't dead when we put him in the car. They've taken him in to Chatterham."

Both of them stood silent for a while, listening to the crickets. The doctor took a flask from his pocket and held it out. Cherry brandy went down Rampole's throat with a choking bite, and then crawled along his veins in a way that made him shudder.

"You've no idea who the man was?" Dr. Fell asked.

Rampole said, wearily: "Oh, to hell with who it was. I didn't even get a glimpse of him; I just heard him running. I was thinking about what I'd seen down there. . . . Look here, we'd better get back to the dead one."

"I say, you're shaking. Steady on—"

"Give me a shoulder for a second. Well, it was this way—"

Rampole swallowed again. He felt that his nostrils would never be free of the odour from that well, or from crawling things. Again he saw the rope curling down from the balcony, and felt the stone against his corduroy trousers as he swung himself over the edge. . . .

"It was this way," he went on, eagerly. "I didn't have to use the rope very far. About five or six feet down there are stone niches hacked into the side, almost like steps. I'd figured it wouldn't be very far down, because heavy rains might flood out any hiding place Anthony had made. You had to watch yourself, because the niches were slimy; but there was one big stone scraped almost clean. I could see an 'om' and a 'me' cut into a round inscription. The rest was almost obliterated. At first I thought I couldn't move the stone block, but when I braced myself, and tied the rope round my waist, and put the edge of the trench-mattock into the side, I found it was only a thin slab. You could push it in fairly easily, and if you kept it upright there was a hole at one side where you could get in several fingers to pull it back again. . . . The place was full of water-spiders and rats. . . ."

He shuddered.

"I didn't find a room, or anything elaborate. It was just an opening hollowed out of the flat stones they'd used for the well, and a part of the earth around; and it was half full of water, anyway. Herbert's body had been squeezed into it along the back. The first thing I touched was his hand, and I saw the hole in his head. By the time I had hauled him out I was as wet as he was. He's pretty small, you know, and by keeping the rope tied round my waist to brace me I could hoist him on my shoulder. His clothes were full of some kind of overblown flies, and they crawled on me. As for the rest of it . . ."

He slapped at himself, and the doctor gripped his arm.

"There wasn't anything else, except—oh yes, I found the handkerchief. It's pretty well rotted, but it belonged to old Timothy; T. S. on the edge, bloody and rolled in one corner. At least, I think it's blood. There were some candle-ends, too, and what looked like burnt matches. But no treasure; not a box, not a scrap. And that's all. It's cold; let me go back and get my coat. There's something inside my collar. . . ."

The doctor gave him another drink of brandy, and they moved on heavy legs towards the Hag's Nook. Herbert Starberth's body lay where Rampole had deposited it beside the well. As they looked down at it under the doctor's light, Rampole kept wiping his hands fiercely up and down the sides of his trousers. Small and doubled, the body had its head twisted on one side, and seemed to be gaping at something it saw along the grass. The cold and damp of the underground niche had acted like an ice-house; though it must have been a week since the bullet had entered his brain, there was no sign of decomposition.

Rampole, feeling as though his brain were full of dull bells, pointed.

"Murder?" he asked.

"Undoubtedly. No weapon, and—you know."

The American spoke words which sounded idiotic even to him in the way he felt. "This has got to stop!" he said, desperately, and clenched his hands. But there was nothing else to say. It expressed everything. He repeated: "This has got to stop, I tell you! Yes, that poor devil of a butler . . . or do you suppose he was in on it? I never thought of that."

Dr. Fell shook his head.

"No. No, there is only one man concerned in this. I know who he is."

Leaning against the coping of the well, Rampole groped in his pocket after cigarettes. He lit one with a muddy hand on the match, and even the cigarette smelt of the depths down there. He said:

"Then we're near the end—?"

"We're near the end," said Dr. Fell. "It will come tomorrow, because of a certain telegram." He was silent, meditating, with his light directed away from the body. "It took me a long time to realize it," he added, abruptly. "There is one man, and only one man, who could have committed these murders. He has killed three men already, and tonight he may have killed a fourth. . . . Tomorrow there is an afternoon train arriving from London. We will meet that train. And there will be an end to the murderer."

"Then—the murderer doesn't live here?"

Dr. Fell raised his head. "Don't think about it now, young fellow. Go down to Yew Cottage and get a bath and a change of clothes; you need it. I can watch."

An owl had begun to cry over the Hag's Nook. Rampole

moved through the brush, back along the trampled trail where they had carried Budge. He glanced back only once. Dr. Fell had switched off his flashlamp. Against the blue and silver of the moonlight, Dr. Fell was standing motionless, a massive black silhouette with a leonine head, staring down into the well.

Budge was conscious only of dreams and pain. He knew that he was lying on a bed somewhere, with deep pillows under his head. Once he thought he saw a white-lace curtain blowing at a window; he thought that a lamp was reflected in the window-glass, and that somebody was sitting near him, watching.

But he could not be sure. He kept dozing off to sleep, without seeming to be able to move. There were noises like the shiver of beaten gongs. Somebody was arranging a prickly blanket about his neck, though he felt too hot already. At the touch of the hands he felt terrified, and again he tried to lift his arms without success; the gong-noises and the swing of phantom rooms dissolved in a jerk of pain which ran through him as though it were flowing along his veins. He smelt medicine. He was a boy on a football field, under a dinning of shouts; he was winding clocks and measuring port from a decanter; and then the portrait of old Anthony, from its frame in the gallery at the Hall, leapt out at him. Old Anthony wore a white gardener's glove. . . .

Even as he retreated, he knew that it was not old Anthony. Who was it? Somebody he had seen on the motion-picture screen, associated with fighting and gunplay; and a whole genie-bottle of shadowy faces floated past. Nor yet was it any of these, but some person he had known a long time. A familiar face—

It was bending over him now, in his bed.

His scream became a croak.

Impossible that it should be there. He was unhurt, and this was a fancy coloured with the smell of iodoform. The linen of the pillow felt cool and faintly rough to his cheek. A clock struck. Something was shaken and flashing, thin glass in lamplight, and there were tiptoeing footfalls. Distinctly he heard a voice say:

"He'll live."

Budge slept. It was as though some subconscious nerve had been waiting for those words, so that afterwards sleep descended, and wound him rigid as in a soft dark ball of yarn.

When at length he awoke, he did not know at first how weak he was, nor had the morphine quite worn off. But he did know that a low sun was streaming in at the window. Bewildered and a little frightened, he tried to make a move; he knew with ghastly certainty that he had slept into the afternoon, a thing unheard-of at the Hall. . . . Then he saw that Sir Benjamin Arnold, a smile on his long face, was bending over the bed. Behind him was a person whom he did not at first recognize, a young man. . . .

"Feeling better?" asked Sir Benjamin.

Budge tried to speak, and only croaked. He felt humiliated. A bit of remembrance swirled down into his consciousness, like a rope. . . .

Yes. He remembered now. It swept in such vivid colours that he closed his eyes. The young Yankee, the white gloves, the pistol. What had he done?—it rushed over him that he had been a coward, as he had always felt, and the taste of that thought was like nauseous medicine.

"Don't try to say anything," Sir Benjamin said. "You're at Dr. Markley's; he said you couldn't be moved. So lie still. You got a nasty bullet wound, but you'll pull through. We'll clear out now." Sir Benjamin seemed embarrassed. He fingered the iron post at the foot of the bed. "As to what you did, Budge," he added, "well, I don't mind telling you—well, it was damned sporting, you know."

Moistening his lips, Budge at last achieved speech.

"Yes, sir," he said. "Thank you, sir."

His half-closed eyes opened in wonder and some anger when he saw that the young American had almost laughed. . . .

"No offense, Budge," Rampole hastily put in. "It was just that you rushed his gun like an Irish cop, and now you act as if somebody had just offered you a glass of beer. . . . I don't suppose you recognized him, did you?"

(Some struggle in the brain; a half-face, cut into whorls

like water over sand. Budge felt dizzy, and there was something hurting inside his chest. The water washed out the face.)

"Yes, sir," he said, with an effort. "I shall remember it —soon. Just now I can't think. . . ."

"Of course," Rampole interposed, hurriedly. He saw somebody in white beckoning them from the doorway. "Well, good luck, Budge. You've got plenty of nerve."

At the smiles of the others, Budge felt a responsive smile drawing at his own lips like a nervous twitch. He felt drowsy again, and his head sang, but he was floating pleasantly away now. He was not sure what had happened; but warm satisfaction lulled him for the first time in his life. What a story! If only those housemaids wouldn't leave windows open. . . .

His eyes closed.

"Thank you, sir," said Budge. "Please tell Miss Dorothy that I shall be back at the Hall tomorrow."

Rampole closed the door of the bedroom behind them, and turned to face Sir Benjamin in the dim upper hallway of Dr. Markley's house. He could see the white skirt of a nurse descending the stairs ahead.

"He saw whoever it was," the chief constable said, grimly. "Yes, and he'll remember. What the devil, though, was he doing up there, to begin with?"

"Just curiosity, I suppose. And now what?"

Sir Benjamin opened the case of a big gold watch, glanced at it rather nervously, and shut it up again.

"It's Fell's show. I'm dashed if *I* know." His voice grew querulous. "He's gone over my head completely—mine! I mean to say, he has quite a stand-in with Sir William Rossiter, the High Commissioner at the Yard; he seems to be on intimate terms with everybody in England. And he's been pulling wires. . . . All I know is that we're to meet the five-four train from London, and nab somebody who gets off it. Well, I hope everybody's waiting. Come along."

Dr. Markley was still on his afternoon round, and they did not linger. As they went down into the High Street, Rampole was rather more nervous than the chief constable.

Neither last night nor today could he elicit anything more from Dr. Fell.

"What's more," the chief constable grumbled, in the same tone, "I will not go to Southampton to meet the rector's uncle. I don't care if he is an old friend; the rector is going instead. I have business in Manchester—that's Thursday—and I've got to be away a week at the least. Dash it! Something always comes up. I can't find Payne, either; he has some papers I must take to Manchester along with me. Dash it! Here I've wasted all this time with the blasted case, when I could easily turn it over to the proper people, and Fell takes the whole thing out of my hands. . . ."

He was talking rather desperately, Rampole sensed, talking away at anything that came into his head, so that he would not be forced to think. And the American agreed with him.

Sir Benjamin's grey Daimler was waiting in the elm-shadowed street. It was tea-time, and few people were abroad. Rampole wondered whether the news of Herbert's death had yet filtered into Chatterham; the body had been conveyed to the Hall late last night, and the servants warned with awesome threats to say nothing until they were given permission, but that was no guarantee at all. Last night, to keep away the horrors, Dorothy had stayed with Mrs. Fell. Until almost daybreak Rampole had heard them talking in the room next to his. Exhausted, and yet unable to sleep, he had sat at the window, smoking innumerable cigarettes, and staring with smarting eyelids at the whitening dawn. . . .

Now the grey Daimler swept through Chatterham, and the wind stroked his face with cool fragrance. In the sky the fiery streaks had paled; there were white, and violet, and a smokiness of shadow creeping up from the lowlands. There were a few dark clouds, like slow sheep. He remembered the first evening he had walked into Chatterham with Dorothy Starberth, through this mysterious hour of the gold-darkened sky and the faint jangling bells; when a wind ran across the green corn, and the smell of hawthorn grew stronger with dusk. Remembering it, he did not believe that it had been only ten days ago.

"Tomorrow there is an afternoon train from London," he could hear Dr. Fell speaking in the Hag's Nook. *"We will meet that train."*

The words had finality. . . .

Sir Benjamin said nothing. The Daimler roared against the whipping breeze. Dorothy in New York. Dorothy as his wife. Lord! but it had a funny sound!—every time he thought of that, he thought of himself sitting in a class last year and thinking that if he flunked economics (which, like all intelligent people, he detested), it would be the end of the world. Possessing a wife, he would become suddenly a citizen, with a telephone number and a cocktail-shaker and everything; and his mother would have hysterics; and his father, up twenty-five floors in a law-office at Number One West Forty-Second Street, would drowsily lift an eyebrow and say, "Well, how much do you need?"

The Daimler stopped with a slur of tires in the road. They would have to wait for this respectable citizenship; they would have to wait for a murderer.

In the darkening lane which led to Yew Cottage several figures were awaiting them. Dr. Fell's voice boomed out:

"How is he? Getting better?—I thought so. Well, we're ready." He made a gesture with one cane. "Everybody who was on the scene the night Martin was murdered, everybody who can give evidence, is going to be in at the death now. Miss Starberth didn't want to come, and neither did the rector. But they're both here. I think there will be others waiting for us at the railway station." He added, testily, "Well, climb in, climb in!"

The rector's huge figure loomed out of the lane. He almost stumbled as he assisted Dorothy into the car.

"I'm quite willing, of course," he said. "But I don't understand what you said about *needing* me—"

They had come out of the lane's shadow now. Dr. Fell struck his stick in the dust. He said:

"That's the point. That's the whole point. I want you to identify somebody. There's something you can tell us, and I doubt whether you know it yourself. And, unless you all do exactly as I tell you, we shall never know. Do you hear?"

He glared at all of them. Sir Benjamin was racing his motor, keeping his stiff face turned away. He suggested in a cold voice that they be on their way. In the tonneau the rector was trying to arrange his large plump face along pleasant lines. Dorothy sat with her hands folded in her lap, looking straight ahead. . . .

Rampole had not been to the railway station since he had arrived in that other age ten days ago. The Daimler fled along the curves of the road, its siren crying ahead. Chatterham prison fell away behind; they seemed more in touch with reality now. Up over the waves of corn rose the small brick station, and the rails were shimmering against a low, dull, yellow-gleaming sunset. The lamps along the platform had not yet been lighted, but there was a green-shaded light in the ticket window of the station. Dogs were barking, just as on that first night. . . .

As Sir Benjamin stopped the car they heard, far down the tracks, the thin whistle of the train.

Rampole started. Stumbling on his canes, Dr. Fell had lurched out of the car. He wore his old black slouch-hat and box-pleated cape, which made him seem like a fat bandit; and a breeze waved the black ribbon on his eyeglasses.

"Now, listen," he said. "Stay with me. The only instructions I have are for you." He looked fiercely at Sir Benjamin. "I warn you that you may have a temptation. But, whatever you see or hear, *for God's sake don't speak!* Do you understand?" He was glaring now.

"As chief constable of this county—" Sir Benjamin was beginning, snapping the words out, when the doctor cut him short.

"Here comes the train. Walk up to the platform with me."

They could hear the thin, faint, clicking roar. It was rushing through Rampole's nerves now. He felt as though he were one of a herd of chickens being shooed into a pen by Dr. Fell. The headlight of the locomotive winked around a curve among the trees; the rails were shimmering, and they had begun to hum. . . .

A stationmaster pulled open the door of the baggage-room with a long screech, emitting light on the boards of the platform. Rampole glanced in that direction. Against the eeriness of the dim yellow sky he saw a motionless figure standing near the station. Then, with a shock, he saw that there were several of these motionless figures in corners about the platform. All of them had their hands in the side pockets of their coats.

He turned sharply. Dorothy Starberth was at his side, staring up the tracks. The rector, his blue eyes pinched up, was swabbing at his forehead with a handkerchief, and seemed about to speak. Sir Benjamin looked sourly at the ticket window.

Swaying in a gush of cinders, the small train ground in to a stop, its headlight enormous now. There was a heavy sigh from the engine, and it panted in puffs of steam. A white lamp winked on over the entrance to the station. Past the yellow, grimed windows of the train there were flickers as of people moving out. The only noise was a subdued clanking, above the rumble of the baggage truck.

"There . . ." said Dr. Fell.

One passenger was alighting now. Rampole could not see his face because of the conflicting lights and the heavy backwash of steam. Then the passenger moved under the white station light, and the American stared. . . .

He had never seen this man before. At the same time, he was conscious that one of the motionless men about the platform, his hand still in his pocket, had moved closer. But he was looking at this curious person from the train: a tall man, with an old-fashioned square derby and a grey moustache clipped sharp about a strong brown chin. The stranger hesitated, swinging a large valise from his right hand to his left. . . .

"There," repeated Dr. Fell. He seized the rector's arm. "You see him? Who is he?"

The rector turned a puzzled face. He said: "You must be mad! I never saw him before. What on earth—?"

"Ah," said Dr. Fell. His voice suddenly grew louder. It seemed to boom and echo along the platform. "You don't recognize him. But you should, Mr. Saunders; you should. *He's your uncle.*"

During an enormous silence one of the motionless men came up behind and put his hand on the rector's shoulder.

He said: "Thomas Saunders, I arrest you for the murder of Martin Starberth. I have to warn you that anything you say may be taken down and used in evidence against you."

He had taken his other hand out of his pocket, and it held a revolver. Rampole, even while his wits were whirling, saw that the motionless men were closing in, silently, from all corners of the platform.

Chapter 17

THE rector did not move, nor did his expression change. He continued to swab at his forehead with the handkerchief, that old trick of his; large and black-clad and comfortable, with his gold watch-chain swinging. But his blue eyes seemed to have shrunk. Not narrowed, but shrunk, as though they had really grown smaller. He was mustering up unction, ease, fluency, Rampole felt, as a man takes a deep inhalation before a swim underwater.

He said:

"This is absurd. I hope you realise that. But," a polite gesture, with the handkerchief, "we seem to be—ah—attracting some attention. I suppose you gentlemen are all detectives; even if you are so mad as to arrest me, you hardly needed so large a force. . . . There's a crowd gathering!" he added, in a lower and angrier tone. "If you must keep your hand on my shoulder, let's go back to Sir Benjamin's car."

The man who had arrested him, a taciturn-looking person with heavy lines in his face, looked at Dr. Fell.

"This is the man, sir?" he asked.

"It's all right, Inspector," answered the doctor. "That's the man. You may as well do as he suggests.—Sir Benjamin, you see that man on the platform. You recognize him?"

"Good Lord, yes!" exclaimed the chief constable. "It's

Bob Saunders, right enough. He's older than when I knew him, but I should recognize him anywhere. . . . But I say, Fell!" He was sputtering like a boiling kettle. "You can't possibly mean—the rector—Saunders—!"

"His name isn't Saunders," said the doctor, composedly. "And I'm fairly sure he isn't a clergyman. Anyhow, you recognize the uncle. I was afraid you would blurt out something before I could enquire. There was always a chance that the bogus Saunders would resemble the real rector. . . . Inspector Jennings, I suggest you take your prisoner over to that grey automobile on the other side of the road. Sir Benjamin, you might meet your old friend before the rest of us do. Tell him as much or as little as you like, and then join us."

Saunders took off his hat and fanned himself with it.

"Then you are behind this, Doctor?" he enquired, almost genially. "I—er—it surprises me. It even shocks me. I do not like you, Doctor Fell. Gentlemen, come along. You needn't keep hold of my arm, Inspector. I assure you I have no intention of running away."

In the darkening light, the little party moved across to the Daimler. Inspector Jennings turned his neck as though on a slow pivot.

"I thought I should bring a few of the men along with me, sir," he said to Dr. Fell. "You said he was a killer."

The ugly word, unemotionally spoken, caused a hush which was broken only by the plodding of large feet. Rampole, walking behind the rest of them with Dorothy, stared at the large back of the rector moving in confident strides. The bald spot on Saunders' head shone out of the fluff of yellowish hair. He heard Saunders laugh. . . .

They put the prisoner in the tonneau of the car. Spreading himself comfortably, the rector drew a deep breath. The word "killer" was still sounding faintly in their ears. Saunders seemed to know it. His eyes moved slowly over them, and he was meticulously folding and unfolding his handkerchief. It was as though he were putting on pieces of armour.

"Now, then, gentlemen," he remarked, "pray let's make

this appear to be a pleasant little chat in the rear of a mo-
tor-car. . . . What, precisely, is the charge against me?"

"By God!" said Dr. Fell, striking the side of the car ad-
miringly, "it's damned good, Saunders!—You heard the Inspector. Officially you are charged only with the murder of
Martin Starberth. Eh?"

"Quite," agreed the rector, nodding slowly. "I am glad I
have such a group of witnesses about me. . . . Before I say
anything, Inspector, this is your last chance. Are you sure
you want to proceed with this arrest?"

"Those are my instructions, sir."

Again the other nodded pleasantly. "I rather think you'll
regret it, then. Because three witnesses—excuse, four witnesses—will testify that it would have been absolutely impossible for me to have killed my young friend Martin. Or,
indeed, anybody else."

He smiled.

"May *I* ask a question now? Dr. Fell, you seem to have
caused this somewhat—pardon me—amazing procedure.
On the night my young friend—ah—died, I was at your
house, by your side, was I not? At what time did I arrive?"
Dr. Fell, still resembling a fat bandit, was leaning against
the side of the car. He seemed to be enjoying himself.

"First move," he said. "You're opening with a pawn instead of a knight. Stand by, Inspector; I like this.—You arrived in the vicinity of ten-thirty. More or less. I'll give you
ten-thirty."

"Let me remind you"—the rector's voice had grown a
trifle harsher; but he changed it in an instant, smoothly.
"Ah, no matter. Miss Starberth, will you tell these gentlemen again what time your brother left the Hall?"

"There was a mix-up about clocks, you know," Dr. Fell
put in. "The clock in the hall was ten minutes fast. . . ."

"Quite so," said Saunders. "Well, at whatever time he
left the Hall, I must have been at Dr. Fell's house? You
know this to be a fact?"

Dorothy, who had been staring at him queerly, nodded.
"Why . . . yes. Yes, naturally."

"And you, Mr. Rampole. You know that I was at the
doctor's, and that I never left. You saw Martin coming up

to the prison with his light while I was there; you saw his lamp in the Governor's Room while I was there? In short, I could not conceivably have killed him?"

Rampole had to say, "Yes." There was no denying it. During all that time, Saunders had been directly under his eyes; under Dr. Fell's eyes also. He did not like Saunders' look. There was too much of a sort of desperate hypnosis behind the smile of the big, pink, steaming face. All the same . . .

"You, too, must grant all this, doctor?" the rector asked.

"I do admit it."

"And I employed no mechanical device, such as has several times been suggested in this investigation? There was no death-trap by which I could have killed Martin Starberth while I was not there?"

"There was not," the doctor replied. His blinking eyes had become steady. "You were with us the whole time you say you were. In the brief moments when you were separated from Mr. Rampole while you two ran up towards the prison, you did nothing whatever—Martin Starberth was already dead. Your conduct was clear. And yet you killed Martin Starberth with your own hand, and flung his body into the Hag's Nook."

Unfolding his handkerchief again, the rector wiped his forehead. His eyes seemed to watch for a trap. Anger was growing now. . . .

"You'd better turn me loose, Inspector," he said, suddenly. "Don't you think we've had enough foolery? This man is either trying to play a joke, or . . ."

"Here comes Sir Benjamin with the man you say is your uncle," remarked Dr. Fell. "I think we had all better go back to my house. And then I'll show you how he did it. In the meantime—Inspector!"

"Yes, sir?"

"You have the search warrant?"

"Yes, sir."

"Send the rest of your men down to search the rectory, and come with us."

Saunders moved slightly. His eyes were reddish round

the lids, and had an expression like marbles. He still wore his steady smile.

"Move over," Dr. Fell ordered, composedly. "I'll sit beside you. Oh, and by the way!—I shouldn't keep fiddling with that handkerchief, if I were you. Your constant use of a handkerchief is too well known.We found one of 'em in the hiding-place in the well, and I rather imagined the initials stood for Thomas Saunders instead of Timothy Starberth. The last word old Timothy said before he died was 'handkerchief.' He saw to it that a clue was left behind, even beside that manuscript."

Saunders, moving over to make room, calmly spread the handkerchief out on his knee so that it was in full view. Dr. Fell chuckled.

"You don't still insist your name is Thomas Saunders, do you?" he enquired. A motion of his cane indicated Sir Benjamin coming towards them with the tall brown man carrying the large valise. Piercing across the open space, a high and querulous voice was complaining:

"—about what the devil this means. I had some friends to visit, and I wrote Tom not to meet me until Thursday; then he cabled me to the boat to come down here directly, on a matter of life or death, and specified trains, and——"

"I sent the cable," said Dr. Fell. "It's a good thing I did. Our friend would have disappeared by Thursday. He had already persuaded Sir Benjamin to urge him to disappear."

The tall man stopped short, pushing back his hat.

"Listen," he said, with a sort of wild patience. "Is everybody stark, raving mad? First Ben won't talk sense, and now—who are *you?*"

"No, no. That's not the question," Dr. Fell corrected. "The question is, who is this?" He touched Saunders' arm. "Is it your nephew?"

"Oh, hell!" said Mr. Robert Saunders.

"Get into the car, then. Better sit up beside the driver, and he'll tell you."

In went the inspector on the other side of Saunders. Rampole and Dorothy sat on the small seats, and Robert Saunders up with Sir Benjamin. The rector only remarked:

"A mistake can be proved, of course. But such a mistake

is very different from a murder charge. You can prove no murder charge, you know."

He had got rather white. Sitting with his knee almost touching the rector's, Rampole felt a little quiver of repulsion and almost of fear. The bulbous blue eyes were still wide open, the mouth hung somewhat loose. You could hear his breathing. A deadly quiet hung in the tonneau. Dusk had come on rapidly, and the wheels sang with the word "killer."

Then Rampole saw that the inspector had unobtrusively folded his pistol under one arm, and that its barrel was against the rector's side.

Down the lane to Yew Cottage, wild bumping, and Sir Benjamin was still talking in the front seat. . . . They had just stopped before the house when Robert Saunders sprang out. His long arm reached into the tonneau.

He said: "You dirty swine, where is he? *What did you do to Tom?*"

The inspector seized his wrist. "Steady, sir. Steady. No violence."

"He claims to be Tom Saunders? He's a damned liar. He— I'll kill him. I—"

Without haste, Inspector Jennings pushed him away from the car door as it was opened. They were all around the rector now. With his tonsure and fluff of yellow hair, he looked like a decaying saint; he kept trying to smile. They escorted him into the house, where Dr. Fell was lighting lamps in the study. Sir Benjamin pushed the rector down into a chair.

"Now, then—" he began.

"Inspector," said Dr. Fell, gesturing with the lamp, "you'd better search him. I think he's wearing a money-belt."

"Keep away—!" Saunders said. His voice was growing high. "You can't prove anything. You'd better keep away . . . !"

His eyes were opened wide. Dr. Fell put the lamp down beside him, so that it shone on his sweating face.

"Never mind, then," the doctor said, indifferently. "No

good searching him, Inspector. . . . Saunders, do you want to make a statement?"

"No. You can't prove anything."

As though he were reaching after a piece of paper to take down a statement, Dr. Fell drew open the drawer of his study table. Rampole followed the movement of his hand. The others did not see it, because they were looking at Saunders; but the rector was hungrily following every gesture the doctor made.

There was paper in the drawer. There was also the doctor's old-fashioned derringer pistol. It had been broken open, so that the chambers lay exposed; and as the lamplight gleamed on it, Rampole saw that there was just one cartridge in the breech. Then the drawer closed.

Death had come into the room now.

"Sit down, gentlemen," urged Dr. Fell. Saunders' blank eyes were still on the closed drawer. The doctor glanced over at Robert Saunders, who was standing with a stupid expression on his brown face and his fists clenched. "Sit down, gentlemen. I must tell you how he did these murders, if he refuses to tell, himself. It isn't a pretty story. If you, Miss Starberth, would care to withdraw . . . ?"

"Please go," said Rampole, in a low voice. "I'll go along."

"No!" she cried, and he knew that she was fighting down hysteria. "I've stood it so far. I won't go. You can't make me. If he did it, I want to know . . ."

The rector had recovered himself, though his voice was husky.

"By all means stay, Miss Starberth," he boomed. "You are the one with a right to hear this madman's story. He can't tell you—he, or anybody else, can't tell you how I could be sitting with him in this very house—and still throw your brother off the balcony of the Governor's Room."

Dr. Fell spoke loudly and sharply. He said:

"I didn't say you threw him from the balcony. He was never thrown from the balcony at all."

There was a silence. Dr. Fell leaned against the mantelpiece, one arm stretched along it and his eyes half shut. He went on, thoughtfully:

"There are several reasons why he wasn't. When you found him, he was lying on his right side. And his right hip was broken. But his watch, in the watch-pocket of his trousers, was not only unbroken, but still kept ticking without a flaw. A drop of fifty feet—it can't be done, you know. We will come back to that watch in a moment.

"Now, on the night of the murder it rained heavily. It rained, to be exact, from just before eleven o'clock until precisely one. The next morning, when we went up to the Governor's Room, we found the iron door to the balcony standing *open*. You remember? Martin Starberth was, presumably, murdered about ten minutes to twelve. The door, presumably also, was open then, and remained open. An hour's heavy rain, we must assume, drove in at that door. Certainly it drove against the window—a much smaller space, and choked with ivy. The next morning there were large rain-water pools under the window. *But not a drop of rain had come in at the door;* the floor around it was dry, gritty, and even dusty.

"In other words, gentlemen," the doctor said, calmly, "the door had not been opened until after one o'clock, after the rain had stopped. It didn't blow open; it is so heavy that you can barely wrench it out. Somebody opened it afterwards, in the middle of the night, to set his stage."

Another pause. The rector sat stiffly upright. The lamplight showed a twitching nerve beside his cheekbone.

"Martin Starberth was a very heavy smoker," continued Dr. Fell. "He was frightened, and nervous, and he had been smoking steadily all that day. In a vigil of the sort he had to undergo it is not too far fetched to believe that he would have smoked even more heavily during his wait. . . . A full cigarette-case and matches were found on his body. There was not one single cigarette-stub on the floor of the Governor's Room."

The doctor spoke leisurely. As though his recital had given him an idea, he produced his own pipe.

"Undoubtedly, however, there had been *somebody* in the Governor's Room. And just there is where the murderer's plan miscarried. Had they gone according to schedule, there would have been no necessity for a wild dash across the meadow when the light went out. We should have waited, and found Martin's body after a decently long interval, when he did not reappear. But—remark this, as Mr. Rampole has—the light went out *just ten minutes too soon.*

"Now it was fortunate that the murderer, in smashing Martin's hip to simulate a fall from the balcony, did not smash Martin's watch. It was running, and it had the right time. Let us suppose (for the sake of a hypothesis) that it had really been Martin waiting in the Governor's Room. When his vigil was ended, he would have switched off his lamp and gone home. *He* would have known, at ten minutes to twelve, that his time was not yet up. But, if there were somebody else keeping vigil in his place, and this somebody's watch happened to be ten minutes fast. . . ?"

Sir Benjamin Arnold got up from his chair like a man groping blindly.

"Herbert—" he said.

"We knew that Herbert's watch was just ten minutes fast," the doctor said. "He ordered the housemaid to set the grandfather clock; but she discovered that it was wrong, and left the other clocks as they were. And while Herbert was keeping the vigil for the cousin who was too frightened to do it, his cousin was already lying with his neck broken in the Hag's Nook."

"But still I don't see how—" Sir Benjamin paused bewilderedly.

The telephone in the hall rang with a suddenness that made them all jump.

"You'd better answer it, Inspector," suggested the doctor; "it's probably your men phoning here from the rectory."

Saunders had risen now. His fleshy jowls had the look of a sick dog's. He started to say. "Most preposterous! Most —" in a way that sounded horribly as though he were burlesquing his usual voice. Then he stumbled against the edge of the chair and sat down again. . . .

They could hear Inspector Jennings talking in the hall.

Presently he came back into the study, with an even more wooden face.

"It's all up, sir," he said to Dr. Fell. "They've been down in the cellar. The motor-bicycle is broken in bits and buried there. They've found a Browning pistol, a pair of gardener's gloves, some valises full of—"

Sir Benjamin said, incredulous, "You swine . . ."

"Wait!" cried the rector. He had gotten to his feet again, his hand moving like some one scratching at a door. "You don't know the story. You don't know anything—just guesses—part of it—"

"I don't know *this* story," snarled Robert Saunders, "and I've kept quiet long enough. I want to know about Tom. Where is he? Did you kill him, too? How long have you been posing here?"

"He died!" the other said, desperately. "I had nothing to do with it. He died. I swear to God I never did anything to him. I just wanted quiet, and peace, and respect, and I took his place. . . ."

Aimless fingers were fumbling in the air. "Listen. All I want is a little time to think. I only want to sit here and close my eyes. You caught me so suddenly. . . . Listen. I'll write you out everything, the whole story, and you'd never know it if I didn't. Not even you, Doctor. If I sit down here, now, and write it, will you promise to stop?"

He was almost like a huge and blubbering child. Looking at him narrowly, Dr. Fell said:

"I think you'd better let him, Inspector. He can't get away. And you can walk about the lawn, if you like."

Inspector Jennings was impassive. "Our instructions from Sir William, sir, at the Yard, were to take orders from you. Very well."

The rector drew himself up. Again that weird burlesque of his old mannerisms. "There is—ah—only one other thing. I must insist that Dr. Fell explain certain things to me, as I can explain certain things to you. In view of our past—friendship, will you be so good as to sit down here with me a few moments when the others have gone?"

A protest was almost out of Rampole's mouth. He was going to say, "There's a gun in that drawer!—" when he saw that Dr. Fell was looking at him. The lexicographer was casually lighting his pipe beside the fireplace, and his squinted eyes were asking for silence over the flame of the match. . . .

It was almost dark now. A furious and wildly threatening Robert Saunders had to be led out by the inspector and Sir Benjamin. Rampole and the girl went out into the dim hallway. The last thing they saw was the doctor still lighting his pipe, and Thomas Saunders, his chin up and his expression indifferent, reaching towards the writing-table. . . .

The door closed.

Chapter 18

STATEMENT

6:15 P.M.

FOR Inspector Jennings, or whom it may concern: I have heard the whole story now, from Dr. Fell, and he has heard mine. I am quite composed. It vaguely occurs to me that on legal documents one is supposed to put down "of sound mind," or some such terms, but I trust I shall be forgiven if I do not adhere strictly to the prescribed form. I do not know it.

Let me try to be frank. This is easy, inasmuch as I shall shoot myself when I have finished writing. For a moment I had entertained the idea of shooting Dr. Fell during our talk a few minutes ago. However, there was only one bullet in the pistol. When I confronted him with it, he made a gesture of a rope being put about his neck; and upon reflection I could easily perceive that such a clean exit is better than hanging, so I put away the weapon. I hate Dr. Fell, I confess I genuinely hate him, for having exposed me, but I must think of my own welfare above all others, and I have no wish to be hanged. They say it is very painful, and I could never bear pain with fortitude.

To begin with, let me say in all justice to myself, as a last word, that I think the world has shabbily used me. I am not a criminal. I am a man of education and parts; an ornament, I believe, to any society in which I move. This has been partly my consolation. My real name I will not give, nor too much of my background, lest it should be traced: but I was actually, at one time, a student of theology. My dismissal from a certain seminary was due to unfortunate circumstances—such circumstance as may involve any young man of robust and healthy nature who is not enervated by worship from the appeal of a pretty girl. That I had stolen money I do to this day deny, or that I had attempted to place the blame on another of my fellow students.

My parents, not understanding, refused to sympathize. I could not help thinking even then that the world has a shabby treatment for its most favored sons. Let me be brief: I could not obtain employment. My gifts were such that I could have advanced rapidly had I had the *opportunity,* but I got no opportunities, save menial ones. I borrowed money from an aunt (she is dead now; *in pace requiescat!*); I went about the world, I knew poverty—yes, and for one day I was hungry—and I grew weary. I wished to settle down, to be comfortable, to be respected, to use my powers, and to taste the sweets of ease.

On a liner from New Zealand, something more than three years ago, I met young Thomas Audley Saunders. He told me that the influence of a certain Sir Benjamin Arnold, an old friend of his uncle's who had never seen the nephew, had obtained him this new and splendid position. Knowing theology well, I became his friend on the long voyage. I need not dwell on it. The poor fellow died shortly after he reached England. It was only then that the thought occurred to me that I should disappear and a new Thomas Saunders should appear at Chatterham. I did not fear discovery. I knew enough of his history to take his place, and his uncle never left Auckland. I should have to keep up a correspondence, of course, but by typing my infrequent letters and practising the signature on Saunders' passport until I had an excellent imitation, I was safe from discovery. He had been educated at Eton, but his collegiate and theological courses were taken at St. Boniface's in New Zealand, and it was unlikely that I should come upon an old friend.

The life, while pleasant and pastoral, was hardly stimulating. I was a gentleman, but—like all others—I wished to be a rich and roving gentleman. It was necessary, however, to keep a curb upon my appetites so that my sermons might be really instructive and sincere; I say with pride that I kept the parish accounts straight, and only once—on pain of severe necessity, when a serving-girl of the county threatened scandal for being attacked—did I tamper with these. But I wish to live a more pleasant life; say, in continental hotels, with many servants and a fling at amorousness now and then.

In my talk with Dr. Fell, I have learned that he knows almost everything. I had made the same deductions from old Anthony Starberth's diary—which Mr. Timothy Starberth kindly showed me—as Dr. Fell made over three years later. I determined that there must be money hidden in the well at the Hag's Nook. If it were negotiable—jewels or bullion, say—I could presently resign and disappear.

I need not dwell on this part. Chance, *vile* chance, entered again. Why does God permit such things? I had found the cache, and to my delight it proved to be precious stones. Through my earlier experiences I was aware of a trustworthy man in London who could engineer sales at Antwerp in a most satisfactory fashion. . . . I dislike that word "engineer." It destroys what some have been so kind as to call the Addisonian purity of my prose style; but let it stand. . . . Let me say again, I found the stones. I estimated that their value might be conservatively placed at about five thousand pounds.

It was (I remember it distinctly) the afternoon of the eighteenth of October when I made this discovery. As I was on my knees in the hiding-place, prying open the iron box which contained these stones, and shielding my candle from outside observation, I thought that I heard a noise in the well outside. I was just in time to see the rope quivering, and a thin leg disappear from the mouth of the opening, and I heard Mr. Timothy Starberth's unmistakable laugh. Undoubtedly he had noticed something amiss in the well. He had climbed down, seen me at work, and was now going up to laugh. I may here say that he had always a most inexplicable dislike, nay, hatred, for the church and all holy things, and his attitude had at times amounted almost to blasphemy. He, of all people, could work me the most harm. Even if he had not seen my find (and I did not doubt he had) his mirth at finding me thus employed would wreck all my hopes.

Here I must point out a curious feature of my own character. There are times when I seem absolutely to lose control over my reflex actions, and when I seem almost to enjoy inflicting physical pain. Even as a child I had buried rabbits alive and torn the wings from flies. In maturity this often amounts to a certain bewildered activity—which I find difficult to remember, and strive to conceal, and which has often frightened me . . . But let me go on. I found him standing at the top of the well, waiting for me when I came up, his riding-clothes soaking wet. He was doubled up in laughter and slapping his knee with his crop. The precious box was buttoned up in my coat; in my hand I had the small crowbar.

When his elaborate laughter had turned him almost with his back to me, I struck. I took delight in striking him many times, even after he had fallen. I cannot boast that at this time the plan I conceived was at full maturity; but it took shape presently, and I resolved to turn the Starberth legend of broken necks to profitable use.

I broke his neck with the iron bar, and left him in a thicket at twilight, whistling his horse near me.

My fright may be readily imagined when, later on and in a calmer moment, I learned that he was not dead and wished to see me. Dr. Fell has just recently told me that it was this fact which first made him suspicious of me—*i.e.,* that Timothy Starberth should ask for me to be summoned to his bedside, and that I should see him alone. My natural agitation after that interview, which I could scarcely conceal, did not go unnoticed by Dr. Fell. Mr. Starberth told me—in brief—what Dr. Fell already outlined to us all the other day, namely the plan for putting a statement of my guilt into the vault of the Governor's Room, so that a conviction for murder should hang over my head throughout three years. When I heard him tell me this, I did not know what course to pursue. I thought of flying at his throat, but that would only mean a cry and instant apprehension. Given three years, I thought, and I could surely find a means of circumventing his purpose. When I returned to the others, I was careful to implant in their minds the belief that the old man was mad—lest, in an unguarded moment, he should betray me before he died.

Nor need I discuss here the many plans I evolved for stealing that paper. They came to nothing. Instead of being able to resign and leave Chatterham, I was now powerless. In three years, certainly, I might put a deal of ground between myself and Lincolnshire, but there was this overwhelming reason against flight:

If I disappeared, an inquiry would be instituted for Thomas Saunders. It must inevitably be revealed that the real Thomas Saunders was dead—unless, of course, I could step forward whenever they searched for me, and stop investigations. If I were free, without this murder charge in the Governor's Room vault hanging over me, I could always step forward; I could be merely Thomas Saunders resigned from his pastorate. But if I were Thomas Saunders the fugitive—as I must be always—then they would discover what had happened to the real clergyman from Auckland and I should be thought guilty of foul play against *him*. In either case, I should be faced with a murder charge if I disappeared then. The only course was in some fashion to purloin that paper from the safe.

I therefore set about making a confidant of young Mr. Martin Starberth before his departure for America. Without being accused of lack of modesty, I think I may say that my powers of personality are sufficient to make a staunch friend of whomever I choose. I did this with Martin, whom I found a trifle conceited and headstrong, but otherwise a very amiable young man. He told me about the keys to the vault, the conditions, everything concerning his duties on the evening of his twenty-fifth birthday. Even at that date, some two years ago, he was uneasy. As time went on, I saw by his letters from America that the fear had become almost pathological (if I may use the word), and that I might turn to good account both this fact and the well-known devotion of his cousin Herbert to the more brilliant Martin. My purpose was, of course, to gain possession of the paper; it was unfortunate that I should be compelled to kill Martin in so doing—indeed, I liked the young man—and, as a corollary, to encompass the death of his cousin Herbert; but it will be seen that my position was precarious.

I have already indicated that my plan rested upon Martin's fear and Herbert's hero-worship, but there was a third element. These two young men were, in general build and appearance, surprisingly alike. At a distance, one might easily be mistaken for the other.

Taking them into my confidence, I disclosed the arrangement. It would not be necessary for Martin to subject himself to the terrors of such a vigil. On the designated night, immediately after dinner, they should go to their respective rooms; and—lest either of them be intruded upon to disclose the trick—Martin should make it clear that he wanted no interruptions. Herbert should dress himself in Martin's clothes, and Martin in Herbert's. To avoid a waste of time in resuming identities when the vigil was over (I suggested), Herbert should pack a suit of his and one of Martin's own clothes in a bag, and give it to Martin. This Martin should strap on the rear of Herbert's motor-bicycle, and immediately set out on the bicycle, by a back lane, for the rectory. At the appropriate time Herbert should set out for the Governor's Room, taking Martin's keys and going through the instructions as set down by the Starberth tradition.

This, it is to be understood, is what I told *them* to do. My own plans were different; but let me proceed. At just twelve o'clock Herbert was to leave the Governor's Room; and Martin, having changed into his own clothes at the rectory and driven back at this time, should be waiting for him, with the motor-bicycle, in the road before the prison. Whereupon Herbert would deliver to his cousin the keys, the lamp, and the written proof of the vigil, and Martin should return afoot to the Hall. Herbert should take the motor-bicycle, drive to the rectory, change his clothes, and also return—apparently after having taken only a drive through the countryside to relieve his feelings on the night of his cousin's ordeal.

My own design, I need not say, was: first, to provide an absolute and undeniable alibi for myself; and, second, to make the murder of Martin seem the work of Herbert. To this end I played strongly on family pride, which is in its own way a very admirable sentiment. I suggested that, even though the strict letter of the ordeal were broken, its spirit could be preserved. Herbert could open the iron box inside the vault, *but he must not examine any of its contents*. He must, instead, put them all into his pocket, and deliver them to Martin when they met at midnight outside the prison. Returning to the Hall, Martin could examine them at his leisure. If, on the morrow, Mr. Payne protested that he had removed from the iron box in the vault anything which should not be removed, Martin could credibly plead a blunder. A harmless blunder, since his conduct had in any event proved the purpose of the ordeal, *viz.*, that he had spent the hour in the Governor's Room.

My own course of action was clear. When Martin arrived at the rectory not later than nine-thirty, he could be disposed of there. I regretted that I could not make his death entirely painless; but a blow from an iron bar would render him unconscious while the neck was broken and the other injuries prepared. He could then be conveyed without suspicion in my car to the Hag's Nook, and arranged under the wall. The almanac had prophesied dark and wet weather, which proved to be a true prediction. After doing this, I should repair to Dr. Fell's. Having already suggested a party to watch the window of the Gov-

ernor's Room, I felt that I could have no better alibi.
When—at midnight—the light was extinguished in the
Governor's Room, exactly on time, the uneasiness of the
watchers would be set at rest. They would decide that Martin had come safely through his vigil. Shortly thereafter I
should take my leave. Herbert, I knew, would wait pa-
tiently before the prison for as long as I liked, since he expected his cousin; and he would not let himself be seen.
The longer I delayed, the better. When I left Dr. Fell's I
should leave my car and join Herbert. I should inform him
that, unfortunately, in my absence from the rectory his
cousin had drunk himself into a bad state—a statement
which his conduct would admirably bear out—and that it
was necessary for Herbert to accompany me there and
assist in getting Martin on his feet before Miss Starberth
grew alarmed.

With the keys, the lamp, and the contents of the iron
box, he would return with me to the rectory. There was
no need for subterfuge in his case; a bullet would suffice.
Later on in the night I could safely return to the prison
and make sure that Herbert had overlooked nothing. I had
tried to find an excuse for causing him to open the balcony
door, but I feared lest he grow suspicious, and determined
to accomplish this result myself.

What actually happened I need scarcely recapitulate. Although in one instance (which I shall indicate) my cal-
culations went awry. I think I may say that presence of
mind rescued me from a dangerous situation. It was only
chance which defeated me. Herbert was seen by the butler
while he was packing the change of clothes in the bag;
this indicated flight. Martin—whom they thought to be
Herbert—was seen driving away, down a back lane, on
the motor-bicycle; another indication of flight. Miss Starberth happened to come out into the hall (unforeseen
chance) when Herbert, posing as Martin, was leaving the
house. But he was seen only from the rear, at a distance
and in dim light; when addressed, he merely mumbled
something to simulate drunkenness, and thus escaped un-
detected. Not once were either of these two directly addressed or confronted when assuming the identities of each

other. When Budge took up the bicycle-lamp to Martin's room, where Herbert waited, he did not give it to anyone, as he has remarked; he merely left it outside the door. When Budge, in going to obtain the bicycle-lamp, saw Martin on the bicycle, it was in the obscurity of night— riding away.

I applied lethal measures to Martin. I confess that it was with a hesitation that I did so, for he was almost tearfully wringing my hand and thanking me for rescuing him from what he dreaded most. But a sudden blow, when he was bending over the spirits-decanter, and I felt stimulated to my work. He was a very light weight. I am counted a powerful man, and I had not the slightest difficulty later. A rear lane, behind Yew Cottage, took me to the vicinity of the prison; I arranged the body under the balcony and beside the well, and returned to Dr. Fell's. Though I had toyed with the idea of driving the spikes of the well through the body, as a more realistic detail and to confirm the ancient tale of Anthony's death, I abandoned it as being a trifle *too* apt, a trifle *too* studied a vindication of the Starberth curse.

My only fear was now that Herbert should get out of the house safely. Without wishing to speak ill of the dead, I think I may say that he was a dull, cloddish fellow, not overquick in an emergency. He had even been backward in taking up my plan, having several strong and almost bitter arguments with Martin about it. . . . In any event, Dr. Fell tells me that, while waiting in his garden for the stroke of eleven, I overreached myself. My agitation, and my somewhat inessential question, "Where is Herbert?" at the critical period of the wait, caused him some speculation; but I dare assert that I had been through a period of strong emotional tension, and such manifestations were only to have been expected.

I now can discuss another effort of vile and devilish *chance* to overthrow me. I refer, of course, to the ten-minute difference in the clocks. For some time I have puzzled as to why, since Herbert shut off his lamp ten minutes too soon and thus almost precipitated catastrophe—I have puzzled, I say, as to why he had arrived in the Governor's Room almost on the stroke of the *real* eleven o'clock. But I saw my answer anticipated, I regret to say, by Dr. Fell's questioning of the servants at the Hall. Herbert carried a watch which was fast. But while he was waiting in Martin's room he not unnaturally kept his eyes on the clock there. He had ordered the housemaid to set all the clocks right, according to his own time, and he assumed she had done so. There was, as Dr. Fell discovered, a large clock with the right time in Martin's room. Thus Herbert left the Hall by the right time. In the Governor's Room he had only his watch, and he left by the wrong time.

At this point, through no fault of my own reasoning, but due sheerly to *chance,* the young American (for whom I have the highest respect) had been roused to a dangerous pitch of emotional tension. He determined on a dash across the meadow. I tried to dissuade him; it would have been fatal had he run into Herbert leaving the prison, and it would have proved my own undoing. Seeing, therefore, that it was useless to stop him, I followed. The spectacle of a hatless clergyman pounding through a thunderstorm like a boy at a country frolic did not go unobserved by Dr. Fell, but my mind was on other matters. And I saw what I had hoped for, and what was only natural—he was running towards the Hag's Nook, and not towards the gate of the prison.

Thereupon ensued the inspiration upon which I cannot pride myself, since it is a part of my character and no development of my own. I perceived how this danger could be turned into an advantage. I ran—as was natural for a man with nothing on his conscience—towards the prison gate. I had carefully cautioned Herbert that, while he must show his light in going *into* the prison, he must under no circumstances show it in going out; some stranger might observe him meeting Martin in the lane, and wonder.

It was timed with an accuracy I can only regard as the fruit of my own labours. What with the night and the rain, the American was lost; and I had ample time to meet Herbert. I made sure he had the documents. I told him briefly, standing there in the wild night, that he had miscalculated—happy invention!—that he was ten minutes too early, and Martin had not yet left the rectory. I told him further that the suspicions of the watchers were aroused and that they were all about us. He must hurry back to the rectory on foot, and by devious ways. I was genuinely afraid that he might show his light, so I jerked it from his hand, intending to get rid of it in the wood.

But another ray of imaginative insight showed me a better plan. Save by flashes of lightning, the American could see nothing. I therefore smashed the lamp with my foot, and in hurrying to join him I simply dropped it near the wall. It is in such crises as these that one's brain amazes one with the quickness and finely wrought artistry of its conceptions.

I had now nothing more to fear. Herbert would go afoot. It was impossible that the American should avoid finding Martin's body, but, if he did not, *I* was prepared to stumble upon it. Whereupon I, possessing the only automobile within reach, would be dispatched to Chatterham for either the doctor or the police. I should have ample time to anticipate Herbert at the rectory.

Need I say that so it worked out? I had a more than human task to do that night, but I had set myself to it coolly; and, once I had killed Martin, that deed might have impelled me by its inexplicable stimulus to a dozen others. Before getting Dr. Markley—as I later told the chief constable—I stopped at the rectory, quite naturally, for my raincoat.

I had been a trifle delayed, and I was scarcely a second before Herbert. It would have been more prudent to have come close to him and fired against his body, as conducive to less noise; but the rectory is isolated, without much danger of a revolver-shot being overheard; and it seemed, at that moment more sporting to stand at a distance and shoot him between the eyes.

I then put on my raincoat and drove back to the prison with Dr. Markley.

All our labours were over by one o'clock. I had, then, several hours before dawn to complete my arrangements. Never have I felt so impelled to tidy up everything, as one takes pleasure in meticulously tidying up a room. I could have concealed Herbert's body—at least for the time being—in the cellar where I had hidden the bicycle, the valise, and certain implements I had used on Martin. But I must go to bed with my house (so to speak) swept and garnished. Besides, I had wished to fix the murder of Martin Starberth on his cousin, and I must overlook no *chance*.

All that I did, I did that night. It was not heavy work, since the body was so light. Knowing my way so thoroughly, I did not even need a lamp. So many times I had taken solitary walks through the prison—standing on its walls (often, I fear, seen)—standing on its walls, I say, moving through its historic corridors with some apt quotation on my lips—that I knew my way in the dark. With the Starberth keys in my possession, I now had access to the Governor's Room. For a long time I had been uncertain as to whether or not the door to the balcony had ever been locked; in any case (as I have indicated) it could *be* unlocked. I did this, and my plan was complete.

One thing more. The iron box containing the documents in the vault I later dropped into the well. I did this because I still suspected (nay, I dare say feared) the diabolical cleverness of Timothy, whom I had killed. I feared another document, perhaps, a secret compartment; I wished to be sure.

It amuses me to think that last night I was almost caught. I became suspicious of those conferences at Dr. Fell's, and I watched, suitably armed. Some one tried to intercept me and I fired; I was relieved to learn today that it was only Budge, the butler. Earlier in this narrative I stated that I would be frank; I withdraw that statement now. There is one point upon which I cannot be frank, even knowing that in the next few minutes I must put a revolver to my temple and pull the trigger. Sometimes, at night, I have seen faces. Last night I thought I saw one, too, and momentarily it unnerved me. I will not discuss it. Such matters disrupt the nice logic of my plans. This is all I can bear to say.

And now, gentlemen who will read this, I have nearly

done. My dealings with my friend the diamond salesman have been satisfactorily completed—not too often, lest I rouse suspicion—over a period of years. I was prepared. When, as a climax to the buffetings of evil chance, I received a letter from my "uncle" that he was visiting England for the first time in ten years, I could accept it with quiet resignation. In brief—I was weary. I had fought too long. I only wanted to leave Chatterham. So the news of my uncle's coming, with details, I told freely over all the country; as a subterfuge, I urged Sir Benjamin Arnold to meet him, knowing that he would refuse and insist that I go in his stead. I should have disappeared. For three years I had brooded so long over chance, and the malevolent turns it had dealt me, that a smoothly rounded life, without dangers, seemed no longer essential.

Dr. Fell has left me the pistol as a kindness. I do not want to use it yet. The man has too much power at Scotland Yard. . . .

I wish, now, that I had shot him. When death is so close I think I could stand the idea of hanging, if it were only a few weeks away. The lamp gives not too much life, and I should have preferred to kill myself in a gentlemanly way, with a suitable flourish and at least more prepossessing clothes.

The fluency which has animated me in writing my sermons seems to desert my pen. Have I done blasphemy? A man of my parts, I tell myself, could not possibly do so, since my precepts—even though I am not ordained or likely to be ordained—were of the most approved order. Where was the flaw in my plans? I asked Dr. Fell. That was why I wanted to see him. His suspicion of me became a certainty when I, in a too rash moment, to cover up any doubts in their minds, said that Timothy Starberth on his death-bed had accused one of his own family of killing him. I was rash, but I was consistent. If I had been given the opportunity in this life, some chance for my brilliance —I *am* a great man. I can with difficulty bring myself to take the pen from the paper, because then I must pick up the other thing.

I hate everybody. I would wipe out the world if I could.

Now I must shoot myself. I have blasphemed. I who have secretly not believed in God, I pray, I pray . . . God help me. I can write no more; I am sick.

THOMAS SAUNDERS.

He did not shoot himself. When they opened the door to the study, he was trembling in a fit—the pistol halfway to his temple, without courage enough to pull the trigger.

JOHN DICKSON CARR

The man many readers think of as the most British of detective story writers was born in Uniontown, Pennsylvania in 1906. After attending Haverford College, Carr went to Paris where, his parents hoped, he would continue his education at the Sorbonne. Instead he became a writer. His first novel, *It Walks By Night*, was published in 1929. Shortly thereafter, Carr married and settled in his wife's native country, England.

The Thirties were a highly prolific period for Carr, who was turning out three to five novels a year. Some of these were published under what became his most famous *nom de plume*, Carter Dickson. (Because the Dickson novels contain a great deal of a certain type of comedy, many of their earlier readers attributed them to P.G. Wodehouse. Could an American write like this? Never!)

In 1965 Carr left England and moved to Greenville, South Carolina, where he remained until his death in 1977.

In his lifetime, Carr received the Mystery Writers of America's highest honor, the Grand Master Award, and was one of only two Americans (the other was Patricia Highsmith) ever admitted into the prestigious—but almost exclusively British—Detection Club. In his famous essay "The Grandest Game in the World", Carr listed the qualities always present in the detective novel at its best: fair play, sound plot construction, and ingenuity. (He added, "Though this quality of ingenuity is not necessary to the detective story as such, you will never find the great masterpiece without it.") That these qualities are prevalent in Carr's work is obvious to his legions of readers. In the words of the great detective novelist-critic Edmund Crispin, "For subtlety, ingenuity, and atmosphere, he was one of the three or four best detective-story writers since Poe that the English language has known."